The 39 Deaths of Adam Strand

Also by Gregory Galloway

As Simple As Snow

The 39 Deaths of Adam Strand

GREGORY GALLOWAY

Dutton Books

An imprint of Penguin Group (USA) Inc.

DUTTON BOOKS

A member of Penguin Group (USA) Inc.

Published by the Penguin Group

Penguin Group (USA) Inc., 375 Hudson Street, New York, New York 10014, U.S.A.

Penguin Group (Canada), 90 Eglinton Avenue East, Suite 700, Toronto, Ontario, Canada M4P 2Y3
(a division of Pearson Penguin Canada Inc.)

Penguin Books Ltd, 80 Strand, London WC2R 0RL, England

Penguin Ireland, 25 St Stephen's Green, Dublin 2, Ireland (a division of Penguin Books Ltd)

Penguin Group (Australia), 707 Collins Street, Melbourne, Victoria 3008, Australia
(a division of Pearson Australia Group Pty Ltd)

Penguin Books India Pvt Ltd, 11 Community Centre, Panchsheel Park, New Delhi—110 017, India

Penguin Group (NZ), 67 Apollo Drive, Rosedale, Auckland 0632, New Zealand
(a division of Pearson New Zealand Ltd.)

Penguin Books (South Africa), Rosebank Office Park, 181 Jan Smuts Avenue,
Parktown North 2193, South Africa

Penguin China, B7 Jiaming Center, 27 East Third Ring Road North,
Chaoyang District, Beijing 100020, China

Penguin Books Ltd, Registered Offices: 80 Strand, London WC2R 0RL, England

This book is a work of fiction. Names, characters, places, and incidents are either the product of the author's imagination or are used fictitiously, and any resemblance to actual persons, living or dead, business establishments, events, or locales is entirely coincidental.

CIP Data is available.

Published in the United States by Dutton Books, a member of Penguin Group (USA) Inc.

345 Hudson Street, New York, New York 10014
www.penguin.com/teen

Designed by Gregory Stadnyk

Printed in USA   First Edition

1 3 5 7 9 10 8 6 4 2

ISBN 978-0-525-42565-6

"*The best thing that eternal law ever ordained was that it allowed to us one entrance into life, but many exits.*"
—SENECA, LETTER TO LUCILIUS (70)

"*Lo! I leave corpses wherever I go.*"
—HERMAN MELVILLE, *PIERRE*

"*Men always come back. They're so absurd.*"
—JEAN COCTEAU, *ORPHÉE*

Prologue

("and shall come forth, they that have done good")

Against the dark sky there is a darker shadow. It is motionless for a moment, quiet and still, barely perceptible on the edge of a dark cliff, standing against the dark sky, a black patch on a black background, and then it's gone. It is falling—the camera catches it as it falls and tries to stay with it, losing it a few times, falling behind so there is only the black bluff before the figure reappears again. It is unclear what it is or where it is, but you can tell that it's falling through the air, dropping from some height. You know it can't be good, and maybe, even before the next part, you begin to realize that the falling object is a person—you don't know who it is, but you know it's someone falling and that they have jumped from something solid into nothingness.

There's nothing more than that—the image of a person falling. You don't see the impact, you don't even see the body as it ends its descent even though the camera is right on it—it's too dark, too far away, too many other dark shapes around it—bushes, boulders, the dark hillside and the night swallowing up everything—but the next shot is an image of the body, the camera poised

1

directly over him, over his broken and lifeless body. There's more light, a harsh light thrown on the figure from behind the camera—you can see blood and broken bones as the camera moves quickly across the body before stopping on the face. You can see him clearly on the ground; his face is calm, without a scratch on it, as if he had laid down on the ground, and the camera stays there on the closed eyes and quiet mouth, in stark contrast to the mangled body below. The camera moves position; the light lurches a few times, but the face remains the same. The image jumps and then jumps again; the camera twitches with impatience more than a few times. There's no sound, only the image of the boy on the ground, until suddenly he opens his eyes.

I can't watch it; I can describe it, but I can't watch it. Probably because I'm in it. That's me opening my eyes. I'm the one who jumped. I've done it lots of times.

ONE

I guess I'll just begin again

The summer came for me with unusual and unwanted force, as if I suddenly found myself stuck in a vise and then feel its grip slowly tighten day after day, week after week, an annoying discomfort that becomes painful, almost unbearable. But then, as you will find out, there are a lot of things I find unbearable. Sometimes I'm the only one who feels that way, I think. For instance, I might have been the only person who didn't want school to end. At least it was something to do, some distraction for a few hours during the day. The summer brought nothing but dread and determination. There was nothing I wanted from it, endless days of stale heat and humidity, long nights of dull talk and duller senses. It would be the summer of my seventeenth birthday, the distant looming of our last year in high school, and the knowledge that I was never meant to see any of it, had never wanted it, and would try anything to put a stop to it. It was the summer of illness and death and near-death, the time when I would finally, I thought, for once and for all, for forever, kill myself one last time. It should have been a great summer.

We lived on the edges of town during the long months of summer, spending our days on a small triangle of land we called The Point that stuck out into the river just north of town. It was our own isolated spot, practically an island, cut off from the rest of the world by the river on one side and the railroad tracks on the other. No one bothered us, which was fine by me, and we biked there almost every summer day and did nothing but fish and drink. Then we biked home and waited until after dinner to meet up again at the southern end of town, near the bridge that connected Iowa and Illinois, and drank some more. There really wasn't much else to do.

While there's nothing at The Point except tall grass and a pile of empty cans and bottles, there is a park underneath the bridge at the southern edge of town. There's *The Thorpe*, an old steamboat grounded on the banks of the river near the park, with its white wooden sides stripping off and the large paddle wheel splintering and decaying from age and the floodwaters that attack it every spring. It wasn't always useless, of course. It once had purpose, even when they took it out of the water and nailed it to the ground. *The Thorpe* used to be a museum, a place where people paid to go on board and look around at the small, cramped decks, where they could look out at the river and maybe imagine what a lousy life it must have been to be on board such a claptrap of a boat every day, going up and down the river over and over and where tourists could thank someone that their life was better than that. But once the casinos opened with their flashy, unrealistic replicas of the same steamboats, people seemed to lose interest in the real thing. It's nothing now, closed to the public, can't float, would cost too much to haul away for trash, so it sits and rots like the bleached carcass of some extinct animal. We don't even bother to go there much anymore to climb around inside; everything has been stripped or stolen or smashed. Besides, we like to hang out over by the angel.

She stands across the parking lot from the steamboat, closer to the bridge, with her head tilted up toward the traffic, her arms outstretched as if she's starting to reach toward the sky or the bridge itself, her wings starting to spread behind her. Maybe she's getting ready to fly off, but she hasn't moved an inch since 1921, when she was erected in memory of the World War I veterans. We think. You can read the date, but most of the other words below have been chipped away from the stone by vandals who have been coming here a lot longer than we have. I don't know why everyone has the same thought, to hack away at the base. Maybe they think one piece here or there won't make a difference, but then before you know it, the whole thing is chopped off. There are no new ideas, I guess.

The marble angel was probably white once, like a statuary you'd see in front of a church or in the cemetery, but she has turned a grimy gray, almost black from the pollution constantly spewing from the factories in town: General Mills, which makes corn syrup, and Universal Wheel, which makes wheels for trains, and Union Carbide, which makes . . . I don't know what they make, pollution mostly, it seems. We're not sure what the angel is doing down by the river, standing there with her face tilted slightly away from the water, her eyes hooded and darkened by years of soot and dirt. It's hard to tell where she's looking— toward the bridge, watching it or watching the traffic as it moves back and forth, or is she looking at the sky, toward heaven, or is she looking lower, watching the river move past her, or maybe she's looking across the river at Illinois, waiting for something or someone to arrive on the other bank. Maybe she isn't looking at anything; it's hard to tell. Her eyes seem dead and lifeless in certain light. Maybe she's blind, her arms reaching out to feel her way through the world, blind like Justice or a wounded Greek god. She didn't seem to be in anguish or distress; she seemed sad, wanting something, I thought, but maybe I was wrong. I thought about her too much.

Some people think the angel looks peaceful, raising her arms in a gesture of acceptance and grace, while others think she looks sad, disappointed in her inability to rise off her pedestal. I think she's a little pissed, waiting there to catch someone jumping off the bridge, her arms still empty after all this time. I would like to jump to her, but not to have her catch me. I'd like to land on her and knock her off her perch. It seemed like a good goal, to hit her, to land on her, to be held by her—a morbid game, a strange version of ring toss. It never happened. The closest I ever came was hitting the pedestal. It would have counted only in horseshoes.

I have killed myself thirty-nine times. Usually when I say this—and I rarely do—people misunderstand me. They think I mean that I have tried thirty-nine times, that I have tried and failed. Do not misunderstand me—I have succeeded thirty-nine times; it is not me who has failed. It is something else.

I have killed myself thirty-nine times—which most people think is a lot. It's really a small number when you think about it. I mean, there are a lot more days I haven't killed myself. There are a lot more times I've decided not to try to end it all than days when I have. I've said that before—no one thinks it's funny except me. They're still fixated on thirty-nine, thinking that it's a lot. Maybe it is—all I know is that it's thirty-eight times more than I wanted and one less than I need. I'm still here; that's the worst part of the whole thing, unable to accomplish what should have been one small, inconsequential task but has become a larger failing to shape my own destiny. It is not the story I wanted to tell. The truth of it is, I didn't want any story at all. That was the whole point. Instead, I have had to account for each death and much more. I have become a scholar of death, a student of its various ways, and the more I learn, the less I know.

Thirty-nine. It seems small when I write it and smaller still when I break it down into how it was done. This is how I've done it: eighteen times by jumping (from bridge or building or other high place and once from the back of a truck), five by drowning, five by asphyxiation, four by poison/overdose, three by hanging, one by fire, one by gun, one by chain saw, and one by train. There are reasons for this. I live within a few miles of two bridges and a high bluff that look down to the Mississippi River. I can't go near the bluff or cross either bridge without seeing myself leaping out into the air, free-falling down toward a certain end. It's like a video that starts playing in my head every time I see the bridges or the bluff. I've watched that video thousands of times. It's my favorite, I guess. I'm a leaper.

I know this isn't normal. I'm not normal. I'm not even normal in how I choose to kill myself. Gunshot is usually the way to go—over sixty percent of the people who kill themselves use a gun. More than 18,000 people a year. I don't get it. For one, it's messy, and someone's going to have to clean up the mess you leave behind. Then there's the problem of getting a gun (if you're underage like me, it's a problem—not a big one, but still), then you have to load it (if necessary) and place it to your head, in your mouth, under your chin, and then you have to pull the trigger. There's too many steps, too much thinking involved, too much time to think, and too many times to wait, pause, stop. It's not like jumping—after the first step it's all over, nothing else to do but enjoy the ride down. Maybe I'm a coward, but I couldn't use a gun, not again anyway. Forget the maybe part. I am a coward. I know that. It's part of my problem.

I've been looked at by doctors and more doctors, doctors of every kind. They've poked and prodded at me, analyzed me, examined me, and talked to me—talked and talked and talked—and I have left them, almost without exception, shaking their heads. I don't want anything from them anyway, only to be left alone, but people (my family, mostly) want some explanation, some simple answer. Of course there are no easy answers. I'm a freak. There's something inside me that compels me to do what I do and something that prevents it as well. How screwed up is that? I don't get it. No one does, but mostly they think the problem is in my head. Maybe it is, but for me there seemed to be no other way to go about it. I look at the people around me— my parents especially—and I can't figure out how they can live the way they do, how they can go on day after day. My father is not an unhappy man, but he isn't anywhere close to happy either. He seems to go through the motions, an efficient program of actions—wake, shower, eat, work, eat, watch TV, sleep, repeat—micromanaging his existence to the minute, eliminating any wasted effort or spontaneity. He's the type of guy who thinks there's a right way and a wrong way for toilet paper to come off the roll—he's contemplated the issue, put serious thought to it, maybe even performed a test or two until it's a problem solved and he doesn't have to think about it anymore, unless it's done wrong and then he has to correct it and educate the person who has created the problem (usually me). It's over, by the way, never under.

I understand his desire for control—we are alike in that way. Except I take enjoyment in my actions—some of them—as hard as that might seem. I'm frustrated, restless, bored (very), but I'm not unhappy, depressed, or whatever other label they've tried to pin on me, and I'm certainly not an automaton like my father. I have more control of my life than they give me credit for (and less than I would like, believe me). I see that my father seems to take no comfort in his control, but he has no complaints either. His is a smooth, uninteresting road, which he has carefully, meticulously paved for himself.

While my father has few complaints—and the complaints he does have seem to be the same few repeated over and over—my mother does little but complain. Each day for her is a series of small traps that were set in the night while she was asleep, nothing lethal, only annoying, like getting caught time after time in those paper Chinese handcuffs. The trouble is, everything is a trap for my mother—the weather, the sky, the sun, the clock. She complains about the length of the straps on her purse: one day they are too long, the next too short; she complains about the humidity and its effects on her clothes and hair; she complains about the time it takes to make her morning tea and then complains that it's always too hot, which only traps her deeper inside the clock. While my father seems able to control every tick, my mother seems to always wake up ten minutes too late. She's always in a rush, always behind, no matter what she does—time is conspiring against her. She complains about it every day, and of course it's never anything she's done. Her road is anything but smooth, but she puts no effort into repair. Her job, it seems, is to find fault, not to fix anything. She moves through each day beset with problems, and she is continually providing her own narration in a half-hushed muttering of disappointment and correction. You can never make out exactly what she says, only a word or two here and there, but her cadence is always the same, like some epic blues song she is fated to sing over and over.

There are two things my mother never complained about: my brother and my father. She rarely complained about me, or not nearly as much as I gave her reason. Complaining is her way to feel as if she has accomplished something—the world is against her, but she is not defeated. She knows what's wrong with the world and everyone in it. They might set their traps, but she won't stay caught. She has her reasons—a need to vent her energetic anger or whatever that might help her get through her day—just as I have mine, or don't. I try not to peer too deeply into my whys; it's a tangle I'd prefer not to spend time picking apart, just as the whys of my return time after time seem inexplicable, beyond current understanding and reasonable explanation. No one seems as interested in the why of my refusal to leave this life, not nearly as interested in the why of my desire to leave. That they think they can fix. Why is that? Everybody's got their own disease, I think, but not everyone's got their own cure. I thought I did, but I was wrong.

My father is a loan officer down at the bank. Unfortunately, he's not one of those guys who ruined the economy. He didn't give anyone a loan he shouldn't have, didn't fudge any numbers, take any risks he shouldn't have, didn't do anything one inch this side of illegal or unethical. He's a safe-bet man, limited liability, which is why he works in a small bank in a small town, why we don't live in a bigger house and drive a better car. The most interesting thing I can tell you about him is that he is an amateur efficiency expert. He puts a stopwatch to everything—how long we take to wake up, how long we spend in the shower, how long we take to get dressed, how long to eat breakfast, how long to leave in the morning, how long I spend on the computer. This is where I get my interest in details, I suppose, my fascination with data, all that crap, a trait I only developed because of a certain gene passed down from my father. You can't outrun your blood. I don't try to impose my interests on others, usually. That's all my father does. He has timed it all and somehow developed an "optimal" time for all of these things. Overages are quickly reported. If you are in the bathroom longer than ten minutes in the morning, he's there banging on the door, yelling that you're wasting water or wasting his time.

My mother and I are the prime culprits in the household, make no mistake about that—we travel from room to room wasting something, demonstrating the great waste that seems so infuriatingly obvious to my father but still remains somewhere outside our mind's grasp. He would be better off living alone, with his rooms dark and quiet, his electricity tucked safely inside the walls, the water waiting inside the pipes, the dials on all the meters creeping forward as slowly as possible, not flying as you would think they are in our house. He tries to educate us, but we are slow learners. At least my father is not a stern man; in fact, he thinks he has a sense of humor.

My father likes to quote the best thinkers of his day—Bill Murray, David Letterman, Peter Sellers, everyone from *M*A*S*H*, and especially Woody Allen. "The world is separated into two categories," he said, trying to recite something from *Annie Hall,* "the tragic and the miserable. The tragic are people with handicaps, cripples, mentally impaired, all of that. And the rest of us are miserable. You're definitely not tragic, so you should be happy that you're miserable." The problem was, I wasn't miserable. I knew I wasn't tragic (my father was wrong about the categories, btw; horrible is the other category, according to Woody), but I never considered my life too miserable. We were a solid middle-class family in a small working-class town. My parents loved each other and me and my brother, as far as that went, and we never struggled or faced any hardship that was out of the ordinary. I was lucky; I knew that. It was something else.

"What's wrong with you?" my father asked me after I awoke from number eight.

"I'm bored. I'm the chairman of the bored." I didn't know what to say; I thought he'd like it, think it was funny. It seemed like something one of his guys would say.

"Boredom is just another form of depression," he said. I don't know what movie he got that from.

"If you're bored, do something," my mother said. "Read a book, watch TV, take a walk. Call somebody. This is no way to behave just because you're bored."

I did do something. Over and over. It's not what they had in mind.

Friends introduced, with crème de menthe

If you could pick four people to be stranded on a desert island with, who would they be? I know I wouldn't pick my friends, but then, I spent almost every day of the summer with them at The Point, which is practically the same thing. There's no one else around, our phones don't work, Todd has baseball practice or games, and Jodi won't come there. So it's just me and Ash and Bruce and Darryl and Vern. They remind me that the vise is turning.

I remember my mother once saying something along the lines of "you only find out who your true friends are when you're dead," which stuck with me. I've been dead thirty-nine times and I'm still not sure who my real friends are, and I'm less sure now than ever. I've been with the same hodgepodge collection of different personalities for most of my life. I've known most of them for at least eight years or more. We don't seem to like the same things as a whole, or no longer agree on most things, but it is the few things we agree on that seem to keep us connected. That and the fact that we have been hanging out together for so long, it has become a repetition that has excluded most others, keeping us insulated and isolated, together and apart.

The Point is over a mile from my house, down River Road—we always said "down," even though it was actually north, but the road sloped down from the height of the bluff to level with the river. The railroad tracks were built up on a mound, blocking the view of the river in some spots. We rode our bikes there in the morning and dragged them up and over the raised tracks and then down again and through bushes and tall grass and weeds. There had been a path cut years ago, and every spring we tried to find it again and clear a narrow trail to the end of the triangle.

We spent most of our time fishing, if that's what you could call it; it wasn't really fishing, but mostly just having a line in the water. We didn't really care if we caught anything. Having a fish on the end of a hook was actually more of a nuisance—we preferred to go to the same spot every day and drink and do as little as possible until it was time to go home in the evening.

"You know the only difference between fishing and not fishing?" Ash said. "In one of them you wish you weren't fishing."

We all arrived earlier than usual one morning and waited for Darryl to arrive with another bottle of wine. He'd found (or stolen) a case of it the last week of school, and had hidden the bottles in some undisclosed spot, and arrived every day with another bottle we let cool in the water for a few hours before we cracked it open. It was, we knew, some cheap, supermarket wine, but we treated it as if it were liquid gold, as if the act of drinking it somehow improved us, made us superior to our former selves, elevated us to a better, more refined class. Ash even arrived the second day with legitimate wine-glasses. They weren't anything fancy, old stemware he'd bought at a yard sale, but we treated them with care and carefully measured the wine from each bottle into equal parts, holding the rare drink in our new glasses and swirling it around a few times as we marveled at our good fortune and then guzzled it down with greedy delight. We felt better about ourselves because of the wine, there's no doubt about that, and those days would have been unbearable without it. There were some days when I could have handled an entire case of it and not feel the least bit drunk and other days when a few swallows would have made me unsteady. "It's the sun," Todd said. I don't think so; it was me. The trick was to act the same drunk as you acted sober. You had to maintain composure no matter what. We got drunk to feel different inside, not to behave like morons.

I was the last one to arrive one morning, and all of them, even Todd on one of his rare appearances at The Point, were already there, crowded at the northern edge, intently studying the water. They waved for me to join them and I hurried to the spot to discover a large dead cow that had washed up against our shore and had become entangled in some tree branches that had collected there over the spring. It was a large red-and-white Hereford, lying sideways among the tangle of branches, with a white head and white underbelly. "Beef," Ash said. "It's what's for dinner." Nobody laughed. We didn't know of any farms along the river. "Maybe somebody dumped her," Darryl said. We all

continued to stand on the bank and look at the large body suspended in the water. I wondered if it had fallen in—maybe it
had gotten loose and lost and disoriented and had fallen into the
river in the night—or if it had been dumped into the water, but
it was too big for one person to haul around. I wondered if she'd
jumped. Maybe she just thought to hell with it, she wasn't going
to wait around to get shipped off to the slaughterhouse and take
a shot to the head and have every part of her chopped up and
ground up and shipped who knows where.

The rest of them spent very little time wondering how it got
there, where it came from, and how far it traveled; we all marveled at our luck that this large beast had found us, had made its
way from some spot upriver to lodge directly in front of us. We
thought we were lucky.

The cow was slightly bloated and its hide looked slimy in the
water. Its legs were hidden by the dried tangle of limbs, but it did
not look in distress. In fact, the animal looked gentle and calm; its
mouth was open and the water pushed its way up through the
opening and spilled out over the jaw in a frequent drool, as if it
had laid down in order to take a much needed nap and fell quickly
into a deep sleep. Vern wanted to get a branch and free the dead
animal and watch it float down the river. Darryl wanted to scoop
out the eye and cut it in half to see what it was like inside. Todd
and Ash wanted to leave it alone so we could watch it decay and
turn into a skeleton.

It was huge, over a thousand pounds of literally deadweight—
the largest corpse any of us would probably ever see—washed up

right in front of us for all of us to look at, examine, observe, poke, and prod on limited occasions. We, of course, had to vote on it. You couldn't touch it without everyone being present, and you could only touch it, poke at it, with a long stick if everyone agreed. The main objective, we decided, was to watch it rot, and we were afraid that poking at it too much would somehow disrupt the natural course of things. It was like trying to not pick at a scab—sometimes you don't care about the consequences and you have to pick even if it all turns bloody.

Bruce had already named it. "Strand," he said. "Get it?" I did. We left it there, my namesake, drooling at us day after day, swelling even more in the heat until it began to ooze froth and filth into the water. Vern brought his camera every day and shot a few minutes of video; he tried to stand in the same spot and hold the camera at the same angle so he could make what he called "a poor man's time lapse," but he never got it right. The edited piece was a mess, with the cow jumping all over the place, magically moving from one part of the frame to the other, and of course he had to junk it up by putting shots of the rest of us in the thing—I didn't want him taking my picture at all, but he caught me napping one afternoon and used it in the video with the cow. It was a mess, but it still looked cool and racked up more than five thousand views in the first few days after Vern posted it. It wasn't even the finished video; we were still waiting for the last of the flesh to disappear and reveal the complete skeleton. "I told you I'd make Strand famous," he joked.

○ ○ ○

Vern took it for granted that he was going to be famous. The details were vague, but the end was always the same—somehow, someday, someone would come through town and discover the obvious genius that is Vern and would want to make him a star. He talked about it as if it were already happening, as if that person were on his way right now. It didn't matter that Vern had no discernible talent or that no one like that ever came through town.

"You don't have to have talent," Vern said. "Some of the most famous singers can't sing, some of the most famous actors can't act, and some of the most famous people in the world can't do anything at all except be famous. Any moron can be famous."

"You might be overqualified, then," Bruce said.

"That's a beer," Vern said.

"No it isn't," Bruce said.

"You broke the ban." There had been lots of bans over the past year or so. In fact, it seems as if we've banned everything—jokes about looks ("You can't make fun of something you can't control" is how Ash had introduced it), jokes about mothers, "gay" jokes, "racist" jokes, "sexist" jokes; we even banned swearing for a short while because Todd had heard somewhere that cursing was nothing more than a substitute for action, and that idea rubbed him the wrong way. He wanted action—this is from a guy who sits around most nights doing little more than tipping a bottle to his mouth. That's action.

It took a majority to implement a ban, but only a unanimous vote could lift it. It was becoming very complicated—too many rules and regulations, votes and vetoes. There had even been a discussion about banning bans, but that went nowhere. Sometimes I wondered if we were friends or some horrible society like the Shriners or the city council. We had decided, voted on it, that we couldn't call each other a moron or an idiot or say that someone was stupid. There had even been, a while ago, a debate as to whether you could use the phrase "that's stupid." It had been thrown around a lot (mostly by me, I have to say) and Vern in particular had been on the receiving end of much of its usage, usually referring to all the stupid things he said. Which *were* stupid. Which was almost everything. But without Todd around as much that summer, Vern had the votes, and a lot of stupid bans had been passed. The moron ban was one of them.

"Didn't we lift that ban?"

"No," Vern said. "Bruce owes me a beer."

"Ban or no ban, I don't owe you," Bruce said. "I didn't call you anything."

"We need a vote," Vern said.

"No vote," Bruce said.

"Just pay him the beer."

Bruce handed over the beer. "It pays to be a moron, doesn't it?" Vern didn't ask him for the second beer.

When Vern wasn't talking about himself becoming famous on his own, he was talking about becoming famous by making me famous. His big idea was for me to have my own reality show.

"How would that work?"

"Every week viewers could vote on how they wanted you to die and then you have to do whatever the winning thing is," Vern said.

"That would last two weeks, tops," Bruce said.

"Okay," Vern said. "What if you were a serial killer, but you only have one victim—yourself. I bet we could sell it with that one-sentence pitch."

"That's worse than the other one. How would that play out?"

"I don't know what the show would be, all right," Vern said, "but the concept is still good. They'd figure out the details. I mean, just look at all the people who have shows who have absolutely no talent whatsoever. You can at least do something, something no one else can do. They would give you a show. We should make a video and send it in. I bet you'd get an offer immediately. You'd be famous."

"I don't want to be on TV." I didn't know how to explain to Vern that there was something inherently contradictory about what I wanted and then trying to be famous for it. I wanted to reduce the number of people who knew me to zero, not multiply it. If I could, I would erase all memory of me.

"How about *Let's Kill Adam Strand* for the name of the show?" Vern said.

"Seems too gleeful."

"But it should be fun, right? Or else no one will watch," Vern said.

"How about *Die, Adam, Die*?" Bruce said.

"*Faster, Faster, Adam Strand, Die, Die.*" Vern wouldn't let it drop. "Or you could take over that *1,000 Ways to Die*, so it's just you every time. We should go out to LA."

"I thought your guy was coming here," Bruce said.

"What guy?"

"The guy that's going to make you famous," Bruce said.

"I meant for Adam," Vern said.

"I'm not going anywhere."

"Don't worry, none of us are."

None of us will amount to anything—that's the prevailing wisdom of our parents, teachers, coaches, friends, just about anyone you could ask—no one from here has ever amounted to much, no one famous or noteworthy—everyone has been nothing more than the least they could be, small and subordinate, but no less necessary, I guess. It doesn't bother me, but it bugs the shit out of Vern, and Ash and the rest, even Todd. They all want to leave, get as far from here as possible, do something better, live bigger— they all want it, talk about it, but I think Todd's the only one who would actually work for it. The rest of them are only talk.

It doesn't matter where we are—at The Point or down by the bridge, in the park, on the golf course, and in Todd's brother's car, if he can get it—we always do the same thing. Drink. It's something to do. Personally, I don't like it that much. The rest of them can't wait to get drunk. It's too much out of control for me. I like a drink or two, but I don't like getting stupid. The rest of them seem to want to get as stupid as they can as fast as they can.

The rule is that everyone has to bring something. Todd can buy liquor sometimes, depending on who's working. We usually buy beer. They don't seem to mind as much if you buy beer but get reluctant if you try to buy any hard liquor. That's all right by me; I don't mind beer. Everybody else tries to steal something from their parents' supply, usually some bottle from the back of the cabinet. Archie—who everybody calls Ash for some reason none of us can remember—always brings the worst stuff: Baileys Irish Cream, Drambuie, Tia Maria, an unopened bottle of crème de menthe. The crème de menthe was too much for Todd. "No more back-of-the-cabinet crap," he said. "I'm not handing out beers to everybody if this is what you're going to bring. It's not a fair swap. You have to drink the crème de menthe on your own, Ash. Drink the whole bottle and then go puke on yourself."

That's usually how it went when we were drinking. Sadly, even if we weren't. Unless Jodi was with us.

With Jodi and more often without

Everybody dreads birthdays, don't they? Especially their own. I can't think of a more pointless exercise than celebrating an event you really had nothing to do with—no control, no decision, no accomplishment other than being pushed into something, arriving on a more or less random date and time. I've never liked my birthday, even when I was little.

Of course the first one I remember was a disaster. We had moved from Oklahoma nine days before my fourth birthday. I was born in Norman, Oklahoma, which might be the only place I can think of that's worse than here. My brother remembers Oklahoma. He wishes he didn't.

My father went to the university there and hung around working at one bank and then another until he met my mother, who was finishing school. She's originally from Chicago, so they say that's how they picked here—it's the midpoint between Norman and Chicago, but it's not really. Still, it's what they say whenever the subject comes up, which it almost never does, but at least they have an explanation prepared anyway.

We didn't know anyone when we moved here, but my mother had a birthday party for me anyway, inviting the kids in the neighborhood. Maybe ten showed up. My mother thought there would be a bigger turnout, and she wasn't happy. I remember that. She had three long folding tables set up on the deck in back of the house, with plastic tablecloths that had pirates on them, balloons, colored napkins, and pointed cardboard hats. There wasn't a theme, obviously, only a strange assemblage of party clichés. The kid sitting next to me, Matt Boeringer, peed his pants within the first ten minutes. And never said a word about it. I still can't see him without immediately recalling the smell. At least he tried to keep his mess to himself.

After we had cake and ice cream, Kaitlyn Douglas threw up all over the pirates, which led to a yard full of shrieking, hysterical kids running around gagging, trying desperately to keep their own chocolate cake inside them. I would wish for someone, even Kaitlyn Douglas (who has long since moved away) to come and vomit at one of my parties now—at least it would be a welcome change from the bland, almost-grim rites they have become. I don't help matters, I know, and I can't really blame my parents, but I would prefer if the day passed unnoticed. My mother won't hear of it. So we have the usual cake and ice cream after dinner and my father hands me the same practical gift he has given me since I turned twelve, which is an envelope with a receipt for the amount he's deposited in my college fund.

I hate birthdays. I hate holidays. I hate the calendar, which is both a circle and straight line, a wheel and an arrow, grinding around and shooting forward at the same time, each spin, each anniversary, each day a reminder of my failures, my lost plans, unfulfilled objectives and wishes—the days aren't taken off the calendar, subtracted one by one, but added, another small stone accumulated, another foot moved ahead, the arrow flying forward instead of falling back to earth, when all I want is a complete stop.

The only good thing that happened at that first birthday in town, or at any birthday for that matter, is that I met Jodi. She wasn't from the neighborhood, but, according to Jodi's mom, my mother saw them at the store when she was stocking up on party stuff and invited her. I don't remember her being there that day—nothing remarkable happened, nothing memorable—but we both remember the disaster it was. In fact, the event would have probably passed into the dim shadows of lost history if we hadn't met again on the first day of preschool.

She started crying the second her mother left her in the morning, and for some reason, Mrs. Bradley brought her to me. I was playing with something—Jodi remembers it as a plastic pony, while I like to think of it as a plastic pistol—and whatever it was, or whatever I was doing, seemed to calm her or distract her and she stopped crying. We've been friends ever since. If somebody put a knife to my heart (and they have), I would probably say that Todd is my best friend, but it's really

Jodi. She's known me the longest, knows more about me than anyone else, and doesn't care about the bad stuff. I like it when she hangs out with us, but she usually only comes if she can convince some of her girlfriends to come along. It's not an easy convincing.

I'm not in love with death, but it's the best of my bad options (#1)

As I mentioned, there are two bridges in town, and they're within a few hundred feet of each other. The older bridge is all iron, built almost a hundred years ago or something like that, and hasn't been in use for over five years. It stands there like a carcass picked clean, its bones hung out for everyone to look at and be reminded how inadequate it was. The new bridge is solid, heavy, a massive, soaring, slightly curved concrete that doesn't at all appear to rise out of the water but forcefully sits in it, planted, as if steadying itself for a fight. The old bridge, on the other hand, is airy, frail; the iron gridwork seems too delicate to hold a single car, let alone the hundreds, thousands, the millions that crossed over it. Now it is left, discarded, like the steamboat that sits downriver. It isn't even worth tearing down, I guess, so it has to wait there, forgotten and lonesome, with its middle hanging out open, until it rusts and decays and time and the river can take it. It was fine for decades and decades, and now it's not even good enough for scrap.

It was too low, for starters. The middle section had to swing open to allow barges and larger boats through. This meant that traffic had to be stopped while the center detached and swung parallel to the river, the boats and barges allowed to pass, and then the section swung back in place and the barricades lifted and the anxious drivers started their cars and continued. No one wanted to get stuck on the bridge when it opened—it was a long process, maybe twenty minutes at its fastest, sometimes lasting as long as an hour and a half, depending on the length of the barges, the number of them, and how well they coordinated with the bridge operator, who sat in his box of an office, barely bigger than a phone booth, watching the river and waiting to drop the wooden gates and trap the traffic trying to get across the river. I always thought it would have been a great job, being the man in that box, but no one sits there now.

I loved watching the middle section of the bridge swing open, as easily as a gate, seeming to weigh no more than your arm, bending at the elbow until it stopped perpendicular to your bicep. Few people seemed to enjoy it as much as me; it was a nuisance that had to be endured, and best to be avoided. The problem was, nobody knew when the bridge was going to open. There was no schedule or even much warning. The red lights would come on and the gates would close and that would be it—you were going to be on the wrong side of the bridge for a half hour or more. People would get out of their cars and lean against the railing, smoke cigarettes, talk to their neighbors, throw coins or trash into the river below.

It was nighttime when we were on the bridge, my older brother, Michael, in the passenger seat and my mother driving. My father was out of town somewhere, so Mom had taken us across the river for dinner. We were coming back when the traffic stopped. Everything seemed to stop. My mother and brother were as still and quiet in the front seat as cardboard cutouts. A string of red taillights stretched ahead of us by fifteen or sixteen cars. Cars passed us going the opposite way, but they ran out as the rest of them were left waiting on the other side of the wide gap up ahead. We sat there in silence for at least fifteen minutes until I heard a sound, nothing more than a noise at the edge of my hearing. At first I wasn't sure if it was coming from outside the car or inside, and then I realized that it was coming from inside me, a sound I'd never heard before, a low murmur, maybe a voice. It wasn't in my ears but seemed to be coming from inside my bones. As it grew louder, I realized that it wasn't a voice—I'm not even sure if it was a specific sound; it seemed more like a tone, an enveloping note that filled me, that almost shook me as it emanated inside me, a strange, meaningful roar, like the roar of a crowd at a baseball game, urging a player on, a thousand individual voices making one unified sound, but it wasn't that; it was unlike anything I'd ever heard before, but I seemed to recognize it and knew instantly what it meant. I felt like a tuning fork, vibrating after it's been struck. I rolled down the window to see if that would help, to see if that would let some of the sound out of me, but it didn't change anything. It was an urging, a calling, a beckoning, an invitation and plea.

I opened the car door and walked to the edge of the bridge and looked over the railing into the water. The older bridge was low, close to the water, no more than seventy-five feet above the river at its highest spot. It looked closer than that; I could make out each wave below; the white crests seemed close enough that I could reach down and pet them like a cat. The sound had changed, now it was an action, or a desire for one. I could feel every muscle and every thought aligning to go over the bridge, as if urging me on, convincing me, convincing my mind and my body to go. I wasn't afraid. I loved the way the water looked, dark and peaceful, with tender lights shimmering on the surface. I loved the feel of the bridge, the cool iron railing and the iron grating at my feet. It was sturdy and strong, but my feet wanted to leave, my whole body wanted to go. I didn't look back at my mother or Michael; I climbed quickly to the top of the railing, which was about as wide as a balancing beam, a perfect spot to take an evening leap, so I jumped.

I remember the air was crisp and cold; it tasted like a tart apple. It made me thirsty. I couldn't wait to hit the water. But I don't remember that. The next thing I remember was waking up in the hospital the next day. Everyone was surprised to see me.

"We thought you were dead," my mother said.

"You were dead," my father added.

I felt good, better than I had for a long time, although I remember being disappointed that my family was there. I would have liked to have remembered, or at least tried to remember. They wouldn't let me think. It was a barrage of questions, none of which I wanted to answer. I couldn't explain anything, but that wasn't good enough. Then the doctor came in and he had more questions, then another doctor. I was ten years old; I didn't know what they expected from me.

My mother kept returning to the same question, or a variation on the same theme: "Why aren't you happy?" "How can we make you happy?" "What makes you so sad?" I wish I could have explained to her that it had nothing to do with being happy or sad, that those questions missed the point completely. They still do. No one is "happy" all the time or "sad" all the time, are they? I don't know, they seem like transitory things, like the weather; they come and go; nothing is a permanent state. That's part of the problem. I didn't like the transitory nature of any of it. I didn't like being young, and I didn't like the fact that I would get older; I didn't like the fact that I would gain weight, grow taller, grow out of my favorite shirt, have to get my hair cut, would need to shave one day, brush my teeth every day, graduate from one grade and move on to the next, leave home, go to college, get a job, retire, die. None of it interested me. I never got the point. For me, anyway. I'm sure there are people who are perfectly content with any of those things, and maybe there's somebody who's happy with all of it, but it wasn't for me. I should have been born a rock, or permafrost, a clump of coal miles underground that will never be disturbed, or some molecule on some distant planet that will never be discovered or touched by anyone, that will just stay there frozen in space, isolated and alone, no one even aware of its existence or the possibility that it might exist. That's what I should have been, or not born at all. How do you tell that to your mother?

It didn't make the papers or even the local news. Nobody told them they had a miracle in their midst. Boy Cheats Death. Boy Rises from the Grave. You'd think that would be the type of story they'd like, but nobody said a word. It was just as well. My parents thought the less said about it, the better. They seemed to know that something was amiss, that this was just the beginning, a small trickle compared to the torrent of trouble ahead. My brother was horrified. He's five years older than I am and probably knew that his freak of a brother would cause him a lot of grief. He was right.

It didn't take long for rumors to start, and the entire tenth grade seemed to focus on Michael, peppering him with every rumor that spread through the halls, classrooms, and especially the bath-rooms and cafeteria of the high school.

My brother was popular at school. He was a good student, was on the varsity track team three years, and played the lead in a couple of school plays (*You Can't Take It with You* and *Arsenic and Old Lace*), and got in just enough trouble that no one thought he was a simp. He should have kept his mouth shut, however, if he wanted to keep everything quiet. That's what my parents told him to do—don't say anything. Only a few people had seen my mother rush to the railing of the bridge, looking for me in the dark water below. She'd laid on the car horn, hysterically wanting the bridge to swing shut, but that could be explained away easily enough. Lots of people went hysterical on the bridge waiting for the barges to crawl through, and no one paid any attention to the honking. Nobody, it seems, had actually seen me jump, except for my own family. So, say nothing, that's what Michael should have done; instead, while not saying exactly what had happened, he admitted that something had happened, that I had been in the hospital, and he was just glad to have me back. Well, that just led to more and more questions, rumors, and unwanted attention. He wanted it all to go away. Even though everybody was talking to him, he could feel his popularity slipping away. Things weren't going to be the same. We all knew that. You'd think that it might at least bring us closer together, my brother, my parents, and me. Instead, we drifted apart, imperceptibly at first, like the first ripples from a rock thrown into the still water, still close to the center, but moving.

It wasn't all drifting—I helped push. I remember lying in the hospital, with my brother sitting in a chair next to the bed, looking at me with concern and damp, pleading eyes. "We're all pulling for you, you know," he said.

I didn't say anything for a moment, then, "When you tell me things like that, it only makes me want to do it more."

I know that what I've done is selfish, but only in the same way that a diabetic is selfish about what they eat, that a person who has allergies to cats or dogs is selfish about avoiding those animals, the way an alcoholic is selfish about avoiding people who drink. I know I'm selfish, and I've tried to fix it, believe me.

My brother couldn't wait for high school to end. I'm sure he thought those four years took up his whole life, and when he left, he left for good. And I'm still here, despite my best efforts.

Just a wave, not the water (#2)

After the first "attempt" (is it an attempt if you succeed?), the ringing sound, or tone, that had filled me was quieted, but what was left was a longing, an ache, a lingering that I wanted it back. I wanted all of it back, the sound, the urge, the sensation, the leap, the fall, all of it. I imagine it's like the first time you hit a home run, win a race, hear/play a great song, get good and drunk; it's like how you feel after your first kiss or the first time (or any time, probably) you have sex. You want that feeling back as soon as you can get it. You want to be filled up and emptied out in the same way. I don't know what you call it, but I wanted it back. And I wanted to see if I could do it again, but have it last this time.

This is part of who I am; I know that now, but I wasn't so sure when it first began—it's like if you picked up a baseball for the first time and threw a ninety-mile-an-hour strike. You'd want to see if you could do it again. It was always there; I just didn't realize it.

It wasn't the bridge the next time, but the bluff. The two-hundred-foot bank extends above the dam, rising steeply at first, then leveling along Grand Street, which is lined with huge homes that look out over the river and peer across to the Illinois side. Grand Street is twelve blocks long, almost exactly a mile, and then turns into River Road, which still follows along the bluff, but the bluff has turned into an erratic, rocky ledge that is steep in some spots, almost like a cliff looking down at the railroad tracks next to the river, and more of a slope in other parts, overgrown with bushes, small trees, and brambles in the summer months. This part extends for less than half a mile before the bluff slowly slopes down to the same level as the river.

There is a park across the bluff at the start of River Road (or the end, if you are coming from the north, following the direction of the river), a large garden that has a maze of stony paths that lead through it and a large meadow lined with tall maples and oaks that have been there for a century and a half or more. It was all probably beautiful once—people probably came with their picnic baskets and spread blankets in the meadow and ate their lunch or dinner and then walked to the wooden benches along the bluff and sat and watched the barges and steamboats move down the river. None of that happens now. The meadow is almost always empty, and the garden has been closed for a number of years.

These are places that I knew all my life, places I had passed almost daily, that had become bland and meaningless, almost without shape or definition, like cardboard scenery in some boring grade school play. But suddenly, the bluff was new; every inch of its edge, every outcropping and ledge was full of opportunity and possibility; there was an entire undiscovered world there, a movie, a story, a beginning, and most certainly an end.

There's a low fence along the edge of the bluff, a double strand of rusty cable running through wooden posts that are no more than three feet high, but there's talk of building a taller fence. That talk came about because of me, I'm sorry to say.

I love the river. I love everything about it—the way it looks from the bluff, two hundred feet above, where you can see the path it has cut into the earth as it makes its way south; the way it looks down near the bridge, where it appears to be moving like an enormous beast, one heaving mass of water sliding past; the way it looks in winter when it refuses to freeze, but pushes the ice toward the shore in towers of glass-sharp sheets and a channel still cutting its way through, the water almost clear for once; I love the way it looks, with its murky, muddy color when it's still and a dark blue when it's really moving and clear and white as it slides through the gates of the dam and rushes down to rejoin itself and continue on unvexed to the sea—it never looks the same, but changes all the time—but of course it does; it's different all the time, with new water coming by and replacing the old, whatever was there a moment ago is gone; the way the river spills its banks every spring, shouldering its way across the low parts of the cities up and down the river, frequently extending the floodplain as a warning to us not to get too close, purging itself in an annual ritual as it deposits mud, silt, and our own garbage back to us; I love the legends about the catfish as large as grown men that live at the bottom, old and far too smart to ever get caught, let alone seen; I even love the foul smell that rises from it in the spring and hot summer months; I love the way it holds the pollution close like a shroud it can hide behind for a while.

I like to watch the water and think about the billions of waves that rise and then quickly fall back below, existing only for a minute and then becoming part of the river again. I like to think about the trillions of drops of water that make the river, how you can't see a single drop, you don't even realize that they're there, all huddled together trying to get from Minnesota to Louisiana, losing some, gaining some along the way, but the river keeps going, pushing its way along, the massive tonnage of all those drops, with enough force to wipe out houses and buildings, entire towns.

There used to be severe rapids upriver from the bridges, and it's there that they built the one thing I don't like about the river: the dam. It was built in 1913 and at the time was the second-longest dam in the world—only the Aswan dam on the Nile was longer—with one hundred and twenty gates to control the river. The dam erased the rapids, but it can't control the river. As one Missouri farmer said after he'd lost his house in a flood, "You only need to know one thing: the river is going to do what it wants."

The first time was spontaneous, a flood that rose within me and swept me out of the car and over the railing, but the second time was premeditated. I thought about my jump from the bridge, waking up in the basement of the hospital, and I thought about the blank in between. I thought about it all the time for almost two weeks, wondering if I could do it again, only better. It had to have been a fluke, like guys who fall out of planes and survive, get struck by lightning over and over, freakish stuff. Maybe it had something to do with the water. They say you need about a hundred feet over land to ensure that you won't survive and almost two hundred over water. I had the reverse, a two-hundred-foot-high bluff and a bridge that wasn't quite a hundred. I had to try, if only to disprove a theory that was formulating in my mind.

We were running around the park, playing chase. Todd had invented the game, which was sort of team tag, where you separated into two equal (more or less) teams and one team had a head start of thirty seconds and then the other team ran after them and tried to capture all members of the first team. You had to stay in the park, but if one member could elude capture (being tagged) until dark, that team won, but if all members were captured, the second (pursuing) team won. It was really an excuse to run around like crazy until dark. The bluff, which was technically still part of the park, was out-of-bounds, since its thick undergrowth provided too-perfect cover, but I ran there anyway once I knew I was out of sight. I found a spot under a low bush and hid there until dark. It was probably more than an hour, but it seemed as if only a few minutes had elapsed. I kept thinking about my dive from the bridge, trying to remember how it felt, my feet leaving the railing and then the fall into the water, the air pushing against my legs and arms and chest, the fresh smell and crisp taste of the air—I tried to watch myself, not to see what I saw, but look at it as if I were right there beside me, like a camera following me down. This time would be different—there would be no water, only the rocky bed for the railroad tracks, the ties, and if I was lucky, I might hit one of the rails. And it was higher, over twice as high as the bridge. In the end, it wasn't the same, but it wasn't different.

The Point, the bridge, and the emergence of the pestilence of Mormon flies and Troy Liddell

We had stayed too long at The Point, drunk too much wine in the heat of the afternoon, and we all felt miserable. None of us wanted to get on our bikes and pedal back up the slope to our homes and eat the crap our mothers were making for dinner. We would have called and told them we couldn't make it, but The Point was in a different century, so we sat and complained about what we had to do instead of just doing it and getting over it. "I'd trade places with that cow right about now," Vern said.

Vern had been named by Bruce. The name that had been given to him at birth was Sterling, after his father's favorite actor, Sterling Hayden, but no one called him by his rightful name. Vern was his name, derived from Sterling in a very Bruce-like way: *vern* from *ver* from *silver* from *sterling silver.* Vern. It made complete sense, to Bruce.

Vern always says he's never seen a Sterling Hayden movie,

and we always have to correct him. "Michael Corleone shoots him in the head, remember?"

He remembers.

Why would your dad name you after some guy that gets shot in the head?" Ash asked.

"It's not the only thing he's done," Vern said. "He's in a bunch of movies."

"How would you know; you just said you've never seen any of them," Todd said. "Maybe he gets shot in the head in all of them. Maybe that's his whole career."

"Maybe," Vern said. He always said "maybe" when he was done talking. Nobody wanted to talk about Sterling Hayden anyway; even Vern's father never talked about him, and he never called his son Sterling either. He called him Vern just like the rest of us. Everybody did.

"He's in Dr. Strangelove." I knew that one. I rarely knew about movies, but I knew this one. My father liked to throw around phrases from the movie—"gammy leg," "I'm not saying we wouldn't get our hair mussed," "precious bodily fluids," and his favorite: "I've been to one world fair, a picnic, and a rodeo and that's the stupidest thing I ever heard." He made me watch it a few years ago. I didn't think it was that funny, but I did like the fat cowboy, and it had a young Darth Vader in it. Sterling Hayden plays a psychotic Air Force general who starts World War III. I can't remember if he gets shot in the head.

"I'd rather eat it than what my mom is making," Ash said.

I stood up and felt the earth try to pull me back down. My legs were weak and I wasn't sure I could even make it to my bike, let alone ride the stupid thing. "I'm leaving. Who's going with me?"

"Can't we just stay here?" Vern said. "Let's not go home; let's not go to the bridge."

It was a good idea—it really was—but we went anyway. It's what we always did.

I took my time getting to the bridge after dinner, meandering along the homes along the bluff on Grand Street, taking my time, trying to get in touch with Jodi to see if she'd come, trading texts with Todd, who was once again running late. I was still the first one to get there.

It was just me and the angel and the first appearance of the summer of the Mormon flies, disgusting bugs that looked like dark, slender shrimp with wings. They came out of the river almost every summer, millions of them flying around for a day, breeding another batch for the next season and then dying, dying everywhere, on the houses, the lawns, the trees, the roads, the bridge. They smelled like rotting fish and were road hazards where they collected and were squished into slick patches—there was a report in Burlington that they had collected almost eight feet deep on a road during one particularly hot and humid summer. It was called the "black snowstorm." The old bridge was built with iron grating so the flies could fall back into the river instead of building up on the road, as slippery and dangerous as ice. The new bridge, with its concrete deck, has to have the snowplow come out in the heat of summer and scrape the mess off the road.

When we were little, we would grab a board and swing at the flying Mormon flies because they would make a bubble-wrap-like pop if you hit them just right. With millions of them flying around, a broad enough board, and a strong enough swing, you could get that sound by the hundreds.

I sat and waited for the rest of them, suddenly too sober, but content to look at the bridges. My bridges.

While we Americans prefer to blow our brains out more than any other populace, five of the top-ten places to kill oneself in the world are bridges:

10. Jacques Cartier Bridge, Montreal, Quebec

9. Aurora Bridge, Seattle, Washington

8. Eiffel Tower, Paris, France

7. Coronado Bridge, San Diego, California

6. Prince Edward Viaduct, Toronto, Ontario

5. Clifton Bridge, Bristol, England

4. Beachy Head, East Sussex, England

3. Niagara Falls, New York–Ontario border

2. Golden Gate Bridge, San Francisco, California

1. Aokigahara Forest, Mount Fuji, Japan

Nine of the ten spots include jumping. Not bad, but I like my own bridges. Both of them. I don't know what I like better—the bridge, the water, or the air on the way down.

I wish I could have seen the new bridge while it was being built, seen the first pilings driven into the river, seen the span extended foot by foot as it turned empty air into a road, watched as they curved it slightly to the south, an unnoticeable bend as you travel across but one you can see from the side or at either end. Instead, I remember it only in leaps, large sections of completion, too much work accomplished from one time to the next. Honestly, I barely remember it being built at all. It wasn't there, and then suddenly it was, with cars moving across as if it had always existed and I had not noticed it.

If the new bridge is artful efficiency and grace, the old bridge is a stoic essence, the raw nature of what a bridge is—a functional conveyance, with its pieces all on display—welded metal, grids and angles, a mechanical sweep from one bank to the other with a movable midsection, which few people appreciated as it swung away from its primary purpose and brought all car traffic to a halt in order to let barges full of coal or corn or who knows what move up and down the Mississippi. And now it stands mostly useless, useless to everyone but me. It is there for me, only for me, I think sometimes, my bridge.

There's something inviting about water, whether it's a pond, a stream, or a river, whether you see it up close or far away. I like the way the water looks, like a distant foreign world, or when it reflects like a mirror—it's different every time you look at it, always holds your attention. The river water is ugly, I guess, brown and gray in the daylight, but it's still better than land. I prefer the water at night, when the sludge brown color of day becomes a thick black. The water, especially from the bridge, looks as if it is all one piece, a solid mass of darkness moving downstream, quietly prowling like some nocturnal animal.

The air smells like an animal sometimes, especially on humid nights in the summer, and it leans heavy against you. Other times it is thick and damp, like trying to inhale a soaked towel that someone has set on fire, and then other nights the air feels as if it is trying to pull you down, trying to pull you off the bridge with its hot and heavy arms. And in the winter the air is as sharp as a frozen sword, where every breath stings and hurts, or it whips down the river and feels like a fire hose as it comes over the dam and barrels into you on top of the bridge, anxious to give an unnecessary push. And on the best of nights, standing there on the rail of the bridge, right before I jump, the air smells the way it does before a spring storm or before a tornado, calm and heavy with expectation, an eerie, electric anticipation, a cleansing air, clear and fresh and promising something new.

The world is perfect when you're dead. There are no problems, no grief, no distress, disgust, no disease, discomfort, or disappointment; there's no shame, sadness, betrayal, or boredom; nothing is lost or gained, nothing is wasted or wanted, nothing is said or left unsaid, nothing is remembered or recalled or reminded, nothing lingers. Nothing is nothing, and everything is quiet and calm. It's perfect. Maybe that's what heaven is, a perfect nothing, an emptying out of everything until you are as clean as the moment before your first breath, a serene absence of everything. Maybe it's not even a place, but I've been there, traveled there many times. I know what it's like. The world is perfect there. Or maybe you're perfect and the world is the same.

The river, the bridge, the angel—they were almost perfect for me, the three of them collected there in a holy trinity below the dam, but the river above the dam, as looked at from the height of the bluff, was almost perfect as well. The river there, depending on the light, looked like a sliver scar scratched into the earth, a trail of liquid gold, a dirty skid mark, a comfortable ditch of dirt, and at night it looked like a slice of the Milky Way, cut off and fallen from the sky, a flat asphalt road, a dark meditation, a deep abyss staring blankly up past the bluff and right at me. And the bluff was long enough and overgrown enough that you could find a secluded spot, a private, undisturbed place away from everyone else, while the spot below the dam was, if not popular, at least well known and frequented by people I did not like and did not want to be around. Part of me wanted to leave it all alone, and another part wanted to keep going back, if only to keep others away.

The others were scurves, white trash from the south side of town. They were led by Troy Liddell, one of the three or four feared people in school. He liked to pick fights, and he usually won. He didn't look like much of a threat: he was tall and thin and goofy-looking with an almost-cartoon aspect to him. But he was not cartoonish, he was terrifying—a local terrorist who scared the shit out of most of us with beatings, threats, and a small group of scurves who he needed around, the kind who would have hijacked planes if Troy told them to. I thought he looked like a coyote, and he seemed to fight like one, all thin arms and elbows, thrashing away with nothing to lose. He would sit on the hood of a car before school and ask questions as we passed by. "Do you smoke pot?" If you answered yes, you got beat up; if you answered no, you got the same. There was no rhyme or reason to it, only Troy's sense of fun and whatever mercy he decided to mete out that day or night.

Troy and his following, mostly underclassmen who had decided to join Troy instead of being beat by him, liked to drive around and look for trouble. Troy had an old van that you knew was crammed with scurves waiting for a fight, and he would go up and down Main Street looking for someone who wanted to fight or didn't, depending on his mood and how much he'd had to drink.

The usual spot to turn around on the southern end of Main was the Holiday Inn parking lot, where cars accumulated to watch the traffic go past. The street diverged after that, with some of the traffic merging onto the approach for the bridge and some of it (usually none) going down the hill to the statue and steamboat and us. We usually had the place to ourselves, but Troy was one of the few who would come down. Troy and his group mostly stayed over by the van or by the old steamboat, but there were times when they would come over by the statue. We would slowly retreat away from them, moving under the bridge or walking up the hill to the populated and safer parking lot or, on very rare occasions, we would offer some crème de menthe or other horrible liquor to Troy and his crew. They always took it.

Troy Liddell was a senior, for the second time. The rumor was that he flunked on purpose because his father had threatened to ship him off to the army when he graduated, so Troy was going to stay in high school another year until he turned eighteen. I didn't believe it. He failed because he was stupid and lazy. He might have failed again if he'd had the chance. Instead, he went to prison, or the boys' home, or somewhere else anyway.

I don't know what Troy's father did; no one seemed sure about his line of work. Everybody said he was a drunk, and the only times I'd ever seen him (twice), he was drunk. The first time was one winter. We were playing football in the park. The snow was about a foot deep on the field, which we liked—it made for a slogging, tiring, low-scoring game. At some point we started getting bombarded by snowballs from behind a small hill, and we abandoned our football game and began to return fire. We had no idea that it was Troy Liddell and his friends. The minute we found out, we stopped throwing with much frequency or accuracy. It was better not to hit any of them, we thought; they'd be on us like a pack of, well, coyotes. They eventually seemed to grow tired of pelting us with snowballs and stopped their fire, and we returned to our game, but after a couple of plays they started pelting us again. Suddenly a pickup truck screeched to a halt on the road near their cover and this man jumped from the back of his truck as if he'd been hiding there and rushed toward the hill.

We saw Troy dash out from behind the hill and he ran straight toward us, with the man chasing him. "You better run," the man was screaming. "I'm going to kill you as soon as I catch you." He had a stocking cap perched on a wild thatch of dark hair, his face red with cold and more—we could smell the alcohol hang in his wake. He was a short, burly man and ran with his legs splayed wide apart as he bobbed and weaved through the snow while his coyote son moved in a thin dash, his legs seeming to slice through the drifts like whips. They ran past us and down the hill, both of them falling frequently in the deep snow and then rising like white ghosts as they dashed off, the snow flung from them in dissipating clouds.

"Who is that guy?" Todd asked.

"That's Troy's dad," Ash said.

"If he'd run to the road, he'd catch him," Bruce said, applying logic to an illogical situation.

We noticed that the truck had driven off, leaving the father and son to find their own way or maybe circling around a different way. We never found out, and in about fifteen minutes, none of us really cared. We hoped that Mr. Liddell would catch his son and kill him like he promised or at least beat him, the way Troy had beat some of us. But we also suspected that whatever beating Troy received, he would give plenty more in return. And sure enough, he was there the next day, sitting in a different spot outside of school, picking on somebody else, asking them some stupid question and then chasing them down the sidewalk before giving them a pounding before first period. That was before he turned eighteen. He didn't do the actual beatings anymore. Now he had one of his little troop of thugs do it for him. It couldn't have been nearly as satisfying, we thought, but that was little comfort to those on the other end.

A ban of brothers

None of us had girlfriends. Well, Ash always claimed to have someone. Never anyone from our high school, of course, but always some girl we didn't know, "some girl from across the river" (Illinois? Missouri?) was about as specific as he'd ever get. There weren't too many people who would admit to dating somebody from Missouri.

And Ash liked to give a lot of advice. Mostly about all the sex he'd had. "When the woman's on top, never let her sit straight up. She's going to want to, but don't let her. Make sure she's still leaning down. Grab her by the back of the neck if you have to."

"What woman is on top of you? Your mom?" Vern said.

"That's a beer," Ash said.

"No it isn't. We lifted that ban," Vern said. He knew it wasn't true. Ash always voted to keep the ban to protect his own mom. Vern owed Ash a beer. It was hard to keep from saying something; there was plenty to say about Ash's mom. Whenever they show those videos to demonstrate how fat Americans are, you know, those shots of only women's bellies, thighs, asses, well, Ash's mom is always in there.

I honestly don't think I would care as much that she was fat if she wasn't such a miserable sow. She has a face like a cauliflower, pale and sour, with bulging blossoms all over it. She's really the only parent in the group I can't stand. None of us can. She has an open disdain for us and never wants us in the house. She always makes a comment or two when we're over there. I had my feet up on the coffee table one time—Ash had just had his there a second before his mom entered the room—and she said, "I chopped off the legs of the last kid who did that," and God forbid she should see you eat or drink something. "I'll add that to your bill," she always said. You might think that she's joking, except that she has told Ash not to bring us around. She thinks that he can have better friends. I want to tell her that no, he can't. We're as good as he's ever going to do. And believe me, we're all sad about it.

I'm on fire (#15)

There's a rule in high school that if your parents are gone for the weekend, you have to host a party. It wasn't a choice or consideration; it was an obligation. Michael was a junior when it happened. Our parents left on the first weekend of October, left us alone for the longest they'd ever left us alone, and headed up to Chicago. Michael knew what it meant and tried to keep it a secret, but he was terrible at that. Our parents had told us on Tuesday, and by Thursday everybody seemed to know, and by the end of the school day on Friday everyone was talking about the party my brother was going to have on Saturday night. Michael had never planned a party, had never wanted one, but it was going to happen anyway. It was the price you paid for having parents leave town.

The host didn't have to do much except let anyone show up at the party and provide the beer—although you could collect money from anybody who came. Most parties were out of town, in a field somewhere or down by the river—ragged, feral affairs that seemed to attract people for miles and miles, and not just kids. There were usually fights or the threat of fights, people not paying for beer or sometimes even stealing the keg and driving off with it. And then there was the weather, with us standing around in the rain or the cold. So it was always a big deal when a house was left unguarded by its owners. People really showed up for these parties. Of course the person who hosted the party was usually caught by his/her parents—it's impossible to have a hundred or so high school kids come in and out of a house unnoticed and usually enter sober and loudly leave drunk. Neighbors tend to notice; sometimes the cops get called. Nothing good comes from it, but there isn't much you can do about it. Michael wanted none of it, but it was too late. Everything was already in motion, gathering momentum as each day, then hour, then minute, passed.

We had a house on the corner, with a large backyard that was edged with tall bushes and four spruces. Saturday was an unseasonably warm day, and Michael decided that if people were going to come over, they could stay in the backyard, but they weren't coming inside. He had one of his friends go buy a keg, and he set it up underneath the back deck and put out some folding chairs he dragged up from the basement. He didn't even want anyone on the deck, but he knew that was too much to ask. He kept the front door locked all day, and when the first "guests" starting arriving around six, he went out to the yard and locked the back door behind him. I went with him. I didn't want to miss my first high school party.

It was almost ten o'clock before I had my first beer. Todd

and Ash had left by then—Michael had sent us inside at one point to patrol the house, looking for anyone who might have picked the locks, I guess, or entered through the keyhole like smoke. By nine, however, Michael didn't care. He was drunk and enjoying himself. Everyone was outside, and the one person he should have worried about had been inside with me. Ash would become notorious for pulling stupid stuff—emptying all the bottles in the medicine cabinet, putting stuff in the beds (frozen foods were a personal favorite), disconnecting TVs, changing the clocks, mostly idiotic stuff that would need explaining when the parents returned. The worst thing he did was unplug the freezer over at Claire Vandever's house, which ruined a lot of meat, maybe a full cow's worth. Ash thought it was hilarious, but those pranks were still years ahead of him; that night he poured a box of cereal in Michael's bed. Nothing harmful, just a little nuisance for when my brother crawled into bed later, drunk and exhausted. And funnier if he was with a girl, Ash thought. I didn't know about it until the next morning, and I didn't give Ash up—I told Michael not to worry about that. He had a larger mess to think about.

By the time I had finished my first beer, it was noticeably cooler outside, almost downright cold. Michael didn't want anyone in the house, so he built a small fire on the lawn, thinking it would keep everyone near it and near the beer. There was still plenty of beer left, someone had gone and gotten another keg, so the party wasn't going to break up just because the thermometer had gone south.

What had started as a modest fire slowly grew into a blaze.

Guys started pulling stuff out of their trucks—paper, wood, cardboard, anything that would burn—so the fire expanded in both height and width. It wasn't enough. People drove off to find more stuff to burn and returned with wooden pallets and bundles of cardboard taken from behind the Hy-Vee. Somebody drove up and dumped a picnic table from the park in the middle of the flames. There was an inferno in the backyard, a raging bonfire that burned like a beacon, calling all idiots and turning a quiet party into a bash bordering on frenzy.

Of course the worst of it started with Troy Liddell. He drove up on the lawn in his pickup and started to unload a bunch of paint cans from the back. One of his minions, who was out of school, then tripped trying to get out of the truck bed and flipped over the tailgate and landed on his head. Troy laughed at him, and the guy got up, looking for a fight. He wasn't going to fight Troy, so he had to turn on somebody else. He was either dazed or drunk or both and took a wild swing at the person nearest to him, which happened to be my brother. Even Troy knew better than to beat up the host, so he stepped in and popped the guy on the back of the head, which dropped him quietly to the ground. Troy then had to go after somebody else.

He went over to sophomore Zach Linton and told him to "run through the fire." Zach knew what would happen if he didn't, so he dashed through the bonfire, skirting along the edge. It wasn't good enough. Troy smacked him on the ear and told him to do it again. Zach took the reverse route, with the right sleeve of his sweatshirt catching fire this time, but he kept running, the flames dying as he slapped at them with his left hand as he disappeared around the side of the house. We didn't see him again. Troy continued to torment a number of people, seemingly picking them at random and forcing them to risk being burned or beaten. Most people risked the fire and then left. Troy didn't need anything more to drink, but he kept going over to the keg and rocking it back and forth. I didn't know what the hell he was doing. We just wanted him to leave, but his buddy was still passed out near the truck.

"You know what I think he wants to do?" Michael practically whispered. We shook our heads. "I think he's planning to throw the keg on the fire."

"That would be amazing," someone standing next to us said.

"No, it wouldn't," Michael said. "It would explode like shrapnel."

"How do you know?"

"I saw it on TV," Michael said.

I tried to keep away from the fire, or at least out of its ragged halo of light, standing in the shadows as Troy made his way around, tormenting one person then the next. When he started moving back and forth from the fire to the keg, I heard him asking for me. He became louder and more animated, wanting to know where I was. "Let's throw him in the fire and see what happens." I went inside and locked the door behind me and went down into the basement and hid in the utility room, sitting in the dark, with the hot water heater and the furnace.

I'd never thought about fire before, not in that way. At that time I'd only tried two different ways of killing myself. I knew that people did it that way—self-immolation—but they had gasoline or something; they didn't just jump into a fire, did they? I thought about it for a second, how maybe the fire would burn me up, leave nothing, not even ash behind, but I wasn't going to do it, especially not with Troy Liddell and a yard full of drunken strangers watching. I know what it seems like, that I was a coward, hiding there in the house instead of letting them toss me in like a log; I mean, if I wanted to die, why didn't I let them? If I was really serious about it, really wanted to kill myself, why wouldn't I do it, just jump into the fire or let them throw me in? What was the difference?

There was a big difference. It wasn't what I wanted, not that night, not right then, not that way. Did I have to explain myself? What did I have to prove to them? It wasn't my choice, it was in front of a crowd—which I never wanted—and it was Troy Liddell. Why should I give him the satisfaction? And, to be honest, I didn't know what would happen. I wasn't sure I wouldn't roast like some side of beef, that maybe they'd try and rescue me and pull me out and take me to the hospital, where I'd have to lie around to wait for horrible burns to heal on most of my body and then I'd be scarred or something. Even if they left me there, it wouldn't be quick and it wouldn't be painless. It wouldn't be like flying off a bridge with the taste of fresh air in my face, watching the river as it rose up to greet me or watching as the angel reached out her arms toward me. It wouldn't be like that at all.

So I sat there on the concrete floor, leaning against the furnace, and thought about Joan of Arc, being burned to death at the old age of nineteen, and the image of her standing in the fire that's on the back of one of my father's old albums, one he used to play a lot when we were all younger—I used to sneak looks at it, the image of the young girl, naked, with the flames precisely placed to cover what I really wanted to see. I thought about Shadrach, Meshach, and Abednego, the three guys who refused to bow down to the statue of some king in the Bible and were thrown into a fire as punishment. They walked away without a burn or a blister. If I knew I would be like them, I would have given myself over to Troy, let him toss me in, and then watched his face as nothing happened and I calmly walked back out. It wasn't going to be like that for me—I didn't go unharmed, that was the thing—I would roast and then come back later, maybe days later, as I always did, and I wouldn't be spared burns and blisters. I wasn't going to give Troy the satisfaction of any of it. I wanted everyone to leave, not only Troy. I could have gone upstairs and into my own room—there was no one who was going to bother me, no one who was going to come inside—but I stayed where I was, in my cowardly hiding hole, until I didn't hear Troy's agitated, drunken voice roaming around, and I didn't come out until I heard Michael come inside, after the last guests had gone, locking the door behind him.

Michael was nursing a hangover in the morning when he dragged himself into the kitchen and told me about the cereal in his bed. I was sitting at the table and nodded toward the window. The kitchen was to the right of the deck, and the large picture window had a perfect view of the remains of the party, specifically, the huge burn mark in the backyard. It was at least ten feet in circumference, staring at us like a threatening black eye, with a few scorched paint cans and a charred leg of a picnic table strewn inside the black circle. I hadn't given it a thought, even with the fire burning right there in front of me. Apparently, no else had either, except Michael.

"Somebody told me that if a fire gets hot enough, it burns up completely—so there's no ash, nothing. You'd never know it was there."

"Who told you that?"

"I don't know, some guy standing around."

"And you believed him?"

Michael shrugged. "What was I going to do anyway? The fire was already going."

"What are you going to do about it now?"

"What can I do?" he wanted to know.

"We could move. Or get more fire."

Instead, we went into the yard and cleared away the cans and other debris and threw them into the trees. There was nothing we could do about the black mark, short of digging it all up and replanting the grass. Instead, we waited for our parents to come home.

"How the hell did this happen?" our father demanded to know, no less than five minutes after he'd walked through the front door.

"I have no idea," Michael said. "We've been trying to figure it out. Somebody must have come over and burned the lawn."

"Why would they do that?" his father asked.

"A joke, I guess," Michael said.

"Is it funny?" our mother said.

"It's a prank," Michael said. "The grass will grow back, won't it?"

"Not fast enough," Dad said. "I want to know who would do this."

"Me too," Michael said, thinking that he might have actually pulled it off.

Michael held on to that thought for about ten minutes until one of the neighbors called and asked about the party. It's the only time I ever remember my brother getting into serious trouble with our parents. It wasn't so much that he had the party but that he'd lied about the whole thing. My father gave him a lecture about how he should have spent his weekend looking out for me instead of planning a party and how dangerous a bonfire in the backyard could be and then launched into an extensive monologue about being a man and owning up to his actions instead of lying about them. Michael was grounded for two weeks—one for the fire and one for the lying, he told me. I didn't receive any punishment, and I halfheartedly told my brother, "I would have lied for you, if it had come to that," which I would have, but they never asked me anything. My brother took the hit on his own, which was the natural course for most people who had parties, the bullet you had to bite for letting other people get drunk at your home.

o o o

It wasn't until almost a year later, in late August, just before we went back to school, that I set fire to myself.

I had found a gallon of gas along the railroad tracks at the bottom of the bluff. I used to take walks there after school once in a while, sort of hoping to see a train coming but mostly just to walk along the river. I'd usually enter on River Road and then walk south, the bluff rising on my right and the river staying steady at my left, and continue to walk past the dam and then come out near the bridge, or better yet, near the statue.

This was not after school, however. It was in the morning; the heat and the humidity were already brutal, like being trapped in an airtight compartment where you knew you weren't going to suffocate but you almost wished you would. Anyway, I found the large red container on the side of the tracks closest to the river. It was a five-gallon container, with a handle on the top and one on the side and a long, thin red spout sticking out of it that almost made me laugh because I could hear Ash or Bruce, or both, making a penis joke about it. There was a gallon, maybe more, of liquid sloshing around in it, and I unscrewed the spout and could smell the gasoline. I wondered if it was enough to kill me. That's my brain's fault; that's how it works. Found a gallon of gas? Pour it all over yourself and strike a match, but first you better figure out if it's enough. Not that it ever is.

I walked back north but stopped before the bluff leveled out. I hid the container under the thick brush on the bluff and walked back home. I still didn't know if a gallon would be enough, so I decided to take the container to a gas station the next day and fill it up.

It wasn't easy pedaling my bike with more than thirty pounds of gasoline sloshing in my hand, so I knew I couldn't go as far as I wanted. I had thought I could go out into the country, somewhere where no one would see the large amount of flames and where no one would come and investigate. Instead, I only made it as far as the bluff and then coasted down River Road until I could ride to the railroad tracks. I walked a ways farther and then sat in the middle of the tracks and poured the gas all over myself. I never thought I wouldn't do it, but I understand why it's a method favored by political or religious protesters. It's a commitment.

I'd heard about people doing that sort of thing, but it was mostly monks and protestors—people who wanted to make a point in public. There are videos of it online, of course, and you can see the point they're making. Some guy in Tunisia torches himself, and before you know it, dictators are being pushed out all over. There isn't much of it in America. A University of Wisconsin sophomore burned himself in a concrete culvert in New Mexico a few years ago, and a guy set himself on fire on the Kennedy Expressway in Chicago in 2006 to protest the war in Iraq. His suicide note said, in part, "I only get one death, so I want it to be a good one. Wouldn't it be better to stand for something or make a statement?" I didn't want to stand for anything; I didn't have a statement to make; I just didn't want to start a fire. I thought there was enough space along the railroad tracks, with the gravel shoulders on each side, that the trees and bushes wouldn't catch fire. And I thought that whatever was left of me after the fire might be ground up or scattered or at least run over by an oncoming train.

Instead, the next morning I woke up, brushed myself off, and walked back to my bike and rode home.

If my father ran air traffic control, no one would be going anywhere (#5)

About the time I started wanting to stay out late and run around with my friends was about the time my father implemented curfew—ten o'clock on weeknights and eleven o'clock on weekends. "There's no good going on in this town after that hour," he reminded me from time to time. For every minute I was late after curfew, he would deduct a minute from the next night. He knew exactly when I needed to be through the door. "Nine fifty-three," he'd say, as if it meant something to anyone but him. After a missed curfew for a number of nights in a row, he decided to deduct five minutes for every minute I was late. I kept curfew after that for a while, discovering that he didn't care if I showed up drunk as long as I showed up on time. That was fine for a while until he started to deduct time while I was missing or being recovered.

Once when I was gone for almost seventy hours, he tried to deduct twenty-one thousand minutes from my curfew, almost fifteen days. Even my mother thought that it was excessive.

"You can't punish him for the hours he was dead," she explained. My father disagreed. I ignored him, and the penalty minutes kept adding up; the way it stands now, I'm not supposed to leave the house until I'm thirty. I leave anyway.

"You're off the rails," my father said. "You need to get back on track." I didn't want to get back on track—I didn't want to be anywhere near the track. I wanted to be in some distant ditch—instead, someone had found me at the bottom of the bluff again and had taken me home, had carried me to their car and put me on a blanket in the trunk and delivered me like a lost dog or one of those single shoes you see on the shoulder of the highway, wondering how somebody can lose one shoe and then not go back for it.

Everyone in town knew about me now, knew enough not to trouble the hospital—they had important things to do. I was becoming less a miracle and more of an oddity, less some wonderful fascination and more of a nuisance. So there I was, in my own bed, freshly awakened from my fifth "event" as they began to be known around the house, with a nice, efficient lecture from my father to greet me. Whatever concern my parents had for me in the previous events was now tempered by an itchy annoyance. "You need to get back on track," my father had said. There was no "we" in his lecture. From his perspective, this was now my problem. I owned it. This would have been fine if they had left me to my own solution, but they imposed their solution(s) on my "problem." I didn't want their help—I didn't want their sympathy, either, really—whatever help they could have offered would have been the wrong kind anyway. This was "our" problem, however, as long as we disagreed on the fundamental issue and their idea of a solution. And this was their problem in the sense that whatever was going on with me was deeply instilled, hardwired into my brain and body. It wasn't something that had infected me or had suddenly stricken me from the outside—this was in me, was part of me, something in my blood, in the genetic gunk they'd given to me, passed down from my parents and maybe their parents before them. It was both parts of the issue—my desire to destroy myself and my inability to actually succeed. I was born to be broken, but I couldn't break. The track wasn't the problem at all.

My father's curfew, in reality, was more for him than it was for me. He couldn't sleep if I was out of the house, but once I was inside, he went right to sleep. I could never sleep, not even when I was a child. My mother says that I used to climb out of my bed and sit at the top of the stairs and scream. They didn't know if I was hollering because I wanted to go to sleep and couldn't or if I wanted to be awake, to be with them. They let me scream; they didn't know what else to do. I finally outgrew the yelling, but I never outgrew the sleeplessness. I try to be more productive, or at least quieter. My father sets his limits on how long I can stay on the computer after dinner (no more than two hours, non-homework time, and computer minutes are interchangeable with TV, which I never watch anyway—it's just the same crap over and over, the same commercials about what car to buy, what beer to drink, what pill to take to get hard), how much time I spend on the phone (thirty minutes), and what time the lights should be out (twenty minutes after curfew, which I never make anyway).

My father is always awake when I get home; the minute I start to turn the doorknob, I hear him starting down the stairs, ready to read me the minutes that will be subtracted from my curfew. After that, however, he's back in bed, and no matter what he says, he doesn't know what I'm doing in the privacy of my room, and I'm not sure he really cares, as long as the lights are out—I could be reading, looking at porn, or talking on the phone with Jodi. She can't sleep either. She has bad bouts of nightmares—the same abstract horrors visit her night after night, often the same dream returning and repeating, always waking her at the same point in the story, disturbing her and preventing her from falling back to sleep. She knows I'm probably awake, so she usually sends me a quick text, Wake? and then we'd be off into conversation until one of us drifted into some semblance of rest.

Jodi never tells me the details of her dreams—she doesn't want to recount them, to give them any more space in her life than they have already taken. "They're always boring when you talk about them anyway," she says, "and they're never scary. Because it's more about the atmosphere than what happens."

I don't remember my dreams, if I have any. Maybe I'm never asleep long enough to have one, let alone a nightmare. Maybe I'd like one. Maybe they'd be an entertaining, welcome relief from the real world.

Jodi never likes to have boring back-and-forths, especially in our late-night conversations. "Would you trade me predicaments?"

she wanted to know when I told her I wouldn't mind having a nightmare or two.

"I don't think I would. My brain doesn't torment me or disturb me."

"My brain is not my friend," she said. "You'd think it would want to help me, not scare the shit out of me every night."

"Would you rather have my dilemma?"

"I wouldn't have a dilemma," she said.

"Then it's not the same situation. It's like me saying I'd have your problem if the dreams weren't scary."

"Okay. How about this, then—would you rather be van Gogh, knowing that you'd never sell a painting in your lifetime but would be famous forever, or would you rather be popular, sell a lot of stuff while you were alive, and then be completely forgotten later on?"

She was always asking questions like that and demanded answers.

"If you could get the one thing you wanted but you had to kill a total stranger in order to get it, would you?"

"No."

"What if the stranger was a horrible person, a mass murderer or child molester?"

"No."

"Not even a mass-murdering pedophile? You wouldn't kill him?"

"No."

"But you'd kill yourself?" she said.

"I don't think I have the right to take anyone's life but mine."

Jodi didn't say anything.

"You don't agree?"

"I don't know," she said. "It's not for me to agree or disagree, is it? It's what you believe. Who am I to say? You might have a screwed-up code, but at least you have one."

There's a lot to like about a girl like that.

Keep the kill chain going (#3)

We used to waste our time playing video games before we discovered liquor. My efficient father limited my time after dinner to a single hour, so we raced home after school and spent as much time as we could running around in desolate, mostly concrete landscapes killing each other or working together trying to kill our enemies. Todd, of course, was the best at it—killtastic, or whatever the highest rank was—and Bruce sucked at it. Or else he played his own game. He never followed the rules. Instead, he liked to try and sabotage whatever we were trying to do, constantly fouling things up. Or he would let himself be killed—he liked to watch the screen turn red and hear the gasps and moans that were supposed to be him and then watch himself rematerialize so he could start again. "Look, I'm Strand," he said once, and introduced what became the common verb for it. "I'm Stranding," they would say as they died and respawned on the screen.

I was a pretty good player, at first anyway. I got bored with it fast. I liked the early days the best, when we were all trying to figure out a new game, trying to work together to kill tons of people, which we did—there is something incredibly satisfying about shooting lots and lots of people, even if they're cartoons—but then it became the same old stuff. I mean, how many fake Russians or Arabs or Nazis or zombies does one person need to kill? I'm much happier now that we discovered drinking. Although I have to say that some of our drunken kill fests are still highly entertaining. And Todd can't play drunk at all; it's hilarious. He's constantly complaining that his kill-to-death ratio isn't accurate because of his drunk playing. He's more concerned about his stats than the fun we're all having, so he won't play after he's been drinking anymore. Bruce is a better player drunk—he says he's found his one true talent. "I should do everything drunk," he says. "I'd be a lot better off." I'm the same, drunk or sober; it doesn't seem to make any difference.

I don't know how many hours, days, weeks we've spent killing and being killed, but I know that I've been killed 21,659 times on screen and I've killed 38,274 people, which puts me third in the group. We used to talk about those numbers as if they mattered (to Todd they still do). Sometimes I wish they still did. "Stack the bodies high," Darryl used to say at the beginning of every game. We used almost every weapon known to man, from bare hands to personal nuclear devices and everything in between. Of course no matter how many thousands I've killed in games, no matter how many weapons I've shot, it's nothing like the real thing.

All my friends hunt; all their fathers have guns. We weren't the kind to keep back issues of *Gun World,* the pages tabbed with Post-it notes, but we weren't PETA pacifists either. We knew how to shoot and could hit a rabbit or pheasant with enough regularity to make us want to go back out again in the early morning and tramp around the countryside. My father taught me how to shoot a rifle, a shotgun, and a pistol. He would take me out to the country, to the woods on some farmer's field he knew, and he would set up targets on the trees and then he patiently showed me how to hold the weapon, how to load it, how to aim it and shoot it with accuracy. He taught me how to sight along the barrel of the rifle with one eye and to keep both eyes open with the shotgun and look just past the end of the barrel. He taught me how to clean the guns after we returned home—I think this was my father's favorite part—the guns disassembled on his table in the basement, the rags and oils and rods and brushes carefully arranged in front of him in order of importance, maximizing his efficiency. The guns seemed soft and beautiful as he rubbed the cloth against them, delicate, almost fragile, ready to be put away and almost too fine to take out again. He always kept them loaded—"So you don't have to wonder and so you treat them with respect," he said.

I was ten, almost eleven, the first time he took me hunting. He had hunted a lot when he was younger, had hunted deer and turkey and duck. He had taught my brother the same as he was teaching me, and he had taken my brother a few times—they even went to Canada together once—but he and I never went together. I screwed that up for him. No sooner had I learned how to shoot and hunt than I stuck a shotgun under my chin. That was the end of that. My father got rid of the guns in the house. My friends still go hunting now and then, but I don't. Ash says I should go with them one more time. "You can be the target," he jokes. I wouldn't have a problem with that.

I used the shotgun—the pistol was only a .22 and I didn't know if it would get the job done, and the rifle seemed too fancy. Hemingway had been a hunter, I seemed to remember, and he'd used a shotgun. It had worked for him. I went down to the basement late one night and placed a chair against the concrete wall near the back corner, as far away from the stairs as possible. I took the shotgun from the case and positioned it under my chin. I could barely reach the trigger, so I took the hammer and held it in my right hand so I could press the head against the trigger without straining. I put a garbage bag over my head, thinking it would contain the mess (it didn't), and then fumbled with the gun to get it back in place. Some people say you should put the barrel in your mouth to increase your chances of success, but I didn't want to suck on the metal end of anything, so I pressed my throat on the gun. It was all very clumsy. As I sat there, with the stupid garbage bag over my head, blindly positioning the gun, trying to fit the end properly under my chin and keeping the hammer inside the trigger guard but making sure to not press too hard and make the stupid thing fire before I was ready, I thought about that kid in Reno who thought that Judas Priest was telling him to kill himself and went outside and screwed it all up by shooting off the lower half of his face.

That's the trouble with guns—there's too much that can go

wrong, although they say there's between an eighty and ninety percent success rate with guns, the highest of any method. I'm not so sure. I don't know if I believe the statistics—I know we love our guns, but there's still a large margin for error. There are plenty of cases where guns misfire, cheap ones that explode and blind or maim instead of killing, or bullets that do crazy things—I read about a man who tried to shoot himself in the head with a pistol and the bullet skidded its way around his skull before flying out of the same hole it had gone in. You can't count on a gun, and while there are some people who question the "sincerity" of other methods, overdose and especially wrist-cutting, it's hard to doubt the sincerity of someone jumping from almost a hundred feet and landing on a rocky bank, a parking lot, or a frozen river. I bet there's a high success rate on that, higher than guns. But then, what do I know? I'm only the guy who's done it thirty-nine times.

I feel bad for my father. He had to clean up the basement, then got rid of his guns, although he kept the case, which sits empty in the basement as a reminder of what I took from him, I guess. If I could take back one of the deaths, it would be that one, but I was younger then, and I can't do anything about it now.

There's no place like home (#25)

I was bored with The Point and bored with the same routine, the same people and the same conversations. On top of it, I was also bored with the cow after the first two weeks—about the time the wine ran out—and sick of it after the third. There were the daily jokes about the other Strand—"Strand looks sad today," "Quiet, Strand is napping," or "Strand needs a bath . . . wait, he is taking a bath." It was taking too long to decompose, or longer than we wanted—we had hoped it would be a skeleton by now—but there was still plenty of hide left on it, a rancid, slimy skein that seemed to cling together in desperation, fighting the heat and the sun and the waves as they washed over it again and again and again. The cow's head was the least decayed, but the gentleness was gone from its face, and the skin had retreated enough to make the cow appear to be grimacing. Worst of all, it was beginning to stink—we could smell it long before we reached the end of The Point—and we had to fish in a different spot, far from the blackening body. I wanted to find another spot, at least until the cow was reduced to bones, but no one else wanted to change. I was sick of all of it by the first month of summer and especially sick of my friends, but I kept going back every day. Todd would be finished with baseball soon, and I thought that if I could cut off the rest of the group, if it was just Todd and Jodi and me, then the summer could be almost endurable. But we weren't going to shake the rest of them; it didn't work that way. Maybe they felt the same way about me, wished that one day I wouldn't come back; maybe they all wished it, even Todd and Jodi. If it was true, if they did want it, they almost got their wish.

I was even bored with the river, at least the river at The Point. It was different there—below the bridge the river surged with an unmistakable strength, and at the dam it crashed and thrashed as it rushed headlong on its way, and above the dam, where we usually watched it from the bluff, it was serene and iconic, cutting its way into the earth. But at The Point, almost a mile north of the bluff, we sat a few feet from it, looked at it almost eye to eye, and there it was a timid brownish bore, as tame as a lake, disappointing and dull. Something was wrong and would continue to be wrong as long as we stayed there, but I couldn't convince the rest of them to leave. "We have to keep an eye on Strand," Ash said. They wanted to wait until the cow was all skeleton and then haul it out of the water and wait until the bones were clean and dry and white before they divvied them up as souvenirs.

○ ○ ○

Jodi never came to The Point—it was too far, she said, and "too boring." It *was* boring. The only change in those tedious days at The Point were the baseball games where we went to see Todd play. Not all of us went, thank God, and usually I could leave the rest of them behind and sit with Jodi, and often Maddy, in the stands and forget about the tiresome routine of summer. I usually smelled of sweat and catfish bait and, more often than not, liquor. Sometimes it was even worse and I smelled like the river, fetid and old and dank with decay. I hoped I didn't smell like cow death—that was a smell that took your breath away, made you clap your hands to your face if you weren't used to it and even sometimes when you were. I knew I stank, but I didn't think it was intolerable. In fact, I didn't mind the smell; it was like the secret pleasure you sometimes get from your own farts—you know it smells horrible, but the fact that you made it, that it's part of you, somehow makes it better. I stank from the heat and the fish and the water, but Jodi and Maddy never complained. I wish those games could have lasted forever.

Jodi liked baseball all right, I guess, but what she liked most was being in the sun. She stretched her brown legs across the aluminum bench in front of us and tilted her head slightly toward the sky so she could watch the game but still catch the afternoon rays. She wore a pair of my old madras shorts, which she usually rolled up during the game. Her skin was the color of honey, and every now and then the delicate hairs on her legs would shine yellow or white like electric filament for a second or two. Jodi never seemed to mind the heat, but she made sure that Maddy had plenty to drink. She carried a small cooler, hardly bigger than my mother's purse, large enough to hold a freezer pack, a couple bottles of water, and a bag of grapes. She handed them out to Maddy and me as if they were gold—they were better.

Maddy Leighton is perhaps the smartest person I knew. She reads college textbooks for fun, has probably read more books on science and scientists than all the books I've ever read on everything. She's been smarter than me ever since I've known her, which is about four years, but she doesn't make me feel dumb. In fact, she makes me feel smarter whenever I talk to her, smarter than I do whenever I talk with my own friends. Maddy's ten years old. Jodi babysits her two or three nights a week, and they're together almost every day in the summer. I like Maddy—there's plenty to like. My father says that if she were yellow and had eight fingers, she'd be Lisa Simpson.

Maddy kept her camera at the ready, watching all of the action through the small screen on the back. We never said much to each other during the game, each of us watching in our own way, as if we were seeing three different games that maybe the others weren't interested in or even understood, yet none of us would have gone without the other.

Todd stood on the mound before the start of the game and gave us a funny look—I don't know if it was a "I don't know what I'm doing" look or a "what's the big deal, I've got this covered" sort of look. He wasn't supposed to be pitching that day—the scheduled starter had broken his wrist in the game before and they didn't have anyone else rested and ready, so it was Todd, pitching in a game they needed to win to go to the playoffs and taking time to look right at us with that odd look he gave us.

"What was that?" I asked Jodi.

"I don't know," she said.

That was the trouble with Todd: half the time you didn't know what he was thinking. You also didn't know if he was going to pitch a no-hitter or implode on the mound. In the end, he nearly did both.

I liked watching the preparation and anticipation before every pitch and then the brief disappointment when nothing happened. That's baseball. It's a game of failures—the failure to make the right pitch, the failure to get a hit, the failure to throw in time, throw to the right base, throw to the right cutoff man, failure to do the little and big things. And even when a player does everything absolutely right—makes the perfect pitch, hits the ball hard and square—it can still end in disappointment—a screaming line drive right at the third baseman. Sisyphus would have enjoyed baseball, I think.

Todd had a no-hitter through five innings and the score was still tied at nothing when he took the mound for the sixth. He walked the first batter, hit the next, and then had a quick 0–2 count on the next one before grooving a pitch down the middle that was launched for a three-run home run. It was the only scoring in the game. Todd's season was done.

"One bad pitch," Jodi said to Todd as we walked away from the field. "It doesn't seem fair. You had them."

"It isn't fair," Maddy said. "You looked so good." She held her camera to Todd to show him the pictures she'd taken during the game, but he didn't want to look. He didn't say anything; he repeated the look he'd given us at the beginning of the game.

It was on the way to one of the games that summer that I came to the horrible realization that I was in love with Jodi. At least I was afraid I was. I mean, I've known her practically all my life. I shouldn't have those feelings for her. It's embarrassing. I knew it would ruin everything; I was going to screw this up, I knew it. I couldn't pull it off, even if it was true. I wouldn't know how to transition from friends. It would be so much easier to go up to a stranger and say "I'm in love with you" than it would be with Jodi. I couldn't do it. Not without botching the whole thing. Maybe I've already botched it—Jodi knows me too well; she's been there through the whole thing. She's still here, though. I guess that means something.

The rest of the town grew tired of me a long time ago. They don't even bother to take me to the hospital anymore. I get thrown in the back of a truck, sometimes the trunk of a car—like an animal found on the side of the road, a lost stray or roadside trash—then they drive me home and lay me out in bed and wait for it all to be over. You'd think there was a reward, or at least a deposit stamped on me like on bottles and cans.

It's a bother, I know; the whole town has the eye-rolling

exasperation, the we've-seen-it-all-before resignation I used to see in my parents' faces. I'm not a surprise anymore; they've shrugged me off like an infant's latest tantrum, unwilling to give any satisfaction. What they don't understand is I didn't want a reaction in the first place and I wasn't getting any satisfaction anyway. Any way.

It's like a switch is flicked. I open my eyes and find that I am unfortunately back among the living—no blood, no broken bones, not a scratch, bruise, or any evidence at all that I had drowned or slammed myself into a pile of wet rocks a couple hundred feet below the bridge. It's a fucking miracle.

More often than not, I wake up in my own bed. It happens enough that I'm not surprised when I open my eyes and see all the usual crap I see every other morning, as if I'd awakened from a pleasant dream and had to deal with the typical stuff all over again. It's depressing. I'm like one of those guys you see at the circus or the State Fair, the guy who pounds nails into his face, swallows lightbulbs and broken glass, or holds his breath underwater for half an hour—it's incredible the first time you see it, entertaining the second, interesting the third, and then, all of a sudden, it's boring and you never need to see it again. You'd think it would be more incredible the more you saw it—how does he keep doing it over and over?—but it's not. If a guy hits seventy-three home runs in a season, the seventy-fourth is more interesting somehow, but if a guy takes a hammer and drives seventy-three nails into his head, the seventy-fourth is stale and less impressive. Jump off a bridge once and everyone sits up and takes notice—do it three times and it's annoying. Any more than that is a nuisance. It never got to the point where people ignored me or didn't care, but that was the trouble—it never got past annoying, at least for some. It was as if all the home runs that guy hit went through someone's window every time—the feat was still impressive, but couldn't he stop already?

The only good thing is that sometimes Jodi is there—she has a knack of coming in shortly after I've come back, entering like one of the farmhands at the end of *The Wizard of Oz.* It's a joke with us. "Remember me," she says, "your old pal Hickory." (She likes to say Hickory, even though it's not the right quote.)

"There's no place like home," I say, with as much sarcasm as I can stuff into it.

Everything had changed. I was in love. But with the wrong person. Why did it have to be her? She was one of my best friends; now it was all different. I couldn't be around her, even though all I wanted was to see her all the time. I couldn't tell her. I couldn't tell her anything. So I told Todd.

"Bad idea," he said.

An accident, a coincidence, a scar

like to tell Maddy that I was there when she was born. It's sort of true, and I have the scar to prove it. She likes to think I was right there in the same room, but I was down the hall or probably had left altogether by the time she was born. That doesn't matter; it's just a technicality. The truth is that I was there.

On the evening of the twenty-first of October, when I was six years old, I had run down the stairs to go into the kitchen and missed the bottom step, hit the edge of the small table on the landing, and split my head open. I've walked, raced, run past that table every day of my life; it's still there, and only once have I tripped and fallen into one of its sharp corners. It sliced me open, quickly and almost painlessly. I remember that it didn't even hurt and I got up, more embarrassed than anything, and went into the kitchen, where my mother was sitting, and she started to scream. Blood was pouring down my face and I put my hands up to try and catch it, but there was too much of it and it kept coming. She grabbed the towel from the sink and pressed it against my head and my father came running from somewhere and practically carried me to the car and we raced off to the hospital.

I was spread out on the backseat with my mother leaning over me, pressing another towel forcefully on my forehead. I can't recall if any blood spilled onto the seat; I don't think it did. I remember blood dripping on the floor of the emergency room. We had to wait, I remember that; it seemed like we were sitting there for hours. Carly Marshall was ahead of us with appendicitis, and Mr. Staton was ahead of her with a heart attack or indigestion or something. So we sat there, or I did, pressing the towel into my head as hard as I could, while my mother sat next to me and my father paced back and forth in front of the admitting nurses, as if they were deliberately ignoring us and were going to forget about us.

I was sitting in the emergency room when Maddy's mom came in. I'm not sure if I remember this as it happened or only remember it because the story has been told so many times since then. What I do remember are the lights in the hospital, how bright they were and how they seemed to go on forever down the long hallway that led from the emergency waiting area to all the rooms, one after another that stretched down and down, longer than a few football fields, it seemed to me. All those white rectangles of light, that's what I remember, and trying to watch them, maybe even count them, as they wheeled me down the hall to one of those rooms, where we waited for even longer. My head had stopped bleeding by the time the doctor took a look at it. I remember the doctor even debating whether he should use stitches or just slap a butterfly bandage on my head and let me go. In the end, they put in nine stitches. I'd probably already been stitched up and sent home by the time Maddy arrived in the world, but I still show her the white scar above my right eye as what I got on her birthday. I like my scar—it gives me hope, hope that damage can be done. Maddy likes it; she has a picture of it. She says it looks like the exposed cambium of a tree—she has a picture of that too, more than one, I think. She takes pictures of everything, sometimes up to fifty a day.

Jodi texted me: `u drunk?`
`Plammerrred.`
`ha come c me.`

She was babysitting over at the Leightons'. I didn't want to go. She didn't even wait for me to respond.

`Ive pizza.`
`There.`

"Where are you going?" Todd asked.

"I've got to go."

"Jodi," Vern said.

"Bring her back," Ash said.

"And bring somebody with her," Bruce said, "like Kayla Morton."

"Like you have a shot."

"I don't care," Bruce said. "I like looking at her. Information to use later."

"Gross," Todd said.

None of them were drunk yet, but they were close. Bruce was usually the first one you noticed—his voice would drift into the slight, nasally drawl we all tried to avoid, a hickish speech we associated with scurves and Missouri and other poor trash places downriver. None of them were drunk, yet, but it wasn't going to be a good night. I wanted to leave before the surliness set in. I wanted Todd to leave too, but he wouldn't. He wanted to get drunk and pick on Vern some more. It was fun enough, I suppose—better than anything else, but I wasn't in the mood. Still, it was hard to leave, especially for one person. The group didn't like it.

"Don't do anything stupid," Todd said.

"That's all he does," Ash said.

"Leave the bottle," Bruce said. But there was still some vodka left in it, enough for me to put it back in my parents' liquor cabinet and they wouldn't notice. I tucked it into my bag.

"You're a jerk," Vern said.

"Enjoy the crème de menthe," I said, and left.

When I arrived at the Leightons', Maddy was reading aloud to Jodi from an intro to chemistry textbook. Maddy came and gave me a hug. "You smell like liquor," she said.

"It's Vern's fault. He was drinking and threw beer on me as a joke. That's why I smell."

Maddy scrunched her mouth as she quickly looked at my dry

clothes. "Where did he hit you, right in the mouth?"

"I guess so."

Maddy took my hands and stretched out my arms to their full length; she held on to my arms as she walked up my legs, her stocking feet working their way up to my waist and her head tilting back until she could flip herself backward to the floor. We'd been doing this since about as long as I've known her. "You're getting too tall for this," I said.

"So I should get as many in now that I can," she said, and did another flip and then another until Jodi told her to stop.

"It's time for bed," Jodi told Maddy.

"You'll tuck me in," she said, taking me by the hand. It wasn't a question.

She led me upstairs to her room, which looked more like a college dorm than a ten-year-old's bedroom. Maddy had always been an adult trapped inside a younger body. She probably passed me, maturity-wise, when she was five. She'd certainly been mothering me since she was seven, giving me advice and frequently telling me what to do.

The family cat, an orange tailless creature that usually avoided everyone except Maddy's mother, pushed his way past us on the stairs and was waiting for us as we entered Maddy's bedroom. The cat looked at me, looked at Maddy, then looked back at me and, after determining that there was nothing of interest between the two of us, walked over to Maddy's bed and climbed on. His name, given to him by Maddy's mother years ago, was Whiskers. Maddy refused to call him by his given name, instead opting for other names of equal value—Nose, Ears, Feet, and No Tail. Now she tended to call him Manxcat. She didn't dislike the cat, she said, but she didn't like him either. "I tend not to think about him," she said. "And if I don't think about him, he's not really there."

"I should try that—with a lot of things."

"Don't think about yourself so much," Maddy teased. "That would be a start."

She had a large poster of the periodic table hanging on the wall of her bedroom. The boxes were colored green and red, blue and peach, and pink and purple and arranged in columns and rows. The alkali metals were red and ran in a column on the left side, while the noble gases were a pale blue and formed a column on the right side. The purple and pink rows of lanthanides and actinides were offset from the others and ran horizontally at the bottom. I only knew any of this because of Maddy. Maddy stood in front of the poster and pointed out all sorts of information, literally pointed at the boxes, like a teacher in class. The poster was not new, but she was in full delay mode, killing as much time as she could before Jodi came up and demanded that she go to sleep. She walked over to the end of the table, sweeping her hand across the last few rectangles. "This only goes up to atomic number one hundred and three, see? Some go up to one eighteen and others go as high as two ten, but I don't think that makes much sense. Most of those after one eighteen are hypotheticals. I'd like the one eighteen version, though."

"Maybe you'll get it as a present. For your birthday, maybe."

She shrugged. "I know them all anyway: rutherfordium,

dubnium, seaborgium, bohrium, hassium, meitnerium, darmstad-
tium, roentgenium, then it goes into all the ones that begin with
U: ununbium, ununtrium, ununquadium, ununpentium, unun-
hexium, ununseptium, and finally, ununoctium, which has the
highest atomic mass of any of the discovered elements."

"I'll take your word for it."

"You know what I like about these down at the bottom?"
Maddy said. "Some of them only exist for a fraction of a second
and some of them have never been observed, but they're here just
the same. You know what I mean?"

"I know." I led her over to her bed and pushed Manxcat to
the floor and then pulled the covers up above Maddy's shoulders. Manxcat hopped right back onto the bed and curled up near
Maddy's neck. They were both staring at me with pensive, serious
looks. Maddy was working on something; Manxcat was mad at
me. Maddy used to not let the cat crawl up on the bed, but now
she seemed to like it, or at least tolerate it.

"If you could be an element, anything on the wall, which
one would you be?" Maddy said.

"How about rutherfordium." It was the only name I remembered her saying, but I thought I should be one of those at the
bottom.

"Maybe," she said, but then reconsidered. "Maybe we're
thinking about this wrong," Maddy said. "Maybe you're not like
those elements at the far end, maybe you're more like iodine or
uranium."

"Why's that?"

"They're around forever. Uranium-238 has a half-life of four and a half billion years."

"I don't want to be uranium. Maybe iodine. Maybe something way down there, past one eighteen."

"You have to be on the poster," she said.

"Okay, now it's time to go to sleep."

"You have to pick first."

"You pick."

"You."

I went over to the wall and spent a few seconds looking at the bottom rows of the table. "How about this one?" I pointed to one of the boxes.

"Mendelevium? Why?" she said.

"I like the name."

Maddy laughed. "Do you know where it gets its name?"

I had no idea.

"Dmitri Ivanovich Mendeleev," she said. "He created the first version of the periodic table."

"I did all right, then."

"You did all right."

"Okay, then. Now you have to go to sleep."

"Do you watch me when I sleep?" Maddy asked.

"No. That's creepy, don't you think?"

"Very creepy," she said. "People watch you, though."

"When I'm sleeping?"

"No," she said. "When you're dead."

"I don't know. Maybe. Maybe they see me—they find me,

and then they take me home. I hope they don't watch. I don't really think about it." I wanted to turn the light out and leave her, but she kept looking at me and I could tell she had more to say.

"Can I ask you something?" Maddy said.

"Sure. And then you'll go to sleep and I won't watch." Jodi was going to be at the door soon; I could almost feel her getting off the couch.

"Okay," Maddy said. "Do you feel like a freak?"

"Yes."

"Me too. Sometimes. Do you think that's why we're friends?"

"I wouldn't doubt it. We have to look out for each other."

"But no watching," she said, and turned her face away from me. I turned out the bedroom light and closed the door nearly shut, still letting a slice of light into her room, the way Maddy liked it.

"You're going to break that poor girl's heart," Jodi said when I went back downstairs.

"I'm just an object of her scientific study."

"You should have seen her when she knew you were coming," Jodi said. "But you can't come here anymore when you've been drinking."

"I only had a couple. Besides, what did you think I was doing?" I joined her on the couch. She stretched her legs across the length of the sofa and rested her socks on my knees. Her socks were mismatched, one gray and the other blue. They weren't even the same material—one was thin cotton and the other thick wool.

"Well, you can't smell like that around kids."

"Maddy won't say anything."

"Here, eat something." She withdrew her feet and leaned toward me with something in her hand. She leaned close enough to smell me, and I hoped to God that I didn't stink like shit on fire. I'd rather smell like liquor than something worse. Jodi raised her hand and pressed a peppermint into my mouth. It was one of those red and white ones you get at your grandmother's or in the bank lobby; I don't like them, but I took it anyway. She stayed close, long enough to smell the sugary sweet on my breath. I wanted to lean toward her; I thought she might be waiting for me to, but I didn't move. I flicked the candy from one side of my mouth to the other with my tongue, the hard disk clicking against my teeth. As she moved away from me, just for a split second, I could see down the front of her shirt, see the thin, white edge of her bra, gentle curve of white, as if she had caught a small, shining crescent of the moon (I later described it to Todd as seeing a quarter of a cup and he said, "Yeah, that's about right," which he thought was hilarious). My left hand, which was resting on the back of the couch, began to tremble uncontrollably; my stomach began to flutter—for the first time in my life I was nervous around Jodi Telamon. I didn't know what to do. She couldn't see me all nervous and shaking like a stupid leaf in a storm. I had to get out of there.

"Better?" she said.

"I'd better go before the Leightons come home."

"They won't be home for another hour."

My arms and hands were turning to water, and I thought I would turn into a puddle right there on the floor if I didn't leave. I could hardly even look at her—she didn't seem like the same person, and every time I looked at her, I had thoughts in my head, wanting to rush toward her or say something I knew I couldn't. It was horrible. My mouth was dry, but the rest of me was water. "I should go anyway." She didn't stop me. Maybe she knew. I'm sure it was obvious.

I walked back to the park to look for Todd and the rest of them, but they weren't there. I didn't want to call them, but I walked down to the river, looking for them. They weren't there. I stood in front of the angel, looking at her darkened face that seemed disapproving, her eyes closed, dark and hooded, as if she couldn't be bothered with me. Still, her arms were outstretched. Waiting for someone else, I thought, but not me. No one was waiting for me.

I took my phone out of my pocket and looked, even though I knew there were no messages. I wanted to call Jodi. I wanted her to tell me the things I was feeling, to say them to me first. I knew it wasn't going to happen. I wanted to text her, but I couldn't do that. I had to talk to her. There were very few cars on the bridge; the concrete span was quiet overhead. The old bridge was a black skeleton in the dark, with only a few warning lights blinking red, on and off, on and off. I walked underneath the bridge and sat there for a while, holding my phone in my hands. I wasn't going to call anyone and no one was going to call me. I told myself that if a car came across the bridge in the next five minutes, I would go home. The bridge was still quiet. I walked up the hill and looked out across the river, following the gray line made by the edge of the bridge as it gently arced across the water. As much as I liked hearing the tires move across the deck when I was below the bridge, I loved looking out along the bridge when it was like this, empty and quiet. There was no one on the bridge, but I didn't walk out; instead, I went to the old bridge. There was a hole in the fence, almost invisible, but a place where the chain link had been cut and you could crawl through. Maybe I was the only one who saw it, the only one who knew it was there, like a secret portal.

I made my way through my secret door and walked out about three hundred feet, far enough to be past the shoreline, and I looked down. There was nothing but the black river below, moving imperceptibly from that height. I looked back toward the angel, the dim light from the ground shining up at her, illuminating her like a dark phantom. She wasn't waiting tonight; she was trying to rise, trying to lift off her pedestal. There was nothing I could do to help her. I walked back a few yards and then a few more. I could see the shore below and the dark water to the left. I was standing directly above both, where the water washed against the rocky banks. A few feet to the right and there was land; a few feet to the left and there was water. Her eyes were open now; she wasn't straining to leave, not now. She stood and waited. I was too far to ever reach her from the old bridge; she wasn't expecting me to even try, but she kept looking at me with her dark, expectant eyes. She wanted to watch as I did something she never could. I took a step.

My Therapist Saw Nirvana, but All I Get Is This Stupid T-Shirt

My mother thought I should see a therapist. She didn't want to go to anyone in town, however, for fear that someone might know. I thought it might be more embarrassing if they thought she wasn't doing something for me. Wouldn't most people think I needed to see somebody? Anyway, my mother found a therapist up in Mount Pleasant, where the state mental institution is, about forty-five minutes away. She drove me twice a week. It lasted a month.

The therapist, Dr. Stinchcomb, was nice enough, but like a lot of adults who deal with kids, he tried too hard to prove that he was one of us and dressed and talked too young for his age. He wore a Nirvana T-shirt under his worn blazer—I thought the shirt was funny, but I didn't say anything; I don't know if he was trying to provoke a response from me or if he was too stupid to know what it meant, or maybe he thought I wouldn't know. It's hard to tell with therapists—everything's a game or a test. They like to create conflict and then judge you on how you react. I guess they have to do something; it has to be boring to sit around and talk all day long.

Dr. Stinchcomb didn't seem to mind talking—he did enough of it. Half the time I thought I was his therapist, listening to his life. He liked to make references to stuff he thought I liked—music, movies, games, all that stuff. And he always liked to ask me what I was listening to. I liked to make up names—"I've been listening to a lot of Mike Tyson's Tits," I would tell him—and he'd always say, "I'll have to check them out." He would never come back and say, "You're full of shit; there's no such band." That irritated me.

He wanted to talk about all sorts of stuff, mostly at the edges. I wanted to get straight to the point. "I don't want to exist, plain and simple," I would tell him, "but something is preventing me from that. It's as if there's a huge disconnect between my mind and my body. That's what's messed up. That's what we need to fix."

"I can't do anything about your body," the doctor would say. "But I can help you with the mind."

I didn't want help with that. I wanted help with the other. That was the real problem.

"What do you think of Freud?" I asked him at the last session.

"He was a genius. None of us would have any understanding of the mind if it wasn't for him, even if we disagree with him or think differently about things than he did."

"He committed suicide."

"He was sick. He wanted to die without suffering and with some dignity," he said.

"That's what I want."

"You have your whole life ahead of you. Freud was at the end of his life and he'd already changed the world."

"I don't want to change the world," I said.

We went around and around like this at every session. I would have kept going, but my parents decided to stop it. I'm sure it was expensive, and I'm sure my father thought it wasn't efficient. It wasn't.

And then there were the drugs. What they can't fix with talking, they try to change with chemicals. The drugs didn't change anything, except they made me feel like somebody else, a watery, fake version of myself. I talked too much, slept too much, felt a few seconds behind everyone else, even behind myself, as if I were watching everything instead of participating, like watching a play but talking over it at the same time. I hated it, and the drugs only made me want to kill myself more. I went on a nice little run—jumping, slashing, overdosing, even suffocated myself (which I hadn't done before). They changed drugs, but they didn't change me. Finally, I stopped taking them and found a drug I liked better—drinking. At least I knew what to expect and could control how I felt, and I knew when to stop. I couldn't say the same for most of my friends.

They either didn't know when to stop or didn't want to stop.

The snake that swallows its own tail

Maddy was telling me about Bob. He was a joke between us—a joke that had started almost a year ago—and I was the cause of it, trying to be funny, and here we were still talking about him. I thought Maddy would have grown tired of talking about him by now, but she was still telling me about Bob on every Saturday during the school year and twice a week during the summer, on days she had her riding lessons.

It was my fault—I should know better—I don't do funny or clever very well, and Maddy knew she had the upper hand. She liked reminding me that I am not funny or clever. She was so happy after her first lesson and talked nonstop about it. "I'm going to be a cowgirl," she must have told me a hundred times, so I had to ask her if that didn't mean she'd be riding a cow. That's when Bob appeared.

"I am riding a cow," she said. "Haven't you been listening? That's why I said I wanted to be a cowgirl."

"Tell me about him."

"His name is Bob," Maddy said. "He's brown and white, with a white star on his forehead, and he's fast, faster than most of the horses they have. And I'm the only one who gets to ride him."

"Take a picture of Bob for me."

"He's like you," she said. "Bob doesn't like to have his picture taken." Maddy held her camera to her eye and watched me through the lens. She wasn't going to take my picture. We'd settled on that long ago. She preferred seeing the world through the screen on the back; she liked the shape, the limits of the frame. She took pictures all day long, but she wasn't going to take mine. She already had a few, although you wouldn't really know it was me, not at first. She had a few fragments, parts of me. She had pictures of my scar and a few of my nose. She likes my nose. She says it's a nose that belongs on some Roman statue.

"Nero," I told her, "or Otho."

"No. Marcus Aurelius or Titus."

I knew who they were only because she'd told me about them. I remembered something about Titus. "Wasn't Titus the one who had the insect fly up his nose and pick at his brain?"

"Was it?" Maddy said. "Forget the Romans, then, and all those statues. How about the Sphinx?"

I liked that. I like my nose well enough, I guess, but only when I see it in one of Maddy's pictures. It looks all right on its own but not so great with the rest of the face. Luckily, there are few pictures of that.

I don't know what she does with all the images; I keep telling her to post them online, to make an image diary, but she never does. They're just for her, I think; keeping them isn't the point or having someone else looking at them. Maybe taking them is the whole point—looking and clicking the shutter, having it open and close for a second, a fraction of a second, as it captures a small slice of the world, a small piece of it that is instantly lost. Maybe that's all she wants with it. Maybe that's enough.

My mother doesn't like me bragging on Maddy. Whenever I talk about how smart she is, my mother says that everybody's smart at that age—"annoyingly precocious" is how she put it—and some people are a lot smarter even younger. "That's when you have the most time to know things," she says. "Kids are like sponges, absorbing everything and retaining it, fixating on things. It's easier when you're young because you're free to do it then. When you get older, you have to deal with all the stupid stuff in the world, all the distractions like a job, paying bills, dealing with the unavoidable dumb things, so you get dumber." She tells me that when I was six, I knew all about reptiles—the four orders, all the Latin names, the difference between herpetophobia and ophidiophobia. She says that I was always good with vocabulary and pronunciation—that I used to study all the names and write lists of them—and I used to correct her whenever she tried to say one of the more complicated names. My mother says I had a tenth-grade vocabulary when I was in the second grade. I bet I have a second-grade vocabulary now, so maybe my mother's right. She remembers more about it than I do. All I remember now are the snakes.

My father bought me a Solomon Island ground boa (*Candoia*

carinata paulsoni) for Christmas after my fourth event. Maybe he thought that if I had something to care about, something to care for, I wouldn't be so quick to leave it behind. I named the snake Prinn; he was only about eight inches long when we got him and he never got much bigger. My father hadn't consulted me about the snake before he bought him—if he had, I could have told him that the Solomons aren't great starter snakes. They can be difficult, aggressive, and willful. Prinn wouldn't eat. We tried for weeks and finally we had to go consult with the Snake Boss.

My father should have gone to him in the first place, but he hadn't. He never said where he got Prinn, but he ended up with the Snake Boss. His real name is Mark, but I knew him only as the Snake Boss for years or Skinner, which is what Bruce always called him, from Snake Boss to Snake Plissken, to Skenner then Skinner. He had converted the first floor of his house into his store, which was filled with hundreds of snakes. He kept them in plastic boxes stacked on floor-to-ceiling shelves in small, hot rooms. There were four or five rooms on the first floor, all filled with snakes. The basement was where he bred mice and rats for the snakes, and when you opened the door, you were hit with a solid smell of rodent sex and rodent shit. It sucked all the air out of your lungs. "It's the smell of money," the Snake Boss said to my father. My father thought that was hilarious.

The Snake Boss was younger than my father, a skinny guy with close-cropped black hair and heavy black-framed glasses. He always wore a T-shirt and long cargo shorts that drooped below his knees, no matter what the season. He had tattoos of snakes running down his arms, almost all constrictors, and the snakes were coiled around famous people—Beethoven, Einstein, James Dean, Marilyn Monroe, and some others I didn't recognize— crushing them in their grasps. I don't know what it was supposed to mean, but it looked impressive.

There were two large albino Burmese pythons on display in the front of the store and hundreds of snakes stacked in Tupperware behind the counter—milk snakes, sand boas, gopher snakes, corn snakes, king snakes, and ball pythons in different-color phases. When we walked into the store for the first time, the Snake Boss was helping another customer. He went down the stairs to the basement and we heard a faint squeak and then a hard thump and the Snake Boss returned with a dead rodent in a bag. We became accustomed to that sound.

My father let me explain the problem with Prinn, and the Snake Boss said that he would try to get him to eat if we would let him keep the snake for a week or so. We dropped off Prinn and waited. There's not much difference between an aquarium with a snake and one without, but it seemed like a lonely emptiness while it was unoccupied. Even my father was visibly saddened by the empty aquarium in my room. He would come in and look into it, and wonder how Prinn was getting along without us.

About a week later, the Snake Boss called and said that Prinn had finally eaten. He wasn't sure if he would with us. "You might want to think about another snake," he told my father, and that was almost the end of our relationship with the Snake Boss. "I'm not going to be hustled," my father said, but the Snake Boss told him that he had someone who would buy Prinn, someone who had owned a Solomon before.

"I don't know what you paid for him," the Snake Boss said, "but he's offering a fair price."

My father took the offer—which I'm certain was more than he paid for Prinn—and we bought another snake, a three-foot male king snake (*Lampropeltis getula californiae*). The Snake Boss showed us a few of them and my father let me pick, but I think he might have liked him more than I did. He spent a lot of time with him—I think he admired his efficiency, the way the snake conserved his energy, spending most of his time curled in the corner of the aquarium, only moving when necessary. My father liked to watch the snake feed on the small mice we bought from the Snake Boss, swallowing the pink body whole and then letting it slowly dissolve away, exerting hardly any effort for a couple weeks' worth of food.

I think that in another life, my father would have liked to have been the Snake Boss, watching over his hundreds and hundreds of snakes and rats, his nose filled with the smell of money, or maybe he would have liked to have been one of the snakes. My father would take my snake out of the aquarium and let him coil around his forearm, his triangled head resting on the back of his hand. My father studied him, examined him, as if with full consideration and understanding he could become more like a snake himself. I imagined my father wrapped around himself in the corner of his bedroom, hardly moving, except for the few times when my mother brought him something to eat. It wouldn't be such a bad life, I guess, if you had a snake brain and could lie still for hours and days without all sorts of thoughts constantly churning and spinning inside. Our brains can't rest; that's the trouble. Our brains are not our friends.

I named the king snake Zig. Bruce was the only friend I had who was interested in Zig. Bruce held him and even fed him a few times. Bruce called him "Heil" for a short time before going all in with "Hitler." He told everyone that I had a poisonous snake named Hitler and everybody believed him. Why not?

"What if he was Hitler?" Bruce asked one day as he watched Zig doing nothing in the corner of the tank. "I mean, what if he was reincarnated and there he was right there in front of us?"

"I don't think Hitler would be lucky enough to come back as a snake. Besides, how would we know?"

"I don't know," Bruce said, and pretended to give it some thought for a second. "If he makes a mad dash for Poland, we'll know we're in trouble."

I thought that would be the end of it, but it wasn't. He brought it up later when we were over at Todd's, sitting around his room doing nothing. "What if Hitler was back?"

"Strand's snake?" Vern said.

"What if his snake was the real Hitler? And what if Strand let him reproduce, so his genes get passed on to all these other snakes and then one of them comes back as the real Hitler?" Bruce said.

"Zig's not getting any company."

"What if Hitler was someone's dog, then, or cat, or whatever? And you raised him and fed him and took care of him and let him make babies and suddenly there's a whole spawn of Hitlers and they die and get reincarnated as something else, or worse, someone else and one day you wake up and there's Hitler all over again and it's your fault?"

"Why would he come back as a snake or a dog?" Ash asked.

"Why not?" Bruce said. "Isn't that how it works?"

"Strand comes back as himself," Ash said.

"Why is that?" Vern asked.

"I don't know."

"Maybe he hasn't learned his lesson," Bruce said.

"What's that supposed to mean?"

"I don't know," Bruce said. "Isn't that the whole thing about reincarnation—you get what you deserve based on karma or whatever? If you lead a good life, you move on to some higher stage, and if you lead a bad one, you come back as an insect or a cow or something—but you haven't done anything, so you don't deserve to go higher or lower, so you come back as yourself until you either get promoted or demoted."

"What would you want to come back as?" Todd said.

"Nothing."

"If you had to pick—had to—between a Mormon fly and Hitler, which would you take?" Vern asked.

"The fly."

"I'd pick Hitler, no question," Vern said.

"Of course you would," Todd said.

I began to lose interest in Zig, which, I guess is not so surprising. I was losing interest in everything. My father, however, was finished with Zig before I was. He never came in to handle him anymore, didn't even come in to look at him, and never asked about him, as if Zig had stopped existing. I had to remind him to stop by the Snake Boss's for food. The thing is, I stopped thinking about Zig as well—days would pass and I hadn't looked in on him, hadn't even thought about the animal living there, relying on us for his health and well-being. Zig was like a pile of dirty clothes on the floor—it's glaringly obvious at first, but if you leave it there long enough and walk around it, look at it every day in the landscape of the room, it becomes integrated to the point of invisibility—you don't notice it at all. Zig might have been better off as a bunch of dirty clothes. My father was sick of the trips to the Snake Boss, sick of the thumping and handling the plastic containers of mice. Once or twice a month was too much of a burden for him. He didn't want to do it anymore. My mother refused, and I couldn't, so after almost two years, Zig returned to the Snake Boss and we didn't miss him. The empty aquarium is still in the same spot, which is almost exactly like having a snake in it.

Some days are darker than nights (#20)

`Can I call u,` Jodi wanted to know. It was almost four in the morning. I was awake. I called her.

"My mother creeps me out," she said.

She'd had a nightmare, I thought. And I was right, but it was more than that.

"I guess I was screaming; at least that's what she said."

"Do you usually?"

"I don't think so. I don't know. Maybe they sleep through it, maybe I sleep through it, but I doubt it. You know me, I'm always awake after. Sometimes I'm screaming in the dream, sometimes my mother is doing horrible things to me, like tonight, and then I wake up and she's standing right there, lording over me like a vampire or something. I'm telling you, it creeps me out."

"Maybe she's the bad thing."

"That's what I think sometimes, that she's the reason I'm

having nightmares. She puts them into me and then stands around and waits for them to happen."

"That's evil."

"I'd like to do that to her sometime, see how she likes it."

"My parents never come into my room."

"Do you lock the door?"

"They took the locks off, remember?"

"Oh yeah," Jodi said. "You have those holes in the door. That's also creepy. Do you ever see an eye looking through?"

"Only your mother's." I could make a mom joke; there were no bans with Jodi.

Jodi talked for more than an hour, and when she was tired enough to go back to sleep, I was still wide awake. The sky was a bright gray, getting ready for the dawn. I sneaked out of the house and walked to the park and then down River Road and doubled back along the railroad tracks. The river was gray and pink, reflecting the sky. The water smelled cold and stale, like a wet cloth that had been left out all night. There was almost no sound, everything as still as the railroad tracks. I thought that if the world could be like this, stay like this the entire day, maybe I would like it, maybe Jodi would be able to sleep through the night, maybe everyone would stay asleep, a deep and restful sleep just before morning, and I could walk around, alone, walk back and forth along the river, and then I thought how stupid it was to think like that. It didn't do any good. Not enough was going to stay the same, and too much would.

Our brains are too big for our meager abilities and too small to help us overcome them

After a three-month absence I was back with Stinchcomb. My father didn't care if it wasn't efficient, I guess. Maybe he wanted to make sure that people couldn't say he wasn't doing anything. They did all they could.

I remember my mother and father rolling their eyes when I was little—before all of this happened—and I would get upset. I wasn't like other kids—I didn't throw myself on the floor, or scream and shout and cry, or hold my breath or whatever crap other kids pull—I would look my mother in the eye and tell her, "I think I'll go throw myself in the river," and she would roll her eyes or, if she was angry enough, she'd tell me that I'd just wind up in Quincy or Hannibal and be someone else's problem. She never thought I'd do it. And now I am someone else's problem. Hello again, Dr. Stinchcomb.

Bruce referred to him as "Felthy." "Felthy Stinchcomb, that's a perfect name for him," Bruce said without knowing anything about the man, without ever laying an eye on him, hearing him talk, nothing. And he was right—it was the perfect name for him. Sometimes in our sessions, it was all I could do to not think about it—I could hear Bruce saying it over and over: Felthy Stinchcomb, Felthy Stinchcomb, Felthy Stinchcomb, so many times that I wanted to say it aloud. Yes, Felthy Stinchcomb, no, Felthy Stinchcomb. Other times I had to force myself to think about it—when the good doctor was blathering on about this "cool" band I should listen to or this book I should read or some other boring crap no one could care less about. I would sit and nod and repeat "Felthy Stinchcomb" in my mind until it became a calming chorus, a distraction that almost equaled meditation. I would say the name to myself and let the sound of it sit in my head until it started to fade and then say it again and then again, like playing the same chord on the piano over and over so there's a constant sound growing and filling the inside of my head, filling it so much that I thought I would have to open my mouth to let it out. It became that I couldn't look at Dr. Stinchcomb without thinking of the name; I couldn't think about him without the name; I couldn't even think about the sessions without associating the name. It was the only thing I liked about any of it, but the trouble was that Bruce liked it too. He liked the name so much, in fact, that he tried to take it back so he could use it for someone else. It didn't work, however; everyone who knew about him had called him Felthy for so long that they weren't about to stop just because Bruce wanted to use the name for someone else (someone as yet unidentified, no less). Besides, it fit

Dr. Stinchcomb. It was Dr. Stinchcomb. Dr. Felthy Stinchcomb, MD. He was Felthy, all right.

There is only darkness. There is no light, no soothing glow, no comforting voices, no out-of-body experience where you float above yourself and are filled with acceptance. There is only darkness, except it's not even darkness since that implies that you're seeing something. It's nothingness, a void, the absence of everything. It's exactly what I like about it, the only thing, the thing I want. Everything else is bullshit.

Those people who experience those other things—well, I don't know—I hope they're true and real enough for them, but it's not what I experience. If it were, I probably wouldn't bother trying again and again, or maybe I would. I might, if I was certain that a better life waited for me on the other side, whatever that means. Maybe it's real for them or that they believe it's real, or maybe it's simply a chemical change in the brain or a cultural hysteria, like all those people who are abducted by aliens and the aliens look exactly alike. What are the odds of that? Scientists have been able to re-create the "near-death, out-of-body" experience by stimulating a certain part of the brain. They call the experience "autoscopy." I learned that from Maddy. She also told me that there's a "negative autoscopy" experience, where a person can't see their own image in a mirror.

"Like a vampire."

"Nothing like a vampire," she corrected. "A vampire doesn't have a reflection. With negative autoscopy everybody else can see the image except the person who's casting it. Get it?"

I did, and we went back to me pushing her on the swing.

Dr. Stinchcomb asked me, "Why do you think you're so fixated on death?"

"I wouldn't use the word 'fixated.'"

"What word would you use?"

"Well, 'fixated' has a judgmental quality to it, doesn't it? I think 'determined' better describes what it's all about."

"What is it about?"

"Correcting a mistake."

TWO

The stars are all dead, but their memories fill the sky (#29)

A thousand stars showered the night, rising out of the darkness like the first sparks thrown out of the big bang, hot red darts twisting and turning every which way, flooding the blackness and then returning to it. We witnessed the beginning and the end, all of it right there in front of us, the whole show, and we marveled at it, not because we had witnessed the birth and death of entire galaxies, millions and millions of stars, but because we had made it. In our stupid drunkenness we had made it, and like God we looked down upon it and thought it was good.

Todd had his brother's truck, so we went mobile. "It's good to get out and see the world," Todd joked, which might have even included the back roads of Iowa. We loaded the back of the truck with a couple of cases of beer and left town, driving out along the farm roads, long stretches of freshly planted fields, the thick air rushing past us as we went aimlessly from one part of the countryside to the other, winding north.

I was huddled behind the cab—the night air was cooler than I thought it was going to be and all I had on was a T-shirt and pair of shorts, and I'd been too late in my call for shotgun. Todd and Ash were in the cab, and the rest of us sat in silence in the back. That was the best part—the quiet, at least the quiet among us—there was plenty of noise around us, the sound of the tires on the dirt and gravel roads, the wind whipping around us—no conversations, just the sound of the truck and the night, and when Todd got tired of driving, he would stop the truck and we'd sit and drink in silence, for a while anyway.

"I have an idea," Bruce said. And for once it was a good one.

We drove back into town and into the Hy-Vee parking lot. Darryl and I got out and patrolled the lot, casually making our way to any stray shopping carts that had been left and waited for Todd to come around so we could throw them to Vern in the back. We had to be on watch for any white-aproned stock boys, as they were the ones who were supposed to mind the carts, but they usually are seen helping older customers to their cars with sickening ingratiation—slobbering, bootlicking for tips they weren't supposed to take in the first place.

Vern had stacked five carts in the back when one of the managers came out to the lot and gave us the stink eye. He couldn't see the carts in the truck from his vantage, but he knew we were up to no good, so Todd drove off and Darryl and I faded away in the night, walking behind the store and down the block, where Todd was waiting.

We jumped into the back of the truck and drove out of town to a paved road off Carbine Lane, near the Missouri border. It was a dark, straight piece of road that went about a half mile or so, rarely used except for illegal races back in the day, we heard. It was perfect for us. No one was on it. Todd stopped the truck and turned off the lights and the engine and we sat and listened to the night as it settled around us and then didn't move. Nothing moved, not even the wind in the trees. It was just us and the dark, and Bruce said, "Let's do it," and Todd started the truck and hit the gas and we kept picking up speed and then went faster. I tried to look through the cab window to see the speedometer, but Todd's shoulder kept getting in the way. We were doing better than eighty—that was the last I saw, and we kept going faster and then Todd shut off the lights.

It was like being in space. We were hurtling through the dark like astronauts. There was nothing but the darkness and us accelerating. And then Bruce tossed one of the carts out of the back of the truck and the sparks flew up behind us in the most amazing shower, the big bang, the beginning of our own universe. We were gods. We did it again.

Todd turned on the lights and slowed down the truck and we drove back, making sure the other cart was off the road. We didn't see it at all. Vern wondered if it had disintegrated, smashed to oblivion. We could only hope. "I wish we could film this," he said.

"Let me throw one," Darryl said, but Todd overruled him.

"Let Bruce," he said. "He knows what he's doing."

Darryl would have usually argued. How much do you need

to know to throw something out of a truck? he would have said, but we were all so impressed with what we had just witnessed that he didn't care. We only wanted it to happen again, and soon. So Todd started the truck from the same spot as before—we went through the same thing, trying to replicate everything exactly. And the same thing happened—the explosion of sparks as the cart clattered across the pavement.

Todd wanted to watch the next time, so he had me drive, and Darryl rode in the cab. The third time wasn't nearly as good—the cart skidded off the road too soon, which was just the way it bounced, but I got the blame, from Darryl mostly, so Todd was back in the driver's seat, and I rode shotgun for the fourth time. It wasn't any better, so we went back to our original spots for the final cart.

Todd tried to find the first starting place and he gunned the engine and brought the truck up to eighty or more and then hit the lights just as he'd done all the other times, but something was different. We were hurtling through space, like before, but it felt as if we were falling, as if we were in a rocket ship that was plunging through space, accelerating on a collision course with the earth. It wasn't frightening; it was exhilarating. I would have welcomed the crash, would have wanted it, but I knew it wasn't happening—it only felt like it—so I stood up and could hear Bruce positioning the cart, could see his silhouette in the night, and I was careful to avoid him as I jumped out of the back of the truck.

I hadn't put any more thought into it than that, and when I woke up, I was back in my bed. Jodi was there and so was Todd.

"What happened?" he said.

"I don't know. I wanted to see if I'd throw off sparks, I guess. Did I?"

"You wouldn't be joking about it if you'd seen it."

He meant the aftermath. "I know. Or I can imagine."

"No you can't. If you could, you wouldn't have done it."

"Don't be pissy."

"I'm not. But I think it got to Vern. Don't tell him I said so, but he was shook up," Todd said. "I thought you were having a good time."

"I was. That's why I did it. I don't know. I wasn't thinking about it. I just did it. What can I say? You knew I was coming back."

"I guess so," Todd said. "You should have seen the mess. We had to put you in the back of the truck. It got all over."

"I bet it did." It sounded sarcastic, not how I meant it at all.

"How do you think we got you there?" Todd said, looking down at his hands as if they still had the muck on them.

"I'll take care of it."

"It's taken care of," Todd said.

"It won't happen again." It didn't. Not like that anyway.

THREE

Meet Mr. Coolidge, the angry transcendentalist

I took a book with me every day to The Point, the same book every day, something by William Styron that our Lit teacher, Mr. Coolidge, had given me the last day of school. It wasn't even ninety pages long, but I never made it past the first paragraph. You'd think that The Point would be the perfect place to get something done, but you couldn't get anything done with my friends around. They can't leave you alone. They were like amped-up lab monkeys who'd just broken out of their cages. I'd try to listen to music, but the minute the headphones went on, one of them was either yelling at me about what I was listening to or grabbing the headphones away from me. You might wonder why I went there day after day—it's a good question. But what else was I going to do? Besides, in the end we all wanted the same thing—to waste as much time as possible, to kill the summer as much as we could—and we did; we watched it die every day, slowly rot away just like our beached bovine friend lying there in front of us. I was resigned to wait it out and resigned to the fact that I wouldn't get a single book read, not the one Mr. Coolidge gave me or any on the list he'd stuck inside it. School would start again, not soon enough, but it would come back.

Mr. Coolidge's class was the only one I liked in school, and even it was a struggle. Mr. Coolidge taught Literature the first period after lunch in a windowless room on the first floor that was just dark enough and just warm enough to make it a perfect place for a nap. Some heads started nodding within the first five minutes, and by the end of the period, probably half the class was passed out, their heads flat on the desks and their mouths open, taking in the warm air that fueled their daytime sleep. Mr. Coolidge didn't care.

"It's your time," he would say. "You might as well learn this now because it will be that way in college. No one is going to care if you sleep, do the work, get a good grade, whatever." He acted as if we were all going, even though less than fifteen percent of our seniors ever went to college. We preferred to fill our factories and fast-food counters, to occupy the bars and drunk tanks, pump gas, wait tables, tend bars, and never leave the nest or fall far from the tree—we stay put and live and die where we were born. We didn't go anywhere. So get educated, America; we've got the rest of it covered.

I almost never met Mr. Coolidge because he nearly got himself fired last year when he tried to teach *Fight Club* in his AP class. He handed out permission slips to all of his students and said that they needed a parent's signature before they could watch the movie. That was his first mistake—never ask for permission. I could have told him that. You just do it and then apologize afterward. But once one of the parents got wind of what was going on, they organized their local church and wanted him gone.

The thing of it is, it was Rachel Pasco's parents who threw the shit fit and got everyone riled, even the parents who had signed permission. Rachel Pasco drank and smoked cigarettes, smoked pot, and it was said that she smoked choad on three different guys in the parking lot by the old steamboat one night, drunk on liquor we'd given her, and I doubt if she'd gotten her parents permission for any of that. But she needed to be protected from a stupid movie. And, oh yeah, she'd already seen *Fight Club*, which she told Mr. Coolidge after she nearly got him fired.

So Rachel Pasco had deprived everyone from learning Mr. Coolidge's transcendentalist take on Brad Pitt and Ed Norton (a discovery of the self through fragmentation, anyone?) and now she'd graduated and gone on to college and left the rest of us under her parents' still-watchful eyes and got Mr. Coolidge punished by having to teach us in the fall.

Everybody called him Mr. Cool, some with a lot of sarcasm and others—mostly the girls—actually meant it. I never called him anything other than Mr. Coolidge. And Bruce had to have his own name for him, of course. He preferred Mr. Schoolidge, which never really caught on, or Mr. School. Mr. Coolidge didn't seem to care what people called him—he would stand in the hallway and talk with people between classes and nod or wave whenever he heard a "Mr. Cool" rise out of the steady stream of students passing in the narrow hallway. The only thing that seemed to bother Mr. Coolidge was our class. He wasn't even supposed to be teaching us—he usually taught the juniors and seniors and had an AP class with a handful of students who actually did want to go to college—but the other teacher bailed a week before school started and moved on to something better, I guess, so Mr. Coolidge was stuck with us and we were stuck with him and the optimistic futures he saw for us.

He complained for the first few weeks, grumbled under his breath, cursing his fate, we thought. It wasn't that, it turned out. He wasn't unhappy with us, wasn't unhappy with the class—he didn't like the crap he had to teach. He didn't like the curriculum, the lessons, and especially the books. He hated them. Finally, it was too much. "We're not reading Shakespeare," he said one day, and everyone was awake for that. "We're not reading a play. You have to watch a play." But we weren't entirely done with Shakespeare, it turned out. Mr. Coolidge scrounged a TV and DVD player and we watched Roman Polanski's version of *Macbeth*, which had enough mud, blood, and nudity to keep almost everyone awake for the entire class, even in the dark. The next class we watched some British version—not a movie, a televised play. "If you want the experience of reading," Mr. Coolidge said, "just close your eyes." Plenty of people did.

Mr. Coolidge was unpredictable—you never knew if he was going to criticize *The Old Man and the Sea*, or slam *The Adventures of Huckleberry Finn*, or rant on and on about how much he hated John Steinbeck. Some people in class actually started defending some of the things we read, which Coolidge loved. He liked a good argument, and you never knew which side he would take. He was unpredictable in all things except his clothes. He had two shirts—a dark blue and a pale blue version of the same shirt, and in the winter he wore an oatmeal-colored cable-neck sweater over the shirt. There was a lengthy debate among the girls about whether he owned multiples of the same shirt or if it was only the two, which he wore day after day after day.

"He smells good," Jodi said one night down by the bridge. She had brought a couple of friends with her, including Kayla Morton, who was one of the prettiest girls in school. There was no debate about that.

"Fresh," Kayla said. "He smells fresh, with a hint of citrus, maybe grapefruit. I think he uses Aveda."

This was torture for most of us, especially Ash. They weren't talking about anything we wanted to hear about; they weren't talking about us, and they were talking about school. And they liked Mr. Coolidge.

"So what if he wears the same clothes?" Jodi said. "He works it."

"Straight or gay?" Kayla said.

"That's a beer," Vern said.

"Forget it," Todd said. "She's a guest."

Kayla had no idea what they were talking about. She was the reason they wanted Jodi to hang out with us, and here they were getting ready to scare her away. Kayla only came because we had alcohol, and even that wasn't enough to keep her for long. I can't blame her—I wouldn't hang out with us if I had a choice.

Maybe Kayla knew that all of us—most of us anyway—were

infatuated with her. She used us, and we used her, I guess, as far as that goes. I never really liked it when she and her friends were around. They acted as if they were doing us a favor (and they were) and were constantly texting to see if there was something better going on somewhere else. And Ash and Vern and the rest of them always acted different when they were around, and not different in a better way. They were even stranger, like people who go to fancy restaurants and pretend to know which one's the soup spoon and which one's for dessert, but they screw up everything. That's what Kayla did to them, and maybe me as well. And if there was something better, Kayla and the rest of them were gone. Except for Jodi; she always stayed. When she joined us, she was there for the duration.

"Kayla's sort of a smutty name," Bruce said after she'd left us again. "Sort of suggestive."

"How do you mean?" Jodi said.

"It's a porn star name," he said.

"Is it?" Todd said. "Name a porn star named Kayla."

No one could.

"It still sounds like one," Bruce said.

"Morton doesn't."

"She wouldn't use her last name," Bruce said. "Kayla Cream, now that's a porn star name."

"Only because of the last name," Ash said. "Anything's going to sound smutty with that."

"Not Darryl," Ash said.

○ ○ ○

We had to write an essay every week. Mr. Coolidge announced the topic on Monday and we had to hand the thing in on Friday. It was only a one-page essay, which sounded easy, but it turned out to be the hardest thing to do—you had to cut to the chase, make your argument, and get out. Mr. Coolidge liked arguments; he liked being challenged. That was the point of the essays, I think, to make arguments against the things he said.

The first thing he told us was that he was a transcendentalist. He said it like someone says they're a Republican, or a socialist, a Baptist or a Catholic, or like someone who stands up in a room full of strangers and says, "I'm an alcoholic." "I just want you to know what to expect," he said, and then gave us a list of books to read that were critical of what he taught us.

The first essay I wrote for Mr. Coolidge was on the Edgar Allan Poe story "Never Bet the Devil Your Head," which was (I thought) a clear criticism of the transcendentalists, but I picked it from Mr. Coolidge's list because of the title. I had no idea the entire story was about a leaper like me—but not like me at all. He was a transcendentalist, which for Poe meant that he was a fool and a very bad leaper. The story was funny, and I tried to be funny in my essay, but it didn't work out so well. Poe made decapitation a lot more entertaining.

I had one good essay; after reading "Bartleby, the Scrivener," I decided to hand in a blank sheet of paper. Mr. Coolidge returned it to me in the same condition—none of his usual comments, no grade, nothing. He handed it to me as if it were exactly like every other paper, every other one he casually held out for everyone else in class, and every other one he'd ever given back to me. Not a word about it until the end of the day—when I was walking out, he said, "I liked your paper. It was perfect. For that story. It's going to be hard to top."

"Maybe I won't hand in anything next time."

"If you can come up with a good reason. If not, maybe I won't hand in a grade," he said.

"I could live with an incomplete."

"I'm sure you could," he said, and closed his door behind me.

It sounded good, but Mr. Coolidge knew I was lying. All I had were my grades—they were my pass, my get-out-of-jail-(somewhat)-free card, the only thing I had to give my parents an excuse to let me do all the other stuff. I had good grades—mostly As with a few Bs—which allowed my parents to not go completely hysterical; they didn't care (or not as much) that I went out drinking every night or jumped from a bridge or cliff every once in a while as long as it appeared that my priorities were aligned with theirs.

"At least he gets good grades," they could tell themselves. I was like a celebrity who gets caught with a prostitute or goes on a drug-fueled rampage or the athlete who gets caught using steroids, or cheating on his wife, or slapping her around, or doing some other deviant thing. As long as he keeps winning, keeps making hit movies, the fans will forgive him. You have to figure out what's important, do that, and use it as a cover for what you really want to do. Be productive—that's what my father taught me—and for someone my age there isn't a lot of opportunity to be productive except in school, so that's where I show them what I can do—the rest is extracurricular distractions, things that can be forgiven and tolerated. If my grades ever dipped, then I'd really be in trouble.

Anything you say can and will be used against you

Mr. Coolidge was standing alone in the hallway as I headed to homeroom and I don't know why, but I went up to him and handed him a piece of paper with a list I'd made. Sometimes I share too much.

"My therapist, you know, Dr. Stinchcomb, had me write up a list of my favorite books. What do you think?"

Favorite Books:

Madame Bovary

Romeo and Juliet

The Sound and the Fury

Jude the Obscure

Anna Karenina

Hamlet

The Brothers Karamazov

Crime and Punishment

Antigone

The Picture of Dorian Gray

The Sorrows of Young Werther

The Great Gatsby

Mrs. Dalloway

"It's a clever list," Mr. Coolidge said. "I see it has an obvious theme. What did your doctor say?"

"Nothing. He didn't get it. He's full of shit anyway."

"Maybe he's full of shit because that's all you give him," Mr. Coolidge said. "Have you ever heard the phrase 'crap in, crap out'?"

"Yeah." I wanted my paper back so I could go to homeroom.

"This list is crap. How do you expect to get anything out of your meetings if you don't put anything into them?"

"It was a joke."

"And that's what you got back. You should make a real list sometime. I'd like to see that. Or read some of these; I bet you haven't even read most of them. Or better yet, I'd like to see you write about the ones you have read or write about anything, write about your sessions or whatever you want. Would you do that?"

"I thought you would think this was funny. I didn't show it to you to get more work."

"Fair enough," Mr. Coolidge said. "But don't be so afraid of work. Write me something, anything. I'd be happy to take a look at it." He held the list out to me, and I almost didn't take it back.

"It's not an assignment," he said. I took the list and headed to homeroom.

Mr. Coolidge started to bring me books. The first was *The Loser*, which I told him I wasn't going to read because of the title. Not so subtle. "Take a look," he said, "I think you'll be surprised." I only made it to about page sixty. It was too much—wall-to-wall writing or raving, more like it—no breaks, no chapters or even paragraphs, only the endless accumulation of sentence after sentence for almost two hundred pages, each page wallpapered with words about people and things I knew nothing about and cared to know less.

Mr. Coolidge wasn't disappointed that I didn't finish it. "I wanted you to see a different way of doing it," he said. I saw it. Maybe I'll see it again. I've looked for it in the library; they don't have it, of course. Mr. Coolidge came right back with more—he liked to give me dark books—*Nausea, The Thanatos Syndrome, Death on the Installment Plan*—along with some of his transcendentalist stuff. Of course he thought all of it was transcendentalist stuff. This is the guy who wanted to show *Fight Club*, remember?

The clock has a face I don't recognize (#28)

Sometimes I wonder if I'm even alive. I wonder if maybe I really did die that first time and I'm wandering around like some guy in a stupid movie who doesn't even know that he's dead. It feels like that sometimes, a bad movie. And let me tell you this—if this is what it's like in the afterlife, you're going to be really disappointed.

Of course most people's life is a movie no one would actually want to see, but mine is more like that except it's like the kind in movies or books in one way—it doesn't move from one second to the next, an uninterrupted flow—instead, it is full of jump cuts, flashbacks, flash forwards, scene changes—made up of a series of fades-to-black and the white spaces between chapters. These are my favorite parts. I joked with Mr. Coolidge that I was going to write a book filled with all the spaces between chapters in famous books. I think he thought I was serious for a second and he got all excited. "Here's the stuff between chapters seventeen and eighteen in *Tom Sawyer.*" I handed him a blank sheet of paper.

"You really try to get a lot of mileage out of nothing," Mr. Coolidge said.

"All these people obsessed with death"

Someone has created the online group The Adam Strand Death Pool. It was probably Vern, but I don't say anything to him. It only has two hundred and forty-one fans. Most people don't care, I guess, which is fine by me. I'm sure Vern is disappointed, though.

Oh my God, they killed Kenny

am not immortal. I believe that. Death comes for everything, but not for me. I don't believe that either—death will come for me; death will find me; one day I will meet the same fate as everyone else when the time comes. I believe that. I'll live to a ripe old age and die of "natural causes." I'll fall down the stairs when I'm sixty. I'll drop dead of a heart attack at forty. I'll develop a tumor right behind my nose that will be misdiagnosed as a sinus problem until it grows to the size of a softball and kills me at thirty. I'll die from salmonella or *E. coli* from eating a tainted egg or hamburger or who knows what, be abducted and murdered before I turn twenty-one; my bones will slowly become brittle and break under their own weight too late in life. I'll get hit by a car. I'll get killed by sniper fire in another of our never-ending military missions. I'll go goofy from stroke or senility and drift along for years. Someone will stab me in the throat with an ice pick. I'll die peacefully in my sleep.

There are probably as many ways to die as there are people

who've done it. Whenever our time comes, however, we get lumped into the statistical heap; the specific and unique way is sanded down until it fits into a category. Heart disease, cancer, stroke, emphysema, accidents, diabetes, the flu, Alzheimer's, kidney disease, infection, suicide. Those are the ways we die in America. Take your pick.

People drop dead all the time; it's everywhere, surrounding us, but most people choose to ignore it—more than 170,000 people die in the world every day, about two every second, more times a day than your heart beats. It never stops. A few people have died in the time it takes to read this sentence, and now a few more. They keep dying all the time and someday we'll all be part of it, maybe seconds apart, maybe minutes or years, but we'll all be added to the sheer tonnage of it, the relentless ceasing. I know I think about it more than most, but no one seems to want to talk about it much. Todd doesn't say anything. "Don't you think about it?"

"I think about it," he says, "but not very much; it's a waste of time. There's nothing I can do about it."

And the rest of them are morons. You can't have a serious conversation with any of them. Ash turns it into a sex joke. "All I know is that I'll die in the saddle," he said. There's no point in trying with them.

Jodi's the only one who talks about it. One night, maybe after the tenth or twelfth event, she texted me: 11y curious—y? dy alws kil yrslf @ nyt?

That was easy to answer—I never felt like it in the day,

especially in the morning. But by afternoon, usually three or four, the weight of the day, the accumulation of the hours and minutes and all those seconds gathering like single flakes, gathering and gathering into a giant avalanche rushing toward me—it was all too much, until by the time it became dark, I felt as if I would be crushed by the tonnage of it all. I always thought that maybe I'd be all right if the day began around one or two in the morning and ended around noon. Then I could take a brief nap, have dinner, and then go to bed long before the weight could accumulate and the avalanche start all over again. The world doesn't work like that, however. You have to fit into it; it's not going to fit you.

Maybe I should have tried more, that's what I think. Maybe I tried hard enough to fit in and didn't try hard enough at the other. It's impossible not to think like that, with so many chances left untouched. There are more days that I didn't kill myself, after all, than those where I did. I wasn't going to fit in either way, but at least I tried to keep it to myself.

It doesn't matter where I go;
I'm always home (#18)

I'd had lots of doctors look at me over the years, but they weren't *my* doctor, the one we went to when we needed one. Dr. V. was the one constant, our first call. He was always there, his calm face peering at me when I had a sore throat, when I had measles, the mumps, chicken pox and when I'd come back from being in the river, landed on the rocks, back from a shotgun blast. He never seemed surprised by any of it. He heard it all and then sent us off to the specialists in Iowa City. They didn't know any more than he did. And here I still was, and Dr. V. is gone.

One hot afternoon in August last year, Dr. Vandever was out mowing his lawn—had, in fact, finished almost half of the expansive front yard of his house on Grand Avenue—when he stopped, shut down the push mower, and went inside and blew his brains out. "At least he could have finished the lawn," my father said when he heard the news. I thought that the doctor and I had more in common than I ever realized.

Dr. Vandever, unlike me, however, stayed dead.

So I'm left with Dr. Stinchcomb, who couldn't stop talking about Dr. V. If Dr. Vandever was a calm, quiet pool, Felthy was a babbling brook. "What do you think about it?" he asked me twenty thousand times.

I usually shrugged, which only made him ask it again. "Nobody knows about this stuff. Nobody," he said, answering his own question.

"Nobody?"

"Not really. Because it was all in his head, what he saw and thought and felt, and because he didn't tell anybody about any of it, didn't talk about any of it, nobody knew. What do you think about that?"

"I don't."

"You don't think about it?" Dr. Stinchcomb said.

"No."

"You don't think about Dr. Vandever?"

I shrugged. I didn't like him talking about it; I didn't even like him saying his name. He said it again.

"I think about the good stuff Dr. V. did, all the people he helped. Everybody says he was a good doctor, and now he's gone."

"And you're still here," Dr. Stinchcomb said, which wasn't my point. "It doesn't seem fair to you?"

"I didn't say that. Nothing's fair; everybody knows that."

"What is it, then?"

I wondered what it would be like to say "no more" and have it actually be true, to not have to come back to the unmowed lawn but actually leave it forever, and then I wondered if I could leave and not come back myself but let someone come back in my place. I would go, and instead of waking up in my bed like every other time, someone else would wake up instead. I wondered if I would bring back Dr. Vandever—if I could only bring back one, would it be him? Would I even want to do it at all? If I could bring back anyone, anyone at all in history, who would it be? Maybe I'd bring back Hitler, let him have another run at things, or his doctor—what was his name? Mengele. Here Dr. Vandever did nothing but help people all his life, was a good man, as far as everyone knew, and who will remember him? And Mengele did nothing but evil, tortured people, inflicted death and pain and suffering on thousands and thousands of people, and everybody remembers him. People would probably be happier if I brought the Nazi back.

"Is he the first person you know who's killed himself?" Dr. Stinchcomb said.

"Freud."

Felthy looked away. He was disgusted with me. I could tell, because he always did the same thing—a slight straighten in his chair, a small turn of his head to the left and down, and his eyes pointed to the floor. That was his controlled look of disgust. Maybe he thought people didn't notice. I bet they do. He does it a lot. "I meant that you know personally," he said.

"I guess." We were done for the day. I don't know how I knew that about Freud, but Dr. Stinchcomb was tired of hearing about it, so on the way home I tried to think of other people I could mention to him, other names that might get the same look out of him. I could always go back to good old Sigmund, he was money in the bank, but I didn't want to completely deplete the account. When I got home, I did some research and found there's a treasure trove.

Famous Suicides

Name	title	method	year	age
Mike Awesome	professional wrestler	hanging	2007	42
Prince Alfred of Edinburgh	Prince	gunshot	1899	24
Salvador Allende	President of Chile	gunshot	1973	65
Mark Antony	Roman politician	stabbing	30 BC	47
Diane Arbus	photographer	overdose/slashed wrists	1971	48
Edwin Armstrong	inventor of FM radio	jumped from window	1954	63
Rick Berry	basketball player	gunshot	1989	24
John Berryman	poet	jumped from bridge	1972	57
Eli M. Black	ceo of United Brands (Chiquita)	jumped from window	1975	53
Clara Blandick	actress (Auntie Em in Wizard of Oz)	overdose/suffocation	1962	81
Mohamed Bouazizi	Tunisian protestor	self-immolation	2011	26
Richard Brautigan	writer	gunshot	1984	49
August Anheuser Busch, Sr.	beer magnate	gunshot	1934	68
Vic Chesnutt	musician	overdose	2009	45
Chung Mong-hun	Chairman of Hyundai Asan	jumped from building	2003	44
Tyler Clementi	Rutgers University student	jumped from bridge	2010	18
Cleopatra	Queen of Egypt	poisoning	30 BC	39
Kurt Cobain	musician (Nirvana)	gunshot	1994	27
Ian Curtis	musician (Joy Division)	hanging	1980	23
Rudolf Diesel	inventor of Diesel engine	jumped from boat	1913	55
Michael Dorris	writer	overdose/suffocation	1997	52
Dave Duerson	NFL player	gunshot	2011	50
George Eastman	founder of Eastman Kodak	gunshot	1932	77
Frederick Fleet	Titanic lookout	hanging	1965	67
Vincent Foster	Deputy White House Counsel	gunshot	1993	48
Sigmund Freud	founder of psychoanalysis	assisted overdose	1939	83
Martha Gelhorn	journalist, wife of Ernest Hemingway	drug overdose	1998	89
Arshile Gorky	painter	hanging	1948	44
Shauna Grant	adult film actress	gunshot	1984	20
Hannibal	Carthaginian commander	poisoning	182 BC	68
Ernest Hemingway	writer	gunshot	1961	61
Leicester Hemingway	brother of Ernest Hemingway	gunshot	1982	77
Margaux Hemingway	actress	overdose	1996	42
Adolf Hitler	dictator	gunshot	1945	56

Preston King	senator from NY	jumped from boat	1865	59
Primo Levi	writer	jumped from building	1987	67
Meriwether Lewis	explorer	gunshot	1809	35
Ron Luciano	baseball umpire	carbon monoxide poisoning	1995	57
Richard Manuel	musician (The Band)	hanging	1986	42
Vladimir Mayakovsky	poet	gunshot	1930	36
Donnie Moore	baseball player	gunshot	1989	35
Nero	Roman emperor	stabbing	68	30
Frank Nitti	gangster	gunshot	1943	62
Otho	Roman emperor	stabbing	69	36
Sylvia Plath	writer	gas	1963	30
Felix Powell	songwriter (Smile, Smile, Smile)	gunshot	1942	63
Nathan Pritikin	longevity pioneer	slit wrists	1985	70
George Reeves	Superman	gunshot	1959	45
Roh Moo-hyun	President of South Korea	jumped from cliff	2009	62
Mark Rothko	painter	slit wrists	1970	66
Junior Seau	NFL player	gunshot	2012	43
Seneca	philosopher	slit wrists and poison	65	66
Anne Sexton	poet	carbon monoxide poisoning	1974	45
Socrates	philosopher	poisoning	399 BC	71
Hunter S. Thompson	writer	gunshot	2005	67
Kokichi Tsuburaya	Olympic marathon runner	slit throat	1968	27
Alan Turing	mathematician/computer scientist	cyanide poisoining	1954	41
Vincent Van Gogh	painter	gunshot	1890	37
David Foster Wallace	writer	hanging	2008	46
Andre Waters	NFL player	gunshot	2006	44
Virginia Woolf	writer	drowning	1941	59

This list could have been twice as long, three times longer—I didn't include any names my father or I didn't recognize, so maybe I left off some really famous people or sort of famous—I'm not even sure what that means—famous—how many people need to know you before you're considered famous, and for how long? The guy who used to host a TV game show thirty years ago killed himself—is he famous? My father couldn't remember his name, but when I said *Family Feud,* he remembered the story. Or the reporter who shot herself on live TV—my father couldn't remember her name, the TV station, or when it happened, but he remembered that someone had shot themselves on TV—is that fame? Is that what it means to be famous?

I wonder if it was in them from the beginning, ticking away like a bomb waiting to go off, maybe even unknown to them, or if they thought about it all the time, or if the idea came to them suddenly. I wonder if they were like me, but I don't know if you could accomplish something, anything, if you thought about it the way I do. Everybody on the list accomplished something; they did something with their lives before they decided to end them. I don't understand that. If I could do something, was good at something, had some sort of talent, any trace of it, it might be different. I don't know. The only talent I seem to have is in coming back, which keeps me from everything from I want.

It's a long list, I know, covers almost every age, occupation, nationality, method. I'd like to think there's not a pattern, but if you're the type that's worried that you might be susceptible, here's some advice—don't be a writer, a Roman, and whatever you do, don't be a Hemingway.

Out on Highway 61

My mother is a quiet person, quieter than most, I suppose, until she gets behind the wheel of a car. Then she wants to talk; she demands conversation. Maybe it keeps her alert— or maybe she thinks it does, when it's really a distraction. She's not a good driver. But she's a good talker when she's driving, and every week we had our nonstop talks to and from Mount Pleasant and Dr. Stinchcomb.

"*Pretense* is an odd word," she said one time, starting as if we had been talking about it, dropping me into some conversation she'd been having in her head. It didn't matter; there wasn't much opportunity to respond sometimes during her monologues. "*Pretense,* 'before tense.' It doesn't mean that, I know, but it seems like it should have something to do with time. How many verb tenses are there in English? I think there are twelve. Is that right?"

I shrugged.

"I think there are twelve," she said, and went on to name them, "and then our new one, pretense, which should be used for verbs that don't relate to time at all."

"Everything relates to time."

"I don't think so," she said. "I think some languages don't have any tenses at all. The verb is just the verb. *To drive* is just that. *I drive*—it doesn't mean now or then or in the future or doesn't necessarily mean any of those. Do you think if you didn't have tenses, you would think differently about time? I mean, it might be Chinese that doesn't have any tenses—let's say it is—do you think that helps them think about the past and the present differently than we do with our twelve? And what about languages that have more than twelve? It has to affect the way you think about time, the way you experience time, don't you think?"

"You're not going to test me on this later, are you?"

"I might," she said.

I wasn't really interested in what she was saying half the time, but my mother wasn't rambling, or not entirely. She was warming up or practicing. She stayed in the car during my session. She always brought a puzzle book with her, one of those brightly colored pulpy things you find at the supermarket, filled with word games, crosswords, acrostics, jumbles, cryptograms, word searches. They all had names like *Mega-Jumbo Puzzle Pack*, or *Miles and Miles of Mind Benders*, or *WTF Lo-Tech Ghetto-Looking Crap Bag of Time Wasters*—titles that were barely English and seemed as if they would repel the intelligence required to solve the challenges inside. She was good at them, and my father didn't really approve—you could see the annoyance on his face whenever he saw my mother "wasting" time with them at home—so she had an hour every week where she could do them in peace. She liked talking about tenses and words and all that stuff with me on the ride up to Mount Pleasant because it helped her in that hour alone in the car.

She never talked to me about Dr. Stinchcomb and what I said to him. She respected the fact that it was private, she said. I could tell her if I wanted, but I never wanted to tell her. What was there to say? So *she* talked, stream-of-conscious commentaries on whatever passed through her mind—words, the weather, the countryside, the road.

One time as we were leaving town for my session, she said, "This is Highway 61. Does that mean anything to you?"

"It runs north and south. North to Minnesota and south to New Orleans."

"That's it?" she said. "That's all it means?"

I shrugged.

"It's also called 'The Blues Highway,'" she said. "Robert Johnson sold his soul to the devil on Highway 61, and Bessie Smith died in a car crash on it."

I didn't know who those people were. "I don't like the blues."

"You would like them," she said, undeterred. "And Bob Dylan was born way up there near the tip of the highway. You have to know 'Highway 61 Revisited.'"

"I don't like Dylan."

"You will," she said. "But you know that album."

I shrugged.

"'Like a Rolling Stone'? You know that. 'Ballad of a Thin Man'? You know that."

"Okay."

"Well, they're on that record. And then there's the song 'Highway 61 Revisited,'" she said, and sang the first verse of it. My mother has a pretty voice. She sang in the choir in school and church when she was my age; she played the piano and flute and guitar. She doesn't do any of that anymore, but she'll still sing every now and then, when she's folding laundry or cleaning. I don't know any of the songs, and she has a good voice, but she's no Bob Dylan.

"That's too good. Sing it like Dylan."

She tried to wheeze and twang like him but stopped when we both started laughing too much. "You're going to make me wreck like Bessie Smith," she said, and then laughed some more. "Out on Highway 61," she sang again in her best Bob imitation, and then gave up. "You try," she said.

"I don't know the song."

"Just sing that part, that one line."

"No." I was done with it.

"Sing it one time," she said. "Sing it like Dylan."

"We're not even on the stupid highway anymore." We were over on 218 by this time.

"Sing something else, then," she said.

"I'm not singing. Just shut up about it."

She did shut up. We drove the rest of the way in silence. It was the only time. I wanted to say something, but I didn't know what to say to her. I looked out the side window at the fields and fields of corn and knew that somewhere there wasn't corn and somewhere there wasn't a Dr. Stinchcomb and somewhere there was another road, running along the river north and south, and there was someone dying in a car wreck and someone else waiting for the devil and somewhere else someone killing his son. And maybe she was thinking the same thing—or maybe she was thinking about how she wished she didn't have to be trapped in a car with me, wishing she didn't have to haul me back and forth on this road, back and forth to see a doctor she didn't want anyone to know about. Maybe she thought about driving down some other road, in some other part of the world, where she didn't have a loan officer husband and a son in college who never came home and another son who was still there, always there. Maybe she wished that I was gone. You couldn't blame her if she did.

I didn't say anything, but when I came back to the car after my session, I told her that I'd made Dr. Stinchcomb sing like Dylan. "You should have heard him sing," I said. "He makes Dylan sound good."

She talked all the way home.

Camus and Coolidge try a trick

"Do you know who Sisyphus is?" Mr. Coolidge asked in the hallway before class.

"Some guy who had to roll a rock up a hill over and over."

"Do you know why he had to do it?"

I did not.

"He thought he was smarter than Zeus," he said, "so the rock was his punishment, and the futility of always having to take it up the hill over and over. So that's Sisyphus. Do you know who Albert Camus is?"

I did not.

"He was a French philosopher and writer. There's a couple of books you might want to check out, but you should also know about an essay he wrote, called 'The Myth of Sisyphus.' In it, he writes that there's only one philosophical question: Should you commit suicide? What's the point of dragging that rock up the hill if it's only going to roll back down again? It doesn't matter, he says, so why not kill yourself? That's the question."

"What does he say?"

"You'll have to read it." He handed me a thin paperback. "I think you'll be surprised."

I read it. I wasn't surprised. It's a trick. Camus starts off all right; he says a lot of stuff I've been thinking but better. He knows the world is fucked ("absurd" is his word) and that Sisyphus is doomed to his futility, but his solution is to imagine that Sisyphus is happy. Imagination? Really?

I took the book back to Mr. Coolidge. "What did you think?" he asked.

"Camus chickened out."

"Okay, but don't you think he has a point, I mean, for those who are looking for an alternative?"

"We have to imagine happiness, he says. Isn't that the same thing he criticizes when he talks about people running to religion, drugs, whatever other ways to delude themselves?"

"He means it in a different way, a more meaningful way."

"He also forgets one huge point about Sisyphus."

"What's that?" Mr. Coolidge asked.

"Sisyphus is already dead. He couldn't kill himself if he wanted. He's doomed with that rock."

"You're right. Camus was trying to apply the myth to the rest of us. He didn't know you were out there waiting."

"That's all right. How did Camus die?"

"Car wreck."

"Perfect."

I like Mr. Coolidge. I think he's younger than he looks. He only has the one outfit, but it matches his personality, no nonsense. You know what you're getting. That's the difference between him and Dr. Stinchcomb—he's old and tries too hard to look young. Everybody wants to be young now. They can have it.

The Myth of

asked Dr. Stinchcomb if he'd read any Camus and he told me that he hadn't. I didn't know whether to believe him or not. I think he keeps too quiet; he acts dumber than he is so that I'll do more talking. It's not a conversation with him. I can't believe he's never read any Camus.

"You know about the myth of Sisyphus?"

He nodded.

"Do you think he's a hero?"

"What would make him a hero?" Dr. Stinchcomb said.

"I don't know, perseverance, I guess. Isn't that what we're supposed to think about him, stoically enduring his fate?"

"Is that what you think about him?"

"Not really. I think he's stupid. And I think if he was doing something other than rolling a rock up a hill, other people would think he was stupid too, or crazy."

"Why is that?"

"Isn't the definition of insanity doing the same thing over and over but expecting different results?"

"That's just a saying, not a definition. Is that even true?"

"Didn't Einstein say it?"

"No," Dr. Stinchcomb said. "Definitely not. And what difference would that make?"

"I don't know. None, I guess."

"Why do you think Einstein said it?"

"I don't know. I thought that's what someone told me the first time I heard it."

"But you don't know yourself?" he asked.

"No," I said. I was sorry that I'd brought it up.

"You should find out who said it."

I didn't really care.

"Have you ever heard the saying 'If at first you don't succeed, try, try again'?"

"I've heard it."

"Do you think that is insane?" I think Dr. Stinchcomb was enjoying himself.

"It's not the same. It doesn't mean do the same thing over and over; it means try it another way, maybe. I don't know."

"Do you know who said it?"

"Not Einstein."

"No," he said, "before him. I think it first appeared in schoolbooks in the mid-1800s to encourage students to do their homework."

"It figures."

"So is Sisyphus stupid or crazy?" he said.

"What if he was a guy who went to work and every time he arrived at the office, his boss punched him in the face? People would probably say he was both. Or what if he was a surgeon and every time he operated on a patient they died? What would people think of him then?"

"That's not the story, though," Dr. Stinchcomb said.

"I'm trying to apply it to today; isn't that what we're supposed to do?"

"Okay," he said, but I'm not sure he was that interested.

I tried a different approach. "I think I'm like him."

"How do you see the similarities?"

"I keep trying to leave but keep coming back. I'm the rock that keeps rolling back down the hill."

"So you're more like the rock than you're like Sisyphus?" he said.

"I wasn't being serious."

"Okay."

I didn't want to talk about it anymore. I shouldn't have talked about it at all with him. He hadn't read the book anyway, so what was the point? I'd already talked about it with Mr. Coolidge. That was the serious conversation. I was just wasting time with the doctor. Maybe he knew it. He didn't seem to care one way or the other, which is the only thing we had in common.

Everybody needs a sign (#19)

The town wanted to do something. They were annoyed with me. I was told that they talked about putting a better fence at the old bridge, high fences along the railings of the new bridge, but all of that was money they didn't want to spend just for me. If there'd been more people jumping off the bridge, maybe they would have done something, but not for one person. In the end, they put up the sign, but that was all—a nice green sign about the size of a No Parking notice with Life Is Worth Living printed in white letters. It was a nice sign and I know that they were only trying to help, but the sign meant nothing. The words said nothing—they were empty and hollow—life, worth, living—they are meaningless generalities, I thought. At first, anyway, then the more I thought about it, the more those words started to bother me. It was "worth"—it implied value, money. What is life worth? How much? Is it all the same? Is my life worth just as much as yours? Is your life worth more or less than that of the person next to you, across the room, across the street, across the world? There are more than six billion people on the planet; are their lives all worth the same? And how much is it? Is the baby born six seconds ago worth as much, more, or less than the ninety-five-year-old who just had a stroke? Is a fireman's life worth the same as the arsonist's, the girl in a coma on life support as much as the doctor, the murderer on death row as much as the woman dying from cancer? Are all those lives worth living? I wish it were true. But it's their sign.

My conversations with God are just as boring as all the rest

The voice of God calls me almost every night. I call him the voice of God because he's only a voice. I've never met him; I don't know what he looks like. There's only the voice—a nice, comforting voice on the phone, a voice you wouldn't mind listening to, reading to you, or talking to you if he had something to say, but mostly he says the same thing, every night. God's name is Don Lemley and he works as the dispatcher at the police station—he's been there almost twenty years and worked the graveyard shift. He called me four or five times a week, usually before he went to work, wondering how I was doing, if I needed anything, did I think I was going to jump that night? Don Lemley was a nice guy—I thought about having him call Jodi and talk to her about her nightmares, but she didn't want that, and maybe he didn't either. So I had him all to myself—it didn't hurt anything, but it didn't help either.

"How are you doing?" is what the voice of God says every time he calls. We talk for a few minutes and then we're done and he's not sure whether I'm going to jump that night or the next, and half the time I don't know myself, but he's done his good deed for the day, I guess is what he thinks, and the rest is up to me. Over the years, I've slowly learned a lot about Don Lemley. He is a religious man, but he doesn't preach to me. He has never once told me not to kill myself. He mostly asks about me and asks me about my family and school and the usual crap except when he asks, I think he actually wants to hear about it. He doesn't talk about himself much, but I have learned a lot.

He was born in Council Bluffs. His parents were devout Jehovah's Witnesses, who believed that the world would end sometime in 1975, so they moved the family to Brooklyn to be near the church's headquarters. Don was a teenager. He says he knows what it's like to want the world to end. He and his parents prayed for it—they believed it was going to happen; they wanted it to happen so Christ could come back and everything would be better. When it didn't happen, they were broke and out of work, out of school, out of everything. So they came here. His parents remained in the church, but Don didn't. He says he never lost his faith, but he didn't believe in the church. He asks me if I've ever read the Bible and I tell him a little. I tell him that I know that there are at least six suicides and that dead people get up and walk around all the time in the Bible, which made the voice of God laugh. He sends me Bibles and copies of *The Watchtower*, with Post-it notes stuck all over the place. Don Lemley might have the voice of God, but he has the handwriting of a drunk with Parkinson's, and half the time I give up trying to figure out what he's written. He never asks me about it anyway. In fact, he rarely brings it up and usually only talks about it when I ask. I ask him if he thinks I'm going to hell, and he says no. The Jehovah's Witness, according to the voice of God, does not believe in heaven or hell but believes in a nonexistence after death, at least until the end of the world, when the witnesses will be selected to live again in some paradise on earth. There's always a paradise in the end, isn't there?

One more thing about time

"**B**old are the hands of time that creep along relentlessly, destroying slowly, but without pity, that which yesterday was young," my father has said many more times than once.

"Who's that, Shakespeare?"

"Close—the Wienie King in *The Palm Beach Story*," he said when I asked, referring to a black-and-white comedy nobody, not even my mother, thought was funny except him.

One day is the same as the next. This week was the same as last week, which was the same as the one before that. I wake up with the sound of my father knocking on the door, saying, "Okay, campers, rise and shine," every single morning, which he thinks is hilarious, then he tells me exactly how many minutes I have before school. It's always the same. I eat the same breakfast, wear the same clothes, go to the same school, sit in the same classes, see the same friends, and then do the same thing the next day and the one after that. It's all the same. It doesn't help that there are only seven days and the week always starts on Monday; it doesn't help that the months only go from one to thirty-one and then start back at one. It's designed to repeat, to be repetitive, to wear you down with its incessant regularity and circularity, turning and turning on itself, chasing its own tail like a stupid dog. It would be better if every day had a different name, a different number, every month a different name—keep things moving forward instead of around and around. The clock turns, the second hand spins, chased by the minute hand chased by the hour until they catch the end of the day and then start all over until they catch the end of the week and take another turn and then another until they catch the end of the month and on and on and on—no wonder I'm dizzy half the time. It's not a straight line; it's a vicious circle—the world turns on its axis as it makes a circle around the sun as it all moves in a larger circle in the solar system, so everything is moving in one meaningless mess, a merry-go-round that I never should have gotten on in the first place and every day is one turn too many.

Every object in the universe has its own gravitational force, from the smallest particle to the largest sun. At least that's what they try to teach you in science—what they don't teach you is that it doesn't have anything to do with mass. I know because I have my own satellites, shadowy objects that circle me in irregular orbits. I've seen them; I've observed them, like any good scientist would, watching them come and go, draw closer and then move farther away in their parabolic paths. I'm a regular fucking Galileo when it comes to observation. Todd and Vern and Ash and the rest of them see them too, and they know they're not there for them. They're mine, and I do little but disappoint them.

The satellites and I are only down by the angel. Most people know that we're down there and people come down hoping to see something, I guess. They're the type of people who go to races hoping to see cars smash into each other and flip over and over, the same people who go to football games and hope to see a quarterback hit so hard he breaks his leg or arm or whatever. These are not the people who slow down when they see a car wreck on the highway; these are the people who are looking around when there's no wreck, hoping they'll see one. I don't give them what they come to see. I've only jumped a couple of times in front of people—once when no one was expecting it and back when I didn't think I'd be coming back to have to answer for it. I stick to hours when no one's around—from places where most people can't see—but there are still those who think something's going to happen just because I'm down by the river, just because I'm walking around. They keep their distance, strolling back and forth across the parking lot or hanging out over by the steamboat until they get too bored, until whatever force drew them there weakens and they drift off, only to come back another night. They don't bother me; in fact, I sort of like the fact that I'm wasting their time. I wish they would calculate how much of their lives they've wasted watching me, waiting for something they'll never see.

Some people pass like clouds, unnoticed, until they turn dark and begin to storm

"**W**hy are you such a freak?" she said from behind me. I didn't even know she was there. I was walking home after school and she'd sneaked up on me. You weren't supposed to let anyone sneak up on you, especially not lunatics like her—you didn't know if she would spit on you or punch you in the back of the head. She had a bad temper, a bad reputation, and arguably the best body in school. She was scary, sadistic, sexy, menacing—like the way some women find Hannibal Lecter sexy; that's how she was. She was the sort of girl who would set you on fire as you sat in your car; she would kiss you, then take half your tongue with her. You know the type. She was a freak.

"Born this way, I guess."

"Most freaks are," she said, looking at me as if she'd never seen me before. "I was wondering if you could help me."

○ ○ ○

Her name was Violet Courtland, which she hated so much she refused to acknowledge it. She went by "V" or, when she absolutely needed more, "VC." She even preferred the vulgar nicknames that had been assigned to her—Bi-let (if you believed the rumors thrown around about everyone's sexuality in school, there would be an inordinate percentage of homosexuals, far higher than anywhere on the planet, I'm sure). Everyone knew about Violet's sexual behavior, primarily because she talked about it so much. She didn't seem to care.

She was also called Violent Cuntland, which was the predominant name among my friends whenever she was discussed, always safely out of her earshot. Bruce, for once, didn't have a nickname—he wasn't going to call her anything. He knew that Violet would (and could) kick his ass if one of his clever names ever got back to her. "I don't want her biting off anything of mine," Bruce explained.

She liked me, however. Or, I should say, she liked me to the point where she didn't punch me in the throat or spit on me, which she did to Todd and at least four other people. She liked to spit on people in school, either in class or walking down the hall. She would curl her tongue behind her top teeth and flick a small stream of spit out of her mouth, like a snake spitting venom. She did this mostly to boys—never to any of us except Todd, who always tried to avoid her, and never said or did anything when she spit on him, never acknowledged it at all. "I don't want her biting off anything of mine either," he said when we asked him why he tolerated it.

She was not random in her behavior, but strategic.

Everything was revenge, and she gave no warning and made no threats; she acted.

She wore jackets and coats almost all the time, even in gym, when she could get away with it, leaving her covered body the subject of speculation and supposed eyewitness accounts from the girls' locker room. We only knew what we saw, which was usually a well-used blue gas station attendant's jacket with a red Pegasus on one side of the front zipper and the hand-stitched name "Frank" on the other. No one dared to call her Frank. She was a fighter, or had been.

Her reputation rested mostly on a few fights in the eighth grade, one of which was legendary and was a constant reminder to Hannah Clauson. No one remembers what the fight was about (and if Hannah does, she's not saying), but they remember that it spilled from school over into a vacant lot down the street from the old middle school building just off Main. A large crowd followed the spitting and yelling that quickly erupted into slaps and a few good punches before turning into a taut wrestling match with opportunistic hair pulling. It seemed as if it was going to wind down into the usual standoff, with someone either breaking it up or each girl giving up to exhaustion, except that Violet Courtland suddenly went crazy, thrashing and spinning and flailing her arms and then Hannah started doing the same, except she was shrieking. We could see blood on Violet's face and Hannah was free, except she was still shrieking and jumping up and down, then bent over, holding her left hand. Violet had bitten off the tip of her left pinkie finger. She wiped the blood and took the severed end from her mouth and threw it as far as she could and walked off. Someone took Hannah to the hospital while a few of her friends stayed behind looking for her finger. They were there almost two hours, combing through the grass and the dirt, the bushes and the bricks before somebody said that it was too late, that even if they found the finger now, it would be no good. No one questioned whether or not it was true; they simply gave up and went home, leaving Hannah waiting at the hospital thinking that one of her friends was going to rush in any minute with part of her finger on ice, waiting to be reunited.

Hannah lost her finger and Violet Courtland earned a reputation, proving that if you go crazy once, people will think you're crazy all the time.

The sky was filled with dark clouds. It was going to storm soon and she stood there, now blocking my way forward, expecting an immediate answer on her vague statement. It hadn't even been a question.

"I don't think so." I started to move around her, but she laid her hand on my shoulder and stopped me.

"You see a shrink, don't you?"

"I have."

"So do I," she said. "But it doesn't do me any good. We have a lot in common—more than you know."

"I wouldn't recommend mine, if that's what you're looking for."

"It isn't," she said, and started walking. I followed her.

The sky was so dark that the streetlights came on, but it hadn't started to rain. It was going to, though, and soon.

We walked a block, with her glancing over at me. She had softened—she was no longer her usual aggressive, confrontational self and actually appeared like someone who wasn't going to spit on you in the next two seconds or bite off your finger. "I want to go with you," she said.

"Where?"

"You know."

"No."

"Why not?"

"It's not a team sport." I'd spoken no more than a dozen words to her in my life and she sneaks up and has this conversation? I thought it was a joke or a trick, but I wasn't sure. It didn't make much sense. It wasn't like her, not like what I'd heard about her anyway. When she wanted something, she didn't ask, she took.

"Come on, freak," she said.

"I can't help you."

We'd been walking a few more blocks together, and I realized that I was going out of my way. I'd been following her. I was so worried about how she was looking at me, so careful about what I said and how I said it, that I hadn't paid attention to where I was going. The sky had turned from black to a still, strange green, like the inside of an aquarium.

"That's a tornado sky," she said. "We should get inside."

She started to run. I stayed put and looked at the eerie calm water green overhead. I imagined a funnel cloud coming out of the sky and descending on top of me, churning me up like a blender—I imagined the strong winds tearing me apart limb by limb or driving me headfirst through a tree, sticking me like an arrow, or a house dropping on top of me and leaving nothing but my pretty red shoes. I imagined the tornado carrying me away, hundreds of miles—out of town and out of Iowa, away from Missouri and Illinois, away from every place I ever knew or ever saw, and dropping me somewhere I'd never been, where no one knew me, somewhere safe.

Once Violet realized I wasn't with her, she stopped and looked back at me, disappointed. "Are you just going to stand there?"

I stood there.

She grabbed my hand and began to run. I followed her as we cut through unfamiliar backyards and the wind started to whip through the trees. We made it inside her house as the sky opened up with a heavy downpour. We could hear it slamming into the house in heavy sheets. She crossed the kitchen and opened a door and hurried down the stairs into the basement. She hadn't said anything, hadn't invited me or ordered me to follow her, but I did anyway.

My father's big on the basement in a storm. Whenever there's a thunderstorm or high winds, he'll yell at us to get down to the basement. I remember during one particularly bad storm, we were huddled in the cold concrete room and my mother looked around at the hot water heater and the furnace, the old paint cans, lawn mower fuel, and all the other stuff that could blow up or burn, and she turned to my father and said, "Are you sure this is the safest place to be?"

"It's the safest place in the house," Violet Courtland said as I reached the bottom of the stairs.

Our basement was a tiny, cramped hovel—the Courtland basement was an expansive two rooms, joined with a giant cutout in the middle. One room was a makeshift den, with a Ping-Pong table and bumper pool, which were now both covered with taped-up boxes that contained Violet's victim's heads for all I knew. There were a couple of old couches around the game area and a full bath in the far corner. The second room was a workroom, with a table saw, a wide range of tools, ladders, sawhorses, and a large work space—a tall, long metal table with drawers and cabinets underneath. It was big enough to butcher a horse on, I thought. She led me into the second room.

We could hear the rain, and then the hail, pound against the house—it was muffled and distant but still loud, as if not quite real. It wasn't going to be a tornado, just a bad thunderstorm. That's the way it usually went. I'd never seen a tornado—there had been plenty around town, but they stayed away from us. Some people said it was because of the river, while others said that the bluff protected us. It didn't matter; we all headed to the basement anyway. "A thunderstorm can be just as bad," my father had explained, "sometimes worse."

This was a bad one, and I was glad to be inside, but not with Violet.

She looked at the tools hanging on the wall—hammers, pliers, saws, screwdrivers, hatchets, the usual stuff, but a lot of it. "What would you use?" she said.

"What?"

"What would you use? To kill yourself."

"None of it."

"Why not?" she said.

"There are better ways."

"How do you know? You're still around."

I went to the other room. There was a small window in the middle of the side wall of the house. I could look up and see a small sliver of the sky, like you see prisoners in the movies looking up from their cells, trying to see freedom. It was still storming. I could hear the strong wind pushing everything around.

"What are you doing?" she said from the other room.

"Looking outside."

"You can't leave," she said.

"Ever?"

She laughed. "We'll see. Come here."

I had started to return to her when the lights went out. It was completely dark—even the window behind me was a dark patch in the darker basement. I couldn't see anything.

"Where are you?" Violet said.

"I don't know; near the door, I think."

"What door?"

"The door to the room you're in."

"There's no door," she said, laughing. "It's just a big opening, remember?"

I didn't know where I was or where I was going or how to get there. I took a step in the darkness and tried to feel around me. There was nothing. I didn't know if it was a step toward her or away from her. I looked back toward the window. It was behind me at least. I took another step and then another. The floor felt sloped, as if I was going down, and the whole room felt as if it was shrinking, closing in on me in the dark.

"Where are you now?" she said.

"I don't know. Why don't you come to me?"

"You're doing all right," she said, obviously enjoying my dilemma. "You're closer already. Just keep walking toward my voice. Follow my voice."

She sounded to the right of me, so I turned and slowly walked in that direction. I held my hands in front of me like Frankenstein and shuffled my feet on the concrete floor, afraid I was going to run into something, like a screwdriver she was holding at my eye level one step ahead of me. I was also afraid that the lights would come back on and she would see me staggering around like an idiot. "You stopped talking."

"Did I?" she said. "I'm out of things to say. Where are you now?"

"I don't know."

"You veered to the left," she said. "Come back this way."

I shuffled to the right. The room felt smaller still and I was sure that I was going to hit my head. It was impossible, I knew—the ceiling wasn't shorter—but I kept waving my hands over my head and then would force them back in front of me again, arcing them side to side until I finally felt the metal table in the dark.

Violet reached for my hand and said, "I knew you'd get here." She didn't let go of my hand; instead, she pulled me to her and kissed my neck and face until she found my mouth. I wondered if she had planned it all—the sky and the storm and the blackout, all of it, and just for this. She knew what she was doing.

Maybe all you think about is that moment—you're there in the dark, just the two of you, and that's all there is—nothing exists before it and nothing after, just that one experience all by itself, a shared secret set apart from everything like a diamond in a plain, tarnished ring. And isn't that what people always say, "You have to live in the moment"? Except that no moment is isolated. It's connected to everything after it, and they're all linked together in some sour sameness, a heavy, continuous ironbound chain you have to carry around, all built on top of each other like a rickety Jenga tower that's ready to topple any minute. Maybe you think that, or maybe you're like me and don't think about any of that—you only know what you want and it silences, suffocates everything else. There's no chain, no tower; there's only this.

I was afraid a little—afraid of Violet Courtland, afraid of what she wanted, afraid of what I wanted, afraid of the place and the time and what I was going to do and how I was going to do it, and none of it mattered. Five seconds ago, the thought never entered my mind—I hadn't wanted it to happen, never thought it would or could, and then it seemed as if I always wanted it to happen, that there was no other way for it to go. I didn't think about the strangeness of it all—the basement, the dark, the table—I didn't care. And that, my friends, is how mistakes are made. Live in the moment, just do it—those are phrases thrown around by people who don't know what they mean. Just do it—it's idiotic. You could slap that slogan on a picture of Hitler and it would make as much sense. He did it, all right.

She pulled my shirt over my head and helped me climb onto the table. I fumbled with my shoes and pants—not wanting to let go of her in the dark, afraid that she might move, leave me there alone. Maybe that was her trick. So I held on to her as best I could. I heard her belt unbuckle and the rustle of clothes as they were pushed across the metal table and fell to the floor, and then I wasn't holding her and I couldn't find her. "Where did you go?"

"I'm right here," she said, and I felt her hand on my shoulder. "I had to grab a hammer. What do you think of that?"

"If you think you can live with it, then go for it."

She pushed me back onto the cold surface and pressed her mouth to my ear.

"Do you think I'll be the only one?" she said.

"I don't know."

"I do. Who else would? You're a freak, you know."

"I don't know. I mean, I don't know about the first of it. I know I'm a freak."

"You're not going to meet many people like me," she said.

"Same here."

"I know that," she said. "I told you we were a lot alike."

She told everyone at school. I didn't get past second period and Todd and Ash and Vern all knew; by lunchtime everybody knew. That's all she'd wanted—to brag about it. She'd had sex with the freak and nobody else had, and because of her, no one else would. She'd poisoned the well.

"How was it?" Vern asked.

"Dark." That's all I said about it. I didn't feel bad about it—I didn't really care if she used me or not—in fact, I wouldn't have minded if she used me like that again (and again), but there was no point in that for her. She'd gotten all she wanted and she wasn't about to let me repeat my mistake. And it *was* a mistake—I felt bad, only because Jodi was so disappointed in me.

> `Boys r all alike,` she texted.
> `I guess.`
> `How cud u w her?`
> `I didn't plan it. Just happened.`
> `Nothing jst hpns.`
> `Everything jst hpns. That's the`
> `problem.`
> `Dum. Dumb. Dumb.`

About an hour later my phone rang. Jodi wasn't finished. "You know," she said, "for someone who's always talking about leading an anonymous, private life, you sure are a public figure."

"I would undo it if I could, believe me."

"That seems to be your solution to everything—and how's that working out?"

"I get your point. You're mad."

"Disappointed. I didn't think you were like this," she said.

"I have bad judgment. I always have. You know that. I screw up everything."

"Evidently." She wasn't as angry. I could hear it in her voice. She hadn't forgiven me, not yet, but she would. She couldn't stay mad at me, and I thought I could never stay mad at her—although I would try. There would come a time when I would try.

"You're screwed up" was what Todd said about it. "And when you're screwed up, you attract other screwed-up people. You think somebody normal is going to like you?"

I couldn't even get Violet Courtland to like me again—*like* is absolutely the wrong word—I didn't need the talk and the bragging, but I would have gone back to the basement with her, but she was done with me. So I avoided her, or maybe she avoided me, or both, like hands on a clock hoping they never have to touch again. The next time I saw Violet, I was walking in the hall, heading down to Mr. Coolidge's, and saw her walking toward me. I looked right at her, but she didn't look at me; then, as she started to walk past, she turned her head and did that creepy thing with her tongue, and a small stream of spit flew out and hit me on the neck.

Summer is saved not by the dam but by a dyke

I rode my bike to The Point every morning. The houses along the river were covered with Mormon flies, entire sides blanketed with their slimy black bodies. Mr. Camp, a retired judge, had the third house along the river as I glided my way down River Road. He was out every morning, standing with his overtanned bare stomach sagging over his khaki shorts and black rubber boots, flushing the insects off his house with the garden hose. He always had a lit cigar clamped between his teeth, if nothing else to keep the smell away. The dead bodies were heaped along the side of the house like a ridge of coal or a black snowdrift. I liked to imagine him as an evil Nazi guard, delousing his captives or torturing them with some poisonous spray. He always waved whenever he saw me, and I would give him a big nod (I couldn't take my hands off the handlebars, not without losing my grip on either my fishing pole or the tackle box), thinking, *Guten Tag, mein Campf,* and wondering how many he was killing today. However many, it wasn't enough. They'd be back tomorrow, and so would he.

The stench of the cow was gone; the hide and meat were gone, and the muscles and tendons and whatever else held the large body together were starting to go. The skeleton was breaking apart, with parts of it pushed against the shore. Some of us wanted to collect all of the pieces. "Maybe we could put it all back together," Bruce said. There was a discussion about where we could keep the reconstituted skeleton, and when it was determined that we couldn't keep the whole thing, we moved to a conversation about what, if any of it, we kept. I didn't care. I was content to let the whole thing go, let it be broken into bits by the river, dragged out into the current and gone down the river forever. We had said we would watch it, that's all. In the end, however, we couldn't leave it alone.

One morning when I arrived at The Point, Vern and Ash were already there, searching around through the tall grass as if they'd lost a contact lens or something. "Somebody stole it," Vern said when he saw me.

I instinctively began to scan the ground, as if I knew what he was looking for. "What are we looking for?"

"The head," Ash said.

Someone had taken our cow's skull.

Vern and Ash seemed (momentarily, anyway) convinced that it was someone else, but I'm still sure it was one of them. I wouldn't be surprised if it was Vern. No one had bothered the cow since we discovered it, and almost no one came out to The Point. It was one of them. They just won't admit it.

It was a perfect moment for us—we all suspected each other of taking it, but none of us talked about it directly, just as none of us had talked about wanting it directly. We all wanted it, at one time or another—it was the only really cool thing about the cow, and we hadn't suffered through the rot and stench and all of it just to let the thing be taken away. We had joked about taking all the bones and putting them back together in front of the school or in one of our lawns, but no one had claimed ownership or even outright wanting this piece or that. Darryl had talked about creating some kind of monument, putting the head on a spike at the end of The Point, some communal *Lord of the Flies* type crap. That wasn't going to happen; we all knew that, so now we were left with silent suspicions and vague theories in our own minds. I had, for a brief time, wanted the stupid thing for myself; after all, it had been named after me. I thought I could keep the skull on my desk, maybe talk to it like Hamlet—"Alas, poor Strand! I knew her, a cow of infinite jest, most excellent. She hath bored me with her stench a thousand times, and now how abhorr'd in my imagination it is!" Or something like that.

Now it's probably hidden away in Vern's room, buried in the back of his closet or under his bed. He won't do anything with it, and he won't dare have it out in case any of us sees it. It might as well have floated down the river; it's as good as gone now anyway.

It was stagnant at The Point, with no breeze, leaving a couple of tons of hot air sitting on us, crushing us as the morning turned the corner and moved to the hottest part of the day. Bruce couldn't take it anymore. He stood up and practically clawed at his T-shirt to get it away from him, then he stepped out of his shoes and shorts and before anyone could say anything, he jumped into the river. We couldn't remember the last time we ever saw anyone go into the river. We fished on it in the summer and skated on it in the winter; we sat by it and stood over it, sometimes even got in a boat on top of it; we watched it and admired it and envied it, but we never went into it (except me, of course, but that was different)—we were in favor of all the prepositions—by, near, beside, atop, over, even under—except in and into. No one went into the water. The river was disgusting, especially above the dam, a liquid turd that oozed along in the summer—brown and ugly and with a smell you would never want on you.

Bruce pulled himself out of the water and stood on the bank and let the foreign, filthy brown water drip off of him.

"You have the whitest ass ever," Darryl said.

Bruce pulled on his shorts and picked up his T-shirt from the ground and looked at Darryl and said, "You're such a dyke."

We collectively dropped our jaws in admiration. Everyone was silent, everything was quiet, as if the sound had been sucked out of all the air. Even time stopped; nothing moved except us as we glanced at each other, wondering how we would react. Bruce had affected time and space, brought everything to a welcomed, noticeable pause, a held-breath anticipation, a gasp of awe and wonderment, and then we all started laughing, even Ash, who was always baiting people to break the bans so he could get a free beer, but the bans had been bested. Bruce logic had beat the ban, and we could feel the gears of the world shift into that rare, perfect alignment where everything is as it should be.

We knew it couldn't last—it never does—but at that moment, we didn't care. The summer had been saved, rescued from stank doldrums and grinding predictability. There was something new for a change. None of us had thought of it—we couldn't say "gay" or "fag," so Bruce calmly dropped a synonym that immediately became a favorite for the rest of the summer. The phrase became The Phrase and was used extensively, even coming close to being banned itself, but we all knew it was too good to ruin and we held back. Even the phrase had a phrase—it was called "dropping the *d*." It might have been the highlight of the summer, beating out a dead cow and a free case of wine—it was that kind of summer.

I couldn't wait for it to be over.

A time for work and time enough

"Do your parents want to send you away," Jodi said.

It was Hy-Vee talk, gossip that they were going to put me in Mount Pleasant, let Dr. Stinchcomb and the rest of them deal with me for a while. I wasn't so sure it wasn't a good thing. I could use the change, I thought. I didn't tell Jodi that; I didn't say anything. And nothing happened. No one sent me away, but they didn't leave me alone either.

My father told me to get a job. It wasn't a suggestion or a request. "Time for work," he said. I wouldn't have minded a job, I guess, but the only problem was there weren't any. Unemployment was almost fifteen percent in the county—I knew this stat from my father. Two manufacturing plants had closed in the past year or so: a school bus factory that used to have its core principles, "integrity, trustworthiness, and reliability," prominently printed in the lobby had moved to Mexico without warning, and a tractor-trailer company had headed north to Canada. Or maybe it was the other way around. All I knew was that they were gone after decades of being in the same spots well north of town. It didn't matter where they had gone; there were a lot of people looking for work.

It was too late in the summer already, but they wouldn't have hired me anyway. Who was going to hire me? Everyone knew me and seemed mildly put out when I asked for a job application. There was nothing; I couldn't even get hired to detassel corn, which is about the lowest job on the ladder. At first, I enjoyed the "you've-got-to-be-kidding" looks I got when I asked about work, but even that quickly lost any satisfaction through tiresome repetition. No one had any other reaction.

My father could have helped, I'm sure—he had plenty of connections. I don't think he really wanted me to work; he only wanted me to waste my time looking for work and to get rejected. That was my lesson for the summer. He asked every day where I had gone, how many interviews I had, how many applications, what was I doing to "follow up," where was I going tomorrow. He nodded at each response and then said nothing, no advice, no words of wisdom, no suggestions, as if he were judging my actions and silently grading my efforts.

I fear that I have given the wrong impression of my parents. It's not what I intended. They love me—I know this, or at least I think I know this. They're distant and probably not too pleased with me most of the time, but why wouldn't they be? I mean, put yourself in their place. How thrilled would you be to have me as a son? I don't listen to them, don't care if I'm punished, and wish I'd never been born. What more would parents want in a son? I don't blame them for having me—they probably didn't want to have me specifically, they only wanted a baby (or maybe not, I don't really know), and I came along. I don't wish I had differ-ent parents—I wish I never existed. To never be born is best—or something like that, from the ancient Greeks, I think. Now they can't get rid of me even if they wanted. I'm like the boy who's always running away from home only to make it back in time for dinner. Actually, I'm nothing like that. I'm far worse. But I like to think that my parents are more comfortable with me, in a strange way, more confident that nothing terrible will happen to me. Isn't that what most parents worry about, especially at night, when they're lying in bed with no idea where their son or daughter is and what they're doing? At least my parents know the worst. I die. And then I come back. Safe and sound. They've seen it over and over, so they can rest easy, at least in that regard. I'm not going anywhere. Or if I do, I'll be back.

There was nothing to do but waste days until school started and hope my father would forget about work and let me get back to what I did best.

Why there are worse places to be than the ditch

Bruce told us all to meet him in the parking lot by the angel. He sounded like a little girl trying to be secretive but dying to tell. So we all stood around and waited for him to show. "I bet he's bringing a girlfriend," Vern said.

"I bet he brings nothing," Ash said.

"He has a car," Todd said.

Bruce pulled up in his brand-new car and we stood silent in the parking lot until Ash said, "It's a car, all right," and we all turned around and went back by the angel as if we couldn't have cared less.

It was, in fact, a big deal for all of us. We didn't have to rely on Todd's begging his brother. We could drive around whenever we wanted. We could leave town, go over the bridge, do whatever we wanted. Or so we thought. It turned out that instead of having more freedom with better transportation, we had less. Bruce's parents didn't want a carload of drunken kids driving all over who knows where and at all hours. Bruce now had a curfew, and if he screwed up, they wouldn't add imaginary time to an unenforced punishment, they'd take away his car. They thought it would keep him safe, keep us all safe.

Bruce was allowed to drive his car only during the day and Friday and Saturday nights and one night during the week. He had to have the car parked at his house by ten on the weeknight and by midnight on the weekend. Those were the rules, and Bruce lived by them. "I'm not screwing this up," he said when we tried to get him to take one more lap up and down Main Street, one more beer, a few more minutes. He wouldn't listen to us.

"We might as well be in the car with my mom," Vern said.

"We'd have a better shot of getting some," Darryl said.

"That's a beer," Vern said.

An argument and a vote were cut short by Bruce driving straight home, pulling in just ahead of his curfew. We had to walk home.

"You couldn't even drop us off?"

"I'm not screwing this up," Bruce repeated.

He could try to not screw it up, but it was only a matter of time before he failed. And not much time, it turned out.

Bruce had owned his car less than a month when we wrecked it. Technically, he wrecked it, but it was all our fault. Here we'd been talking about how great it was going to be to have a car for the winter, no more shivering down by the river, or worse, not going outside at all, how great it would be to drive around in comfort and style, but we never made it to winter; we never even made it to the end of the summer.

The first sign of trouble was a bounty of riches—we had two cars for the weekend. Todd's brother had offered him the use of his car, and Todd wasn't about to turn him down. Bruce wasn't going to not use his, however. "That's the whole point of me having a car, isn't it, so we don't have to borrow anyone else's?" he said. "Those days are done."

"We all don't have to go in the same car," Todd said, and so the beginning of our Friday started out like team-picking time in PE.

Bruce of course wanted to teach Todd a lesson and have all of us ride with him and leave Todd to drive alone. Todd had a trump card—he'd bought the beer. In the end, Darryl and I went with Todd and Vern and Ash went with Bruce. Why the night had so quickly turned into a competition, I don't know, but it quickly escalated.

Todd tried to be the lead car as we drove up and down Main, but Bruce took every opportunity to move in front, so they jockeyed back and forth for the first few circuits. Main was four lanes wide and ran the entire length of town, leading onto the bridge at the southern end and changing into Highway 61 almost three miles later at the northern end. It was a perfect straight stretch to drive back and forth and see other people, and almost every Friday and Saturday night saw a stream of high school kids from all over Illinois, Iowa, and Missouri parading past each other, just driving or looking for a party or whatever.

Todd, however, was determined to stay in front of Bruce,

and he thought the best way to do that was to leave Main. As we headed north and passed the Kmart parking lot, where everybody turned around, Todd kept going north, and Bruce followed.

"Where are you going?" Darryl asked.

"How far do you think he'll go?" Todd said.

"He'll turn around," Darryl said.

"I bet he won't," Todd said, and kept heading north.

We were on Highway 61 when I got a text from Vern. We all got them.

Wtf r u going?

Todd turned off the highway, down some dark dirt country road. All we could see were the two cones of light in front of us and the headlights from Bruce's car behind us. CHASE! Bruce texted, and crept up behind us before Todd sped up and regained some distance.

Todd snaked around for almost twenty minutes, turning down one road and then another until I'm not sure any of us knew where we were. Bruce stayed right behind us, and as we hit a long straight section of road, Todd jumped on it and turned off his headlights. Bruce's car disappeared in the dark behind us.

"Turn your lights back on," Darryl said.

"In a minute," Todd said.

We couldn't see anything; everything was dark around us. The sky was cloud-covered and the same gray as the fields off to each side and the dirt road in front of us and behind us. There were three lights off in the distance, small patches of yellow from farmhouses, I guess. They looked as small as stars, stars that had fallen from the sky and hovered just above the flat earth, foreign and familiar at the same time. They didn't move, but we did. We could feel the road underneath the car and the car gripping into the dirt, digging into it and hurling it up into a dark cloud of dust behind us, building a wall of dust as Todd kept accelerating. We were hurtling through the night, alone on whatever road we were on, a big ship of steel flying blind. None of us said anything; we listened to the road and the darkness and tried to see something, searching in the night ahead of us for something, but there wasn't anything for what seemed like an hour and then finally Darryl said "Turn the lights on" about five times in a row and they came on, just in time to illuminate a turn up ahead. Todd hit the brakes and made the turn and then started to speed up again before I told him to hold up.

Darryl and I looked behind us and waited to see Bruce's car, but it wasn't coming. "Maybe he headed back," Darryl said. Todd slowed to where he was almost at a standstill.

"Should I turn around?"

We saw a pair of headlights for a second and then they were gone.

"He's not stupid enough to shut off his lights, is he?" Todd said, and whipped his brother's car around and turned on his high beams. We could barely see through the dust at first, but we knew Bruce wasn't coming. There was nothing, only the dissolving dust and the night and the empty road ahead of us, stark as a bone in the bright beams of light. We waited a minute or so and then Todd started back the way we came.

We got to the turn and saw that Bruce hadn't made it—his car was smashed into a fence off the road about ten feet. Todd turned his car so his headlights shone on Bruce's wreck. The three of them were out of the car, all standing. Ash had his hand over the right side of his head and we could see blood on the side of his face. We ran down to where they were.

"Are you okay?" Todd asked Ash.

"I'm all right," Ash said.

"Let me see your head. You've got blood on your face."

"It's not blood," Ash said. "It's fucking Campari or some crap."

"Let me see anyway," Todd said.

"I'm all right," Ash said, "but you should see the car."

The passenger door was creased around a fence post. Ash had hit the passenger window with his head and had a nice egg-sized lump over his right eye. Vern was trying to salvage the liquor from the car, and Bruce was walking away from all of us, walking away from his car. He didn't want to look.

"Get his car back on the road," Todd whispered to me, and left to catch up with Bruce.

I got into the wrecked car but couldn't start it. Bruce had taken the keys.

Todd wasn't happy to see me approach him. I shrugged him off. "I need the keys."

"What are you doing?" Bruce asked.

"We're going to get your car back on the road before someone sees us," Todd said.

"I'll do it," Bruce said.

"Don't worry about it; let Adam do it."

Bruce ignored him and went back to his car. He started it and peeled it away from the fence slowly and parked it on the road with the damaged side in front of the lights from the other car. The front passenger door was badly bent and there were bad scratches on the back door and the front quarter panel, but it wasn't as bad as I thought it would be. We all looked at it, walking back and forth, approaching the damaged side and then stepping back as if we knew how to fix it, as if the more we looked at it, the better it would get. Bruce stayed in the car; he didn't want to see it.

Todd walked around to the driver's side and we followed. "It's bad," Todd said to Bruce, "but it's not terrible. You can still drive it. The passenger side is screwed, but it could have been a lot worse."

Bruce took the beer. "What am I going to tell my dad?"

"Tell him you swerved to miss a deer."

"What were we doing out here? He'll want to know about that."

"You don't tell him you were here; you tell him we were on River Road or cutting across Mormon Trek or someplace," Todd said. "It's not that complicated. Just take your time and calm down. It'll be all right."

Ash stepped behind Todd and said, "I'd take it back where you bought it—that car doesn't turn worth a damn."

In the end, we all paid for Bruce's inability to take a turn on a dark country road at an unsafe speed while drinking. It didn't seem fair. If you can't drink and drive, then don't; pick the one that you're good at and stick to that. Instead, we were forced to go over to Vern's house, which was a punishment none of us deserved. Bruce received no punishment from his father—he didn't really believe the story about the deer, but he didn't question it either. He simply told Bruce that he couldn't drive the car until it was repaired and that Bruce had to pay for the repair himself. He might as well have taken the car away from him—Bruce didn't have any money, and he wasn't going to get a job any more than I was. So his car sat in the garage and would continue to sit there, idle and useless.

Vern's father is actually the one who said, "You can't drink and drive, so you need to pick one," and since we didn't have access to the latter, we picked the former. Which is how we all got dropped off at Vern's house the next Friday night.

Vern's father was a thorn of a man—short, pointed, and painfully unpleasant if you got too close. "I should put your head in a vise," he said to Bruce as we all filed into the living room and took our seats in chairs that had been set out like it was going to be a Bible study group. He was shorter than any of us, and he looked up at the group of us with a weak, defensive smile, like a little dog that isn't sure if he should play nice or bite you as hard as he can.

"It was an accident," Bruce said.

"It was stupid," the thorn said, sticking him again. "You're lucky somebody wasn't hurt or worse. What are you doing about the car?"

"I don't know," Bruce said. "Getting it fixed, I guess."

"Who's doing the work?" Vern's father asked.

"I don't know."

"Take it to Hall's. He's the best guy around. It's your car; you should know how to take care of it. And you should know the people who work on it."

He left us for a minute and before we could get the hell out of there, he came back with a six-pack of beer in his hand. He handed out the cans and took a seat in a chair across from me. He raised his can and said, "Here's to thinking."

Here's to thinking? I thought Ash was going to put down his beer and run. Instead, we halfheartedly raised our cans and took a long drink. We hoped there was more beer coming, but each of us knew there wasn't enough beer to make up for this.

Vern's father had graying, stringy hair, which he wore slicked back or tried to—it had come loose above both ears and stuck out in short tufts like you might see on some exotic bird. He was a dentist, which made him the only parent of any of us who was his own boss. All the rest of our folks worked for someone else. We thought that he must be rich, but Vern's house wasn't that much better than the rest of ours. It turns out that Vern's father wasn't that good of a dentist. My father went to him—once. He wouldn't go back. "That guy's better suited as a butcher," he had said. I remembered that as we tried to settle into the room, with three of us on the couch, myself and Todd in armchairs, and Vern's father in a chair he brought from the dining room. He had barely sat down before he was up again, quickly leaving the living room before returning with another six-pack of beer, which he dispensed with obvious enjoyment.

When he handed me the can of beer, I said, "I only drink grain alcohol and rainwater." He looked at me like I was crazy. *"Dr. Strangelove,"* I told him. He chuckled nervously, politely humoring me, handed me the beer, and moved on. Maybe he'd never seen it. Maybe he'd never seen a single one of Sterling Hayden's movies. Maybe that's how big of a fan he was.

"I've thought about being a dentist," Ash said, kissing ass. "What should I know about it?"

Vern's father held up his right hand, curving his fingers close to his thumb until they almost touched in a tight C. "You should know this," he said. "This is about the size of where you'll work every day. If you can do that, look into that small space all day long, every day, then you'll be all right."

Dentists have a high suicide rate, higher than most professions. Maybe that space, looking into those small, dark caves, one after the other, every day, has something to do with it. I should have asked him about it.

Vern's father was a car guy. It's basically all he talked about. He was into muscle cars, sixties cars like Mustangs and Impalas, Barracudas, Cougars, all these animal names that didn't mean anything to me. He kept talking about them as if we were intimately familiar with them. "You remember the '66 Mustang? It had a something with a something something," he said. I don't really know what he said. I wasn't paying attention. I just sat there on the couch in the basement, holding my empty beer can and wishing to hell that we could get out of there.

He didn't own any of these cars he was talking about, never had owned one, never had driven one as far as we knew, and yet he talked about them in intimate detail, like women he'd slept with and was now bragging about, or worse, had never slept with and was still bragging.

I didn't care about his cars; I didn't think about cars in general—I didn't think about them or know the first thing about them. I didn't even know what cars my parents had. Vern's father must have read my mind. It was scary.

"What kind of car does your dad drive?" he asked me, his thorny eyes looking right at me.

I didn't know what to say. "A white one." Everybody laughed, especially the little thorn sitting across me.

They were laughing at me, but at least I stopped all the car talk.

Vern's father glanced around the room as the conversation crept from one of us to the other, from halted small talk to awkward boredom, but his eyes kept coming back to me. I was used to that look—I'd seen it plenty of times before—it was an examination, a scrutiny that was part accusation (who do you think you are?) and part curiosity (how are you still here?). Vern's father had that same look, except I was wrong about his meaning.

"Are you a pole-vaulter?" he asked me.

I shook my head.

"But you were on the track team."

"My brother."

He paused and considered what I'd said and then nodded. "Your brother was Michael," Vern's father said to me as he watched me drink his beer. I nodded. "He was a pole-vaulter."

I shook my head. "He ran the two hundred, the four hundred, and the mile relay."

"I thought he was a pole-vaulter. Didn't he almost set the school record?"

"That was Mike Sheppard."

"I thought that was your brother," Vern's father said, disappointed. For the record, I look like my brother—there's a definite familial resemblance. Mike Sheppard looks nothing like us. Nothing. Not even close.

We could see his next sentence coming from his mouth long before he said it, like a train barreling toward us. "I was a pole-vaulter," Vern's father said. Of course he was. He didn't want to talk about me or my brother; he wanted to talk about himself. I bet it's that way nine out of ten times an adult starts talking to you—they're only saying anything so they can tell you about themselves. So enough about him, let's get back to me.

I was bored. Even with the free beer. I finished it as fast as I could and wanted to get the hell out of there. I could see that most everybody else was the same way except for Vern's father and Ash. They looked as if they were liking it. I couldn't have been more miserable.

My phone shook in my pocket and I pulled it into plain view and read the text: Ban drinks w adults. Vote.

It was from Todd. Every phone in the room—except for Vern's father's—was awakened in quick succession. In turn, Todd's phone was notified of the answers. Unanimous. The ban was on and we quickly ended the evening.

The worst of it was that I only had two beers. They did nothing. Vern's father had three and acted as if he'd had five more. Maybe he'd been drinking before we arrived. He was a little drunk, definitely impaired, but insisted on driving us home. I halfway hoped he'd wreck so he'd have to pick one or the other. You can't do both.

We were barely all loaded in the car when Todd texted: $5 `if u drop the d on dad`. We could barely keep quiet about it. Vern's father pulled up in front of Darryl's house and said, "This was a lot of fun, wasn't it? We should do this again soon." Darryl nodded and closed the door without a word. Vern's father said the same thing to everyone—he had his phrase and we had ours—but while Vern's father used his freely, no one was willing to drop the *d*. Bruce left with a stifled laugh, but that wasn't going to get him five bucks.

Ash, Todd, and I were left, and as Ash opened the door, we knew he wasn't going to say it. He just wanted to get out. "That was a lot of fun," Vern's father said again. "We should do it again soon." Ash hadn't closed the door completely and he pulled it open again, leaned forward into the passenger's side, and said, "You're such a dyke," and then closed the door and walked to his house, not once even glancing back. That was his loss.

Todd and I were in the backseat and could both see Vern's

father's face in the rearview mirror—it was filled with complete bafflement. He had no idea what had happened and he couldn't ask us. I had to look away or else I was going to start laughing. Vern's father sat there for a moment, staring down the dark street in front of him, and calculated his next move or used the time to regroup, collect his wits, and either come to a conclusion about what Ash had just dropped on him or try to dismiss it entirely from his mind as if it had never been said. When he pulled in front of my house, I thought about dropping it again—I wished I had, but I couldn't do it. Once was enough—they only bombed Hiroshima once after all and then moved on. Vern's father used his phrase, however. I looked at Todd and held up my hand. Five. Todd nodded as if he were the one who had made the money, not the one paying. It was worth it.

He that is not guilty of his own death shortens not his own life

Live your dream—isn't that the simple message of every Disney movie, *Oprah* episode, and half the Hallmark cards? Live every day as if it is going to be your last. I've done that, and here I am. Follow your heart, find your bliss. Isn't that the kind of feel-good crap they feed you? Well, what if your dream is a dark one, what if your heart wants to lead you down a dangerous path? What if your bliss is oblivion? Then you have to change, they say. It's the wrong dream, they tell you, the wrong day, the wrong bliss—something has to be wrong and it has to be corrected; you have to be corrected. Because it's really not your dream they want you to live, it's their dream.

To cause injury, contaminate, or corrupt others

The summer dragged on for me with excruciating dullness, like a train squealing along in slow motion, derailed and scraping along the tracks with no end in sight. There was, of course, my birthday ahead—that's where the train would end its pointless journey and not come to rest, but explode.

I turned seventeen on the twenty-fifth of July and the day passed with the same fanfare—dinner at home, with cake and ice cream and another envelope from my father. My mother cried this year, however, remarking, "I didn't think we'd get to see this one." I ate my cake and left. Todd picked me up and we drove directly to the angel.

We had barely congregated and distributed beers when Troy and a party of six scurves showed up. They parked near us instead of their usual spot across the lot, and it was obvious that Troy was drunk. We wouldn't be able to get up and leave with all of our liquor, so Todd sneaked into the shadows and hid it in the trees.

Troy took notice of us but then led his troop down toward the water, where they stayed and drank more.

It was a hot, humid night, with a stillness that was almost unbearably heavy. "Close" is what my mother calls it. It was close. We should have taken our one advantage—distance between us and the scurves—to gather our things and go, or just go, but we didn't. Instead, we stayed and complained about the weather and how much better we'd be elsewhere.

Before we knew it, Troy was back, standing near the statue, looking at us, stopping to examine each face before fixating on mine. We were off to the side of the angel, and Troy stood near her back, a wing dangling above his head like a menacing stalactite, ready to fall and squash him. Only it was no threat at all; it wasn't going anywhere. Troy was the threat, and he began to threaten.

"What are you trying to prove?" Troy said. I wasn't entirely sure he was talking to me; he had turned away from me and was looking more toward his gaggle of followers than he was to me, and when I didn't answer right away, he took a few steps toward me and asked it again.

"Nothing," I said. I was sitting on the grass and I wanted to stand so I could look at Troy, not have him towering above me, but I was afraid that if I stood, he might immediately think that I wanted to fight. I didn't want to fight.

"Do it now," he said, taking a few more steps until he was standing over me.

"It's not like that," I said.

Troy knelt down so he could look directly into my face. "You're a freak," he said, "and gutless."

I shrugged.

"Come on, prove it," he insisted.

"No," I said. "Unless you want to join me."

It wasn't the right thing to say. The small crowd, which had been egging him on a minute ago, now had turned against him, or at least challenged him with me. Troy's face erupted red with embarrassment and anger. He stood and turned away from me, and I thought he was going to leave. I stood up and had started to move toward my friends when Troy suddenly rushed toward me and slammed into me with his hand held above his waist, the force of his body pushing me back. I thought he had punched me in the chest even though he hadn't thrown a punch; his hand had been held close to him the whole time. Maybe he caught me with his shoulder, I thought. Whatever he'd done, it hurt; a small ball of pain gathered in the middle of my chest. I looked down at the front of my shirt—it was becoming soaked with blood. He hadn't punched me; he'd stabbed me, holding his knife close to him in order to hide it from everybody, especially me. I pressed my hand into the wet cloth of my shirt and then held it out for Todd and the rest to see. Troy was already moving toward his car, and his crowd quickly left when they saw my bloodstained hand. Blood was pouring out of me; I could feel it pumping out of a hole in my chest and sliding down my stomach and into my pants. There was a lot of it, and I stood there and watched Todd as he was already on the phone calling for help. I thought I could stand there and wait for the ambulance, but the blood kept coming out of me and my head emptied of all of its thoughts and I fell forward. Somebody caught me—Bruce and Ash, I think. I don't know; I was floating off somewhere else, leaving them with my bleeding body until the ambulance came.

I was in intensive care for five days. My father came every night after work and sat by my bed. He liked to know all the stats, to look at the monitors as they measured my heart rate, my blood pressure, my breathing, temperature, everything. There was plenty to watch, and the machines told more than I did. I had a tube in my nose, and another in my arm, and a bunch of wires leading out of my hospital gown. I remember my father being there, sitting next to the bed, but he seemed far off most of the time, floating somewhere off in the distance, as if he were on a raft in the ocean and I was on another raft and he was trying to get to me, but the waves kept pushing me away. I was in a fog most of the time. I had a fever, or I was hot, or I felt hot, as if my skin was on fire. I kept kicking the thin sheets off of me, aware of only the fact that I was too hot and that no one was going to help me, that they couldn't help me as I drifted farther out into the ocean. That's what drugs will do.

It's hard to remember exactly what happened while I was in the hospital or in what order. They had me on morphine—it was a little button I gripped in my hand the whole time, and whenever the pain became too much, I clicked the button. It looked like the buzzer the contestants hold on *Jeopardy,* and I must have run the board a few times, thinking I had all the answers. A cloud settled over me, a dark fog that hung low and heavy, obscuring clear thoughts and memory, even making me hallucinate now and then. This foggy drugged state was uncomfortable, slow and sluggish. I wanted to move, wanted to get out of the bed, wanted to tell my father much more than I could, but I couldn't; it was as if I were held with weights, both my body and my mind. My thoughts would sink out of reach before I could clearly understand them; my words dissolved on my tongue before I could say them. I always thought that being on drugs would be better than this, that it would be more like being drunk, where I'm happy or at least a little more numb, uncaring. This was nothing like that. I was convinced that people were out to get me, and I wasn't even sure what that meant, which only added to the confusion. It was like watching a good horror movie, but most of the time you don't know if it's a movie—you only suspect that it is, but you can't be sure.

My father did his best to reassure me that everything was going to be okay. He had come to regard me with a tested tolerance, a weary resignation that I was not going to change but that I was, despite my best efforts, safe and sound. Now that I was back in the hospital, fighting for my life, changed all that, shook him out of his resignation and had him there fighting with me. That was the word he used: *fighting*. And he wasn't the only one.

Don Lemley sent me a card with a photograph of a sunrise on the front and a Bible verse, something from Ecclesiastes. I didn't read the verse, but I did read his note inside:

You have a purpose. I don't know what it is, and perhaps you don't know what it is yet either, but God has a purpose for you. There is a reason you are still here, and I believe you will stay here until we understand the purpose He has for you. I am thankful for that. I am thankful for you and the blessings that have been bestowed upon you. They are blessings, Adam, even though it may seem otherwise. You are searching, and I pray that you will soon find what you seek.

Mr. Coolidge came to see me on the last day, when I was finally off the morphine and more lucid. He came with a book, of course, and a guilty expression.

"They said you fought like hell to live," he said.

"They should have left me alone."

"You don't think it means something, you fighting for your life?"

"It doesn't mean anything. I want to, my body just won't let me. It's the one doing the fighting. I've got nothing to do with it."

He didn't believe me, but he pretended to understand. We'd been down this road before. This was different, though. He knew that. There's a big difference between wanting to do it yourself and having some scurve attack you out of the blue.

"What's going to happen to Troy?"

"They say he's going to plead guilty," Mr. Coolidge said. "He'll go to prison."

"At least it will keep him out of the army."

We lapsed into silence, and the guilty expression Mr. Coolidge had carried into the room returned on his face. He was summoning up the sentences in his mind and his throat; I could almost see the one transferring to the other, quickly crafting the words and sending them down to his mouth, where he was storing them, refining them, preparing them for delivery.

"Are you ready for school?" he asked.

"I'm ready for anything now."

Mr. Coolidge shook his head; it wasn't what he'd wanted to say. "I'm not coming back," he said. "I've taken a job at another school."

"Where?"

"Ohio. Union, Ohio."

I wished I still had the morphine. Mr. Coolidge was about the only thing that made school bearable; sometimes he was the only thing that made the whole town bearable. I didn't know what to say. What was there to say? "Everybody wants to leave, so I guess I should say congratulations."

"It was a hard decision," he said. "I need some distance. Distance is supposed to provide understanding; at least that's what they say. We'll see. But I put my address and phone and e-mail in here. I hope you keep in touch." He handed me the book, a collection of Kafka short stories.

I took the book and placed it beside me. I wondered if it was true—about distance and understanding. Maybe that's what I needed. Maybe I should get away, to Ohio or someplace, away from my family and friends and everyone else I knew and who knew me all too well, away from the house and the school and the whole town, away from The Point and the river and the bridge and the angel standing down there. I tried to get away, farther than anyone could, I told myself. That didn't seem to do any good. I could have told Mr. Coolidge that. But I didn't.

"I hope so too," I said.

The guilty expression was gone from him; he'd unburdened himself and was now free to go. I wanted to tell him not to feel guilty, but I thought it would be too presumptuous. I knew what it was like to want to leave; wasn't that obvious? I never felt guilty about it. He wasn't doing me any favors sticking around anyway, I wanted to tell him, but I didn't say anything. I wanted to see if that expression would come back. It didn't.

After he left, I looked inside the jacket of the paperback. He'd written *Let's Go* and then signed his name. That was it. I didn't know what he was trying to tell me. There was a small slip of paper with his contact information written on it stuck inside the book, at the page where "A Hunger Artist" began. I didn't think anything about it, didn't think that he'd put any thought into where he'd marked the book, but then I read the story, about a performer whose act is to starve himself. He's good at it, better than anyone else, but the thing is, he'd eat, he says, but he could never find food that he liked. It was maybe the first thing I'd ever read that I related to, that I completely understood, as if all the words in all the world had come together to tell me this one thing, this one true thing that I couldn't express myself, that no one else had ever told me, but here was this guy, this insurance officer who wrote in his spare time, speaking directly to me as if he knew precisely what I wanted to hear. And, I came to find out, Kafka had two uncles who committed suicide—one to spare himself the fate of a Nazi concentration camp, where the famous writer's three sisters were murdered. I also learned that Kafka never wanted anyone to see his writing, had, in fact, made his best friend promise to destroy all his work, burn it into oblivion, and his friend betrayed him.

Of course I didn't read it there in the hospital, and by the time I did read it, it was too late.

My father and I waited around all morning for me to get discharged. The waiting about killed my father; it seemed way too inefficient for him, nothing happening, nurses coming and not telling us anything useful and then more waiting. He didn't understand what could possibly be taking so long to give us the word that I could go home. I was fine, I didn't need anything else, they had told us I'd be going home, so why didn't they let us leave already? I thought he was going to leave on his own or drag me out of there—he kept pacing around in the room like a caged animal and then he'd suddenly bolt out into the hallway, frequently checking in with the nurses he saw or anyone who happened to be walking past and then would come back into the room, edgier than ever, constantly glancing at his watch. "It's like a hotel around here," he said. "If they keep you past noon, they get to charge you another day."

Finally, they told us we could go. We walked to the car and there was my mother sitting in the passenger seat, working on one of her books of puzzles. She hadn't stepped one foot in the hospital while I was there. It was too much, she said. It was all too much. So there she was, sitting serenely in the car, gazing straight ahead through the windshield at something ahead of her in the grayness of the parking garage as if she were watching TV. The moment she saw me, however, she sprang out of the car and started crying. She held me tight and I forgave her for not coming. It was all right; I didn't need a roomful of people sitting around while I drifted in and out of pain and clarity. But even my brother came to see me, traveling down from school. He (partially) explained my mother's absence.

"She thinks you're to blame for this," Michael told me near the end of his first day with me.

"That I asked Troy to do it?"

"I don't know if she'd go that far, maybe that you provoked it."

"Troy doesn't need any provoking."

"I know that," he said. "And I told Mom that."

"She didn't believe you."

"I think she did. I don't know. It's everything for her, your attitude, I guess."

"It's all right," I said. "Tell her it's all right."

"What are you doing hanging out down there anyway?" Michael asked after a long silence. "Isn't that where all the scurves hang out?"

"We're usually over by the statue. We don't do anything, have a few beers, keep to ourselves. They leave us alone mostly. I don't know why he started it up. I don't really care. I haven't had any trouble with him before, not really since your party." I could tell he didn't like to hear that.

I drifted around the hospital room as I played with my *Jeopardy* buzzer and the pain in my chest radiated like a red coil on the electric stove. My brother spelled my father for a rest and hung in there as I drifted in and out of my morphine fog. I remember my brother asking me at one point, with great seriousness, "Where does it come from?" We had been talking about something before that, I remembered, something drifting back there in my brain like a cloud that once had a distinct shape and had suddenly shifted into a white blob of nothing. I knew what he was talking about; even in my hazy state I knew.

"I was born with it, I guess."

"Do you think it will go away?"

"I don't think so."

"Do you think I have it in me?" he wanted to know.

"Not a chance."

"I wonder sometimes," he said, his face leaning over the side of the bed, floating there in front of me. I was glad to see it, glad he was there. He wasn't like me, not at all. The face hardly looked like mine.

"It's a recessive gene, I guess. You don't have anything to worry about."

"I'm not worried," he said. "Not about me, anyway. I worry about you."

"I'm indestructible. You know that." Only, for once I wasn't so sure.

FOUR

I saw a picture of you

Todd had thrown us out of rhythm. Our routine was always disrupted during baseball, but not like this. Now he hated The Point, so we barely saw him all summer. Now baseball was over, and we were done with our days at The Point, things were supposed to be getting back to normal, but Todd still wasn't around. We would all be down by the angel, or at the bluff, or wherever, and he would show up late or leave early, without reason or warning, and something didn't feel right about the whole thing. It only lasted a couple of weeks, but everything was off track again—I could feel it, like when you get one tire too far off to the side of the road and hits those bumps to warn you that you're headed for the ditch. I could hear them, feel them—maybe I was the only one—but I knew something wasn't good about the whole thing, but I never knew that it was going to be so bad.

○ ○ ○

`Come over,` Jodi texted.

I was close to getting drunk. Another couple of drinks was all I needed, so I ignored her.

`M has x 2 show u.`
`?`
`M says solve for x.`

Maddy would be going to bed soon.

`On my way.`

I hadn't seen Maddy or Jodi much since baseball was over. I wanted to see Maddy, but I really wanted to see Jodi. I took one last drink and handed the bottle back to Ash and left. Maybe I'd be just drunk enough to tell her, I thought, knowing it wasn't true.

I remember how I felt about her—how I wanted to look at her until there was nothing left to see—how I wanted to look at her until she disappears so no one could see her but me, how I couldn't breathe when I wasn't with her, how I waited to hear from her or to see her, how I would have bent time and space to be with her all the time—I don't know if I feel that way now. I don't know if that's still how I feel or if the memory of how I felt is so strong that it still overwhelms the way I really feel. Maybe it will pass, maybe I will feel the same again someday, or never again. We might have missed our chance. That's what I think. Too much has happened, so much to keep us apart, our paths diverging and continuing in different, parallel directions, so close to connecting but never touching.

Jodi was waiting for me when I got to the Leightons'. "Can you do me a favor?" she said. "Take a look at Maddy's eyes."

"Okay." I waited for her to say something else, to explain or give me more instructions, but that was it. That was all.

Maddy was sitting at her desk with Manxcat on her lap. She had her laptop open and pictures were floating across the screen, pictures she'd taken. "These are just from the past couple of days," Maddy said, glancing over to me and then back to the screen. "I'll get them all uploaded and then do something with them."

There was a picture of Manxcat curled on Maddy's bed, a picture of a crack in the sidewalk that looked like the skeleton of a tree, a picture of her brothers fighting with foam noodles in blurs of blues and reds, a picture of paint dripping down a door like yellow claw marks in the wood. "They look good."

"Aren't you proud of me?" she said.

"Any pictures of Bob?"

"You know better," Maddy said.

There was a picture of Jodi lying in the grass with her eyes closed, the sun lighting her face—I wanted a copy of that; I wanted to tell Maddy to send me a copy, to stop the floating and let me look longer, but I watched it slide out of view and there was a picture of Maddy's mother reflected in the Hy-Vee store window, a picture of a bright pink tent in someone's backyard, a picture of a jar of pickle slices smashed on the floor, a picture of Todd and Jodi kissing.

It drifted from one side of the screen to the other, probably at the same rate of speed as all the rest, but it seemed to race past, too fast, faster than I could really see it. But the image stayed; I could see it long after it had gone. It was all I could see. I wanted to see it again, just to make sure, but I knew what I'd seen. What I really wanted was to have never seen it, but you can't un-see something, can you? You have to see it again and again. More pictures floated around, but all I saw were those two faces pressed together.

"That's it," Maddy finally said. "For now. It's a start, anyway." She dumped Manxcat on the floor, who walked between us and jumped up on Maddy's bed, curling himself right on top of her pillow.

"It's great. What made you finally decide to do it?"

"Todd helped me," Maddy said.

"He's good at that." I wasn't even sure what I was saying.

"Jodi made him, I think," Maddy said. "Otherwise he just hangs out downstairs and eats stuff."

"Like pickles."

"That was my mom," Maddy said. "She didn't like that I took that one."

"I like them all. Show me more when you can."

"Maybe tomorrow," she said.

"If it's all right with Jodi and Todd."

"What does he have to do with it?"

"I wouldn't want to get in his way."

When I came back downstairs, Jodi was waiting, almost anxiously, nervously. She was up off the couch and practically standing at the bottom of the stairs in front of me. "Did you look at her eyes?"

"I didn't see anything." I hadn't looked. I'd forgotten all about it.

"You didn't think something looked wrong with the left eye?"

I wanted to leave. "No."

She wouldn't let it drop. "It didn't seem slow, maybe? A little bigger than the other?"

"I didn't notice anything like that."

"It didn't look like something was in the left eye, something cloudy?" she said.

"I'll go back up and look if you want, but I didn't see anything."

"Don't go back up," Jodi said. "Do you think I should say something to the Leightons?"

"Wouldn't they notice if something was wrong?"

"I guess. Aren't you going to stay awhile?"

I left.

I didn't see Todd or Jodi, or Maddy, for the next couple of days. I thought I would do them a favor and stay away since they'd tried so hard to hide everything from me. *Fuck them,* I thought. I could do my own hiding. But I couldn't. Jodi was the first to find me. I hadn't gone anywhere.

`Did T tell u?` Jodi texted.

`M.`

`Sorry. Its nbd.`

`Ok.`

My phone rang.

"We weren't trying to hide anything," Jodi said.

"Okay."

"We didn't know if it was going to be anything. I don't even know if it's anything now. I don't know. It's awkward, I know. Believe me."

"It's all right. I just didn't know what was going on."

"It's not all right," she said. "I should have told you. I know you like me. I didn't want to screw things up between us."

"Okay."

"Is it?"

"You tell me."

She didn't tell me. Neither one of us wanted to talk about it anymore.

I didn't see Jodi for a while after that, but I still hung out with Todd. What else was I going to do? After my days in my room, we drank and did all the same crap we used to do as if nothing had happened, and half the time I wondered how Jodi could have picked him over me and the other half I wondered how could she ever pick me. How could anyone? I remember what Todd said to me after the VC thing—"and when you're screwed up, you attract other screwed-up people." But isn't everybody screwed up?

Todd never said a word about it, and I never asked him. It's the one thing I used to like about him most—you could tell him anything and it wouldn't be repeated, ever. Todd could keep a secret. Maybe he was better at keeping a secret than anyone else, or maybe he never kept it at all. Maybe he forgot about what you told him almost as soon as he heard it. Maybe he wasn't interested enough to remember it—so he had no secrets to tell, even if he wanted. Maybe he kept nothing, nothing that had to do with any-one else, which allowed him to think only about himself. Maybe that's the trick.

Let's Go

finally e-mailed Mr. Coolidge to thank him again for the Kafka book and to let him know how much it meant to me. I told him that I had become a little obsessed with the stories and with the person who wrote them. I wrote Mr. Coolidge that I wished he was still here so we could talk about them and asked him for other recommendations, stuff like Kafka, even though I knew—hoped even—that there wasn't anymore, that what I had was all there was.

I never heard back from Mr. Coolidge. I don't know why he bothered to give me his contact information if he wasn't going to answer when I used it. I thought that maybe he had to turn his back on us, on the whole town—he had a new life, new school, new kids. It was his job. Maybe he was handing out copies of Kafka to a whole new crew of kids just like me.

A helpful smile in every aisle

I had to go with my mother to the store. I hated that. I hated running errands with her, hated the way she wasted time—she didn't simply go in and get what she needed and then leave; she browsed, she dawdled, she explored her options; she examined all the products, read their packages, compared prices, and then bought the same stuff she always bought. I hated it, but I was trapped in the car with her after another session with our friend Felthy, and she insisted on stopping at the Hy-Vee on the way home. I guess I could have stayed in the car and sat there like an idiot, but I went inside with her and hated it.

I hated the store—the endless aisles of crap—five hundred different kinds of cereal, a thousand different brands of detergent—and there was my mother looking at everything as if she'd never seen any of it before, as if she'd never been in a store before. I don't really blame her—she had to be extra careful with Mr. Efficient waiting back home. He probably examined every receipt, knew the prices on everything to the penny, but you know he rarely went shopping, and he never went with her. He couldn't stand it, and she couldn't stand him being with her. He was a bigger baby about it than I was. He would wait in the car sometimes, staring at his watch the whole time.

I didn't care, as long as I didn't have to be part of it—otherwise it was torture. It was almost impossible to move as slowly as my mother did in a grocery store; grapes turned to raisins in the time it took her to move past; day turned to night and back to day again, but she never noticed. I had to wander, to get away from her or else we'd drive each other crazy—the more I hovered around her, the slower she went—I broke her concentration, she said. So I wandered the aisles like a sane man trapped in an asylum, and I hated the other people in the store, all of them. It was a place for blather, a breeding ground for rumors and disinformation, where people talked and talked crap, where they produced gossip like mold, pestilence, and disease. I almost always found myself in the aisle with all the cleaning products, wistfully looking at the rows and rows of detergents, scrubs, sanitizers, soaps, tarnish removers, bleaches, ammonia. I did this because it supported what people thought about me, and it always freaked them out a little. Maybe they thought I was going to start chugging the stuff right there in the store, drop to the tile, and put on a show. Maybe I should have.

The only people who weren't bothered by me were my classmates who worked there as stock boys. "Lysol, that's good, isn't it?" they might say as they walked past me and then look back with a shit grin. The athletes worked at Hy-Vee. The store paid above minimum wage, so it was one of the better jobs in town, and Hy-Vee always made a big deal out of the fact that they hired high school kids, that they hired anyone and everyone from high school, but we knew better. They only hired athletes, and only the good ones; they wore their white aprons and red name tags like another elitist uniform.

That particular day, however, I didn't make it to the cleaning aisle. I saw Maddy instead. She was in her riding gear, reading the back of a box of cereal.

"That stuff will kill you."

"It might," she said, and continued reading.

I stood there and waited for her to say something else, to pay me some attention, but she didn't. "I'm bored. What can we do?"

"I don't know," she said, and put the box back on the shelf. "I have to go."

"How's Bob?"

She looked at me with hard eyes and said, "Bob is dead," and walked off.

I kept hearing her say it—Bob is dead—until it's all I could hear. Jodi hurt me and I turned around and hurt Maddy and she turned around and hurt me back. I'd told Jodi that it was Maddy that had told me, and Jodi must have told Maddy. I don't know why I'd said it—it was sort of true, I guess—but I didn't really care. Let her be mad. I was mad too. I walked back to my mother, who had just turned into the second aisle of the store, and told her that I was going to walk home. It was a long walk.

She passed me in the car and pulled over and gave me a ride the rest of the way. The walk hadn't helped. I was still mad, but not so much with Maddy or Jodi or even Todd. To hell with them, with all of them. I could do without them, I thought. Of course, I couldn't.

Facing all the same tomorrows (#s 32–35)

This is a mistake. I know it is—one wrong word after another, misrepresenting things, I think, misstating how it all really happened. I'm too polite, withholding too much, trying to paint a prettier picture instead of showing the ugliness of it all. I could show you the retch and bile, the jagged bones, the splashes of blood and limbs crushed and splintered, show the way we tore through each other with complete indifference. No one cared. They had stopped caring—we all had—stopped caring that we were no longer friends, family, whatever.

This is spew, blowing chunks, bile, dry-heaved into this mess I left and leave for everyone else. I know why I started this, but I don't know why I should finish. I've made bad choices. I have picked the wrong friends, or they picked me. Maybe I simply wound up with the only people who could tolerate me, attracting a less than ideal type; I mean, what quality of person would want to be friends with me, would deal with all of my crap? I offer little and seem to have gotten less in return. I never lied to them; in fact, I have been more honest than I should have been (perhaps). They can't say the same. I should have expected it—there were more than plenty of enough signs—but I still don't think I deserved it.

So enough of the nice stuff. Stop reading now—it might be better if you did. It will only get worse from here. Because I'm going to tell you what happened, how I stopped creeping closer and closer to the edge, stopped the pointless dabbling, the infrequent experiments, and finally took a real run at it, shredding the polite veil between us, testing the limits of whatever held me back. It was time. It is time for this to stop.

Here's the thing—the secret of it all: remember one of my father's favorite lines, the bit about how there are two categories of people, the miserable and the horrible. Well, here's the real truth—we're all horrible. There is no comfort in the miserable because we're all horrible, grotesque, immeasurably flawed, impaired, repulsive, revolting freaks wandering around with exaggerated awareness of our own misshapen defects or no awareness at all. I don't know which is worse, but make no mistake—Woody Allen and my father were wrong—we're all horrible. We walk through each day with our gross imperfections, blighted, stained, less human than we want to admit. We lie, cheat, steal, kill—either a little or a lot—or allow it to happen; we are perpetrators or accomplices, predator or prey, or both.

There are people like Todd—who has done nothing—I mean, what has he done in the world?—and thinks he has a right to something, is entitled to something, and goes out and gets it, and probably doesn't feel guilty or blessed or anything other than satisfied for the moment that he got his and doesn't give a shit about who got hurt in the process. How many people do you know like that? And then there's people like Dr. Vandever, who, as far as I know, did nothing wrong and tried his best to help others, and yet he couldn't even mow his own fucking lawn; instead he saw his own terrible lack of something, something that maybe no one else saw, something that maybe wasn't really there, but he saw it anyway, and it stood in his way, stood there and kept him from even cutting one more blade of grass. Is it better to know your own shortcomings or have no idea? Maybe being born a moron is the only way to get through life. If you have a brain in your head, all you can see is the ugliness in the world, the fact that we are primitive savages, clawing at each other just trying to make ourselves feel better. We are so much uglier than the dead—the dead are perfect. Their faults are forgotten or at least forgiven; their flaws fade until all that's left is what was good or nothing at all. They don't have any ambitions or regrets; they don't disappoint.

The idea started in my head as soon as I woke up, not waiting for the day to grind on a few hours, an itchy voice I wasn't going to be able to scratch. Today is the day, it said, and tomorrow and maybe the day after that, if necessary. It seemed to go on, all day long—every time I stopped paying attention to something else, it was there. I tried not to think about it, but by afternoon it wasn't a voice anymore, just the rhythm of the meaning, like the melody of a song you can't get out of your head, and by that time I had nothing to do and nowhere to go, nothing to distract myself, and the itchy rhythm was there, itching and itching, and I decided to give it a scratch.

By dinner I could hear the melody phasing into a familiar tone; it was soft, there behind the rhythm. I knew where this was going, but I knew that this would be different. There would be no bridge, no bluff, no angel. The itch wasn't going to get scratched; it was going to get raked, clawed, hacked at until it was gone. I put together a box of stuff—supplies—and rode down to The Point and hid the box among some tall grass near the railroad tracks. I don't know why I put it there—it was an obvious mistake—but I thought I would go up farther on River Road, and The Point would be a halfway spot or something. I guess that was the reason. I should have known better.

Everybody was up on the bluff by the time I got there, around eight thirty or so, everybody except Todd. The rest of them had finished a couple of bottles of wine Ash had stolen from his neighbors—"it was sitting on their back stoop all day," he said, "what was I supposed to do?" We weren't sure we believed him, but we didn't really care where it had come from. Bruce was passing around a bottle of sambuca he'd found in the basement—so they were mostly drunk and I had nothing. I needed something.

I called Todd and told him to bring whatever he could get, something strong. "Whiskey, vodka, anything."

"I'll be there in a while," he said.

"Soon. I can't be sober around here much longer." It's hard enough to be around my friends when we're all sober but almost impossible when you're sober and they're drunk. Vern was talking about how he'd spent most of the day watching their dog.

Why? You might wonder. Because the dog had swallowed a pair of Vern's swim trunks and he watched it "go in one end and come out the other."

"He liked it fine going in," Vern said. "It was a whole different story coming out." He laughed just thinking about it. It took a long time, he said, a couple of hours, with the dog struggling with the twisted hunk of nylon or whatever man-made crap it's made out of, and Vern didn't bother to help him. "I'm not pulling anything out of an animal's ass," he said.

"I bet you'll wear the trunks, though," Bruce said.

"Nothing's wrong with them," Vern said. "They just needed a good wash."

We weren't sure he was joking.

I thought about leaping off the bluff right then and there or, better yet, riding my bike off, getting a nice long start and pedaling up to full speed and sailing off, past the railroad tracks, maybe reaching the river. They'd get a kick out of it, I knew that. Maybe it would have been better if I had, in retrospect, but I did have a plan, one that helped calm the constant noise in my head, and I was going to wait, not much longer, but there was still time. I didn't have all night, though.

It was almost ten and still no Todd. I texted him. Nothing. I called. Nothing. He wasn't going to show. I didn't need a drink now anyway. I needed to get going, to get away from all of them. I got on my bike and rode down River Road. It was dark, darker than the river beside it. All the houses were dark, even Mr. Camp's, not even a porch light on, and everything was quiet, only the sound of my tires on the dark road. Not even the river made a sound.

As I neared The Point, I could see a car parked on the shoulder. It was Todd's brother's car. I got off my bike and stood in the road for a moment. Everything was quiet. I looked around but didn't see anyone in the dim moonlight and still didn't hear anything. I went up to the car and looked inside—no one was there. I called Todd, thinking I would hear his phone, but there was nothing.

I left my bike near the road and crossed the railroad tracks to retrieve the box I'd hidden. I moved slowly and carefully, hardly making a sound, hoping to hear someone. Todd or his brother had to be around here somewhere. As I reached the box, I heard a voice, barely a whisper. It was Jodi. Jodi and Todd. They were out there on The Point somewhere, not far from me, I guessed. I wasn't spying on them, even though I'm sure that's what Todd thinks. Maybe Jodi too for all I know. I don't care. I know why I went there, and it had nothing to do with them. I wasn't spying, but I did see them, and I know what I saw—and they know too—and then I got the hell out of there, tried to leave as quietly and quickly as I could, and got back on my stupid bike and balanced my idiotic box on the handlebars and rode upriver where I thought no one would find me, where no one would look for me, and where I wouldn't be seen from the water, wouldn't be seen from the road, wouldn't be seen from the railroad tracks, but was close enough to the river that I could see it, could be by it, close enough to touch it if I wanted, and I found my spot and sat down and looked at the dark water barely moving in the humid night, just sitting there like me in the low light of a small moon, and I opened my book and took out a large plastic bottle I'd taken from the garage and drank as much as I could get down my throat.

Let me first say that I don't recommend this. I don't recommend any of it. If I could do it all over again (and I can), I wouldn't. This is what I know—more than twenty million people try to take themselves off this planet every year, with more than a million of them succeeding, more than all the murders and all the wars combined—and they usually take the worst way out—poisoning, hanging, guns, all the stuff I'd been avoiding, all the stuff I didn't like. But for once, I wanted pain and misery and hurt, and I got it. It lasted hours and I knew it was a mistake, but it was too late. There was nothing to do but wait.

I thought about a list someone had put in my locker at school, years ago. It came back to me as if it had just been handed to me, retrieved from my memory like some unwanted, unrequested file.

All suicide methods have the risk of severe, possibly prolonged pain if things go wrong:

If you have taken an overdose, you may vomit before you become unconscious.

If you have swallowed caustic substances, you might survive but have severe burns to internal organs, including the gastrointestinal tract.

If you have taken many toxic substances, you might live but have permanent damage to kidneys and liver.

If your brain goes without an oxygen supply for more than about three minutes, you will suffer permanent brain damage.

If you fail to kill yourself with a gunshot, you might be left with permanent disfigurement and disability.

If you do succeed, think about how you will be discovered:

When you die, you lose control of your bodily functions. To put it nicely, you defecate and urinate on yourself.

If you cut your wrists, hang yourself, or commit suicide with a gunshot, you leave a very grisly task for whoever has to clean up afterward.

You will be bloated and purple if you choose hanging or strangulation.

I never would have done it—I wouldn't have done any of the stuff I did over the next four or five days—except that I thought it was time to try something drastic. Desperate times call for desperate measures. No pain, no gain, right? I wasn't tired of leaping—I still liked it, liked it too much maybe—and I would have preferred it, would have gladly gone back to the bluff or the bridge, anything other than the beating I took, but the leaping wasn't working. Nothing was. So I thought I'd go in a different direction. Just do it.

I'll spare us the torture porn details. The problem with pain is that unless it's happening to you, it's either funny, thrilling, or worse, boring. It's like Itchy and Scratchy, NASCAR crashes, or all those Saw movies. I wish it were funny; I wish it had been thrilling, but it wasn't. It was only pain, but at least I had gotten part of it right—no one had found me. I awakened on the small, hidden patch of land next to the river with my box of goodies still there. It was night again. I didn't know what time it was. I'd thrown my phone in the river, thinking maybe that's how they were finding me. Or maybe I just wanted to be done with it, the stupid texts and voice mails and photos and video and links and all that crap that is a monumental waste of time. I didn't want any of it. I didn't want any distractions; I didn't have any time to waste.

I didn't know if I'd been gone a day, two days, or more, but I wasn't back more than a few minutes when I reached into the box and went through it all over again. Then, like always, I was back. It was afternoon this time. The air was heavy with the day's heat and humidity. I was drenched in sweat and my back was sore, but otherwise I felt like I always did. I thought about going home, but only for a minute—I was determined to try again and again. That was the whole point of being here, I told myself. So I went back to the box. Back to the pain. My stomach hurt again, convulsed, and I was sure I was going to lose everything, heave it all back up, but then I was dizzy, the river was twisting around me, thrashing itself in all directions over my head, and I tried to hang on to something, but there didn't seem to be anything there, only the twisting river, and my head spun and my eyes tried to catch up but couldn't. I made my way over to the bank and looked out across the wrinkled water. It heaved, as if trying to catch its breath in the still, humid air. There were a few lights shining over in Illinois; they seemed happy, winking at me, wanting me to finally succeed. Then it hit me. Like the flu and food poisoning all at once, like someone was trying to pull my insides out of my mouth and something else was trying to pull them out of my ass. Vern's dog couldn't have felt worse than this. My insides tightened, constricted in violent spasms. It was horrible. I dived into the water and tried to drink as much of the river as I could.

The Nazi makes pancakes

The edges of the end of everything curled back like leaves or sheets of paper recoiling from fire. I was awake again—the light had returned and everything was the same—except I didn't know where I was. I was in bed, but it wasn't mine. I hadn't opened my eyes, but I knew I wasn't in my own bed, my own room. There was the unfamiliar but pleasant feeling of soft cotton sheets on my legs; there was the smell of smoke, the stale stench of an ancient fire—it was terrible, like the smell from an old diaper burning. There was the dull comfort behind my head, the thin wafer of a pillow. I knew all of this before I opened my eyes. I knew I wasn't going to like it, I knew it was going to be bad, but I didn't know it was going to be worse.

Mr. Camp was sitting in a chair across the room watching me, the brown diaper of a cigar stuck askew in his mouth, the smoke crawling lazily between us. He was wearing nothing but a pair of shorts—no boots, no shirt—his brown chest and his bulging gut casually on display. I'm in his house, in a guest room, I think, and I wonder what the hell has happened to me, wonder what this Nazi has been doing to me for however long he's had me in this small room with only a bed, a small dresser, and the chair he occupies like a guard who knows he has the upper hand, the only hand. I have my clothes on—I can feel my shorts and T-shirt—but what does that mean? He could have put them on; he could have taken them off; he could have dressed me in a hundred different clothes for all I know. Maybe he's been experimenting on me like some poor patient of Dr. Mengele.

"What's the point?" he said through the smoke.

I didn't know what he was talking about, so I kept my mouth shut and hoped he hadn't violated me.

"What is the point you are trying to make with all of this?" he said. "You're wasting a lot of people's time and energy. Is that what you want?"

"No. I'm not asking anyone to do anything."

"You don't have to ask. It's not about asking." He took the cigar from his mouth and looked at the end of it, as if expecting to see it lit. It wasn't. He rested his right hand on his knee with the cigar sticking up like some extra, diseased finger. He looked at me again. "People have a duty, an obligation, an interest. That's part of life, I guess, why we live among one another, and you're exploiting that, whether you intend to or not, whether you ask or not. It doesn't matter. You are a burden, a tax on us all. So I want to know why. What's the point?"

People always ask me that. What is my point, what am I

trying to prove?—they can't seem to understand that I'm not try-ing to prove anything. They don't want to accept the fact that the only time I really like is the time after my suicide and before I wake up. That's it; that's the point. It's all I want; I only hope that the time gets longer and longer and longer. I don't see the point in asking—it's like asking someone why they keep having sex, or why they watch the same movies or TV shows over and over, or why they keep eating ice cream, or why they keep smoking cigars. What's their point? I couldn't say that to Mr. Camp. He sat there in his chair like a cross between a savage cannibal king and an army colonel gone native, his brown, hulking body blocking my way. I couldn't tell him anything.

Mr. Camp laughed and the smoke shook and fled from him. He stood and removed the cigar from his mouth. "Well, think about it. I expect an answer before you leave. You want some breakfast?"

I got out of bed and followed him. We went into the main part of the house, which was one huge room with the kitchen off to one side of the room, the dining area on the other side, then the living area, and beyond that, another hallway that led who knows where. There was an old jukebox and pinball machine in the liv-ing area, but I didn't dare leave the table to go look at them. I sat there and watched Mr. Camp huddled over by the stove. There were floor-to-ceiling windows all along one wall, looking out to the river. It was a great view. The river was flat and still—you wouldn't think it would be able to carry me from my spot upriver down here. Maybe it hadn't.

"You want something to drink?" Mr. Camp asked. "Coffee, tea, juice, beer?"

"Juice, please."

He brought me a large glass of orange juice and a stack of pancakes with sliced strawberries on the side. They weren't like any pancakes I'd ever seen—dark, almost chestnut brown, with tiny pockmarks over them, thousands of them, as if he'd been jabbing them with a needle, over and over, injecting them with something or trying to get them to confess. Mr. Camp saw me staring at the dark, torture victims.

"They're buckwheat," he said. "I don't use processed flour. That stuff will kill you." He did a double take and laughed. "Well, maybe not you, but you know what I mean. Some people care." They were good, maybe the best pancakes I've ever had.

Mr. Camp sat across from me but didn't eat. There was a noise down the other hallway, but by the time I looked up, all I saw was the fleeting image of long blond hair, a white T-shirt, and long tanned legs disappearing into some other room far away. Mr. Camp didn't look, didn't say anything. He held his cigar in his left hand and sipped on a cup of coffee as he watched me finish my breakfast.

He cleared my plate and glass and set them in the sink and left me without a word. I sat at the table, not knowing if I should leave or not, so I sat there and did nothing. Mr. Camp returned, wearing pants and a blue oxford shirt—talk-to-the-parents clothes.

"I don't need a ride. I need to find my bike."

"I have your bike," he said.

"How did you find it?"

"I know this river about as well as anyone," he said.

At that moment it occurred to me that it had been Mr. Camp who had always found me—he was the one who would come to get me in the woods or in the water, dashed along the railroad tracks, hanging from some tree, whatever. I began to think I understood the nods and waves he gave me as I biked past his house. "I know where you are," he was saying. "I know how to find you." He was my warden and I was the escaped prisoner he always tracked down and brought back and put in the hole.

"You can forget about the box, though," he said. "You ain't getting that back."

I still had more stuff in it, more stuff I could have used. I would have kept going, I thought, I think, if I hadn't fallen in the river or dived in. That was my mistake. I would have gone back to the box one more time and then once more, I thought. But now, I didn't miss the box. It didn't have anything that was going to change anything. I wanted to go home.

"I'll get my bike, then."

"It's in the back of the car," he said. "Come here," he ordered, and I followed him from the house and across the backyard to the edge of the water. You could have stepped from the yard directly into the river.

"Doesn't it flood?"

"Every spring," Mr. Camp said. "But it's only reached the house once." That wasn't why he'd brought me out here—he didn't want to show me the river, and he wasn't showing me his backyard. He was showing me the spot where he'd found me.

He wasn't saying anything, but he was looking right at it. Maybe he could still see me floating there in the water, bobbing up and down like some dead fish. I didn't care. It wasn't my fault I got stuck there. It wasn't as if I had planned it that way. In fact, I had planned it exactly the opposite, that no one would find me.

I turned away from the spot—it obviously meant more to Mr. Camp than me—and looked back toward the house. Standing there, in one of the large windows, was the blonde in her T-shirt and shorts, and like an idiot I stared at her. She must have been in her thirties, maybe even in her twenties— way too young for Mr. Camp. Maybe she was his daughter, I thought, but I'd never heard of him having any kids. She was only there for a second, and as soon as she saw me looking at her, she stepped behind the drapes. Definitely not his daughter. Mr. Camp, with his gut and gray hair, his cigar and black boots, was somehow getting it done.

Here's the oddest thing about the woman at Mr. Camp's—I looked right at her, stared her right in the face, but I can't remember what she looked like. I don't see her. Instead, when I think about her, I always see Violet Courtland standing there. I know it wasn't her, that it was someone else entirely, but I always see Violet in my memory; she's the one in the window looking back at me. Maybe I wish it was her.

"What do you want?" Mr. Camp was still looking at the spot in the river.

"I don't want to be like you." I didn't mean it like that—I didn't mean that I didn't want to be like Mr. Camp specifically. I meant I didn't want to be old like him, fat and pushy and acting like he knew everything. I didn't want to be that person—that's what I meant, but I know how it came out. Now he was pissed.

"You think you're special? You're not special, not one bit. You're going to have to ride this thing out just like the rest of us, and until you realize that, you're wasting everybody's time. I'm not going to get dragged into your mess," he said. "You're like a black hole, sucking everyone in, or a rock that falls into a pile of shit—the rock's fine, but the shit gets thrown on everybody else. What amazes me is that people allow it. Everybody coddles you," he said. "Everybody tolerates your nonsense and either ignores the problem or helps you out, without really helping. If they really wanted to help, really, they'd put a bullet in your brain and do us all a favor. You want me to do that for you?"

"How about a knife? Would that work for you? Because I wouldn't want to put that on anyone, not even Troy Liddell. Remember that?"

That deflated him a little. "I'm sorry about that. And I'm sorry you didn't learn anything from it. You have this tortured logic about the whole thing," Mr. Camp said. "And you know what I think? I think the more you go around trying to prove that you want to die, you're really proving how much you want to live."

"How do you mean?"

"You're still here, aren't you?" he said, looking so pleased with himself. "So what do you want?"

He didn't wait for me to answer; he'd already answered for

242

me. He walked to his car and I followed him and we rode in silence to my house.

Mr. Camp puffed on his cigar and looked at the house as if it might tell him something. Maybe he was debating whether or not he was going to come inside. Finally, he said, "You know, if you'd put half the energy into improving your life, fixing whatever you think is so wrong with it, as you do trying to ruin it, I bet you'd be surprised at how much better off you'd be."

"Yes sir." I couldn't help it. Maybe it helped. Maybe he thought I was actually listening to him. He pulled in front of the house and waited as I pulled my bike from his trunk. I thanked him.

"No sense going all prodigal," he said. I didn't know what he was talking about, but he nodded and started to drive off without talking to my parents. That was the important thing. Then Mr. Camp threw his cigar in the yard like an arrogant ass.

"You're such a dyke," I should have said, but the words didn't even enter my mind. I didn't think of it until days later. It almost made me laugh, the way he'd been gnawing on it all morning, then heaved it right in the grass. I went over and looked at it—I thought about picking it up and waltzing into the house with it, waving it around as I announced my return, like some big shot. Instead, I left it there, figuring that if things went too bad, I could always bring my father out and show him. He'd go through the roof over that. He'd been disrespected; that's what the cigar in the yard would mean to him.

My mother was standing in the kitchen when I walked

through the back door, and she gave me a stern look and set down the spoon she was holding and steadied herself against the sink, as if trying to gather strength to say something.

"Mr. Camp brought me home. He made me breakfast."

My mother nodded. "That's good," she said. "Your father is in the other room. You should go see him."

I stayed in the kitchen. I told her about the buckwheat pancakes. I told her about the small guest room, and I told her about the old jukebox and pinball machine. That's all I said. My father came into the kitchen and placed a sheet of paper on the kitchen table and left. 114,300. That's the number; that's all that was written on the paper. I knew what it meant. It's how long I was gone multiplied by fifteen—it was the new deduction from my curfew. One hundred and fourteen thousand, three hundred minutes deducted from my current total, which I didn't even know what that was, but I'm sure my father knew. That was it; I was back home. I took the piece of paper and went up to my room, thinking that I might have been better off if Mr. Camp had come inside to talk to them.

My old pal Hickory showed up a couple of hours after I was home.

"What did I miss?"

"Nothing," she said.

"How's Maddy?"

"She's still mad. Mad at me and still mad at you. I asked her if she wanted to come; she didn't. There's nothing more stubborn than a ten-year-old girl," Jodi said, and then reconsidered. "Except you."

"How's Todd?"

"I don't know. I haven't talked to him. You haven't?"

"I haven't talked to anyone. Only you. All I know is what you tell me."

"Then I should tell you this," she said. "The world has changed. It's all better now. You'll see."

"There's no place like home." We laughed, but it wasn't the same. She was right: it had changed.

It wasn't like talking to Jodi anymore; it was more like talking to Vern or Ash or Bruce—we talked around stuff now, trying to avoid subjects that we used to have no problems talking to each other about. After we had both grown tired of not talking about things, Jodi finally said that she had to go.

"Tell Todd to call me, or he could come by."

"You call him," Jodi said. "I don't talk to him."

"Okay."

She stood to go and then tried to get in a parting shot.

"Your friend Todd is a lot like you—he doesn't think about anyone but himself."

When I didn't say anything, she continued.

"It was a mistake," she said. "You know a thing or two about mistakes, don't you?"

"If we're so much alike, then why couldn't you make the same mistake with me?"

"I know you don't want to hear this," she said, "but I need you as a friend. I don't need Todd."

"I don't know if I need friends like you."

She left. And I was happy that she was gone. I was happy to

be there alone in my room. I thought that it was the only place to be. I thought that if I stayed in my room, I'd be all right. So I stayed there, stayed off the phone, stayed off the computer (for the most part), stayed out of contact with almost everyone—although my father told me to call Don Lemley. I'd almost forgotten about him, with my own phone being at the bottom of the river.

"How are you doing?" he said.

"Mr. Camp threatened to shoot me in the head."

Don Lemley laughed. "That sounds about right."

"It was after he made me breakfast."

"That's the Judge," Don Lemley said, as if he'd heard the story a hundred times. "Your father said you were gone a few days again," he said.

"I'm back."

"Judge Camp found you."

"Maybe he's tired of finding me. He wasn't happy at the end."

"It doesn't sound like it. He didn't really threaten you, did he?"

"Sort of. He said he wished someone would do the town a favor and shoot me in the head."

"He was making a point," Don Lemley said.

"I got the point. I don't blame him."

"What else do you like to do?" Mr. Lemley said. "And don't say nothing."

"I can't think of anything."

"You like to get drunk with your friends," he said.

"Not really. It's something to do, I guess."

"Well, I'm not saying you should be out there drinking, but as you get older and look back, you'll see that no one regrets the time they spent with friends. They usually regret the time they didn't. You know what I mean?"

"I'm not sure they're my friends."

"That's a different story," Don Lemley said. "I'm not going to tell you what you should or shouldn't do. That's not my place. But at the risk of sounding like an old fart, I'll tell you what I think. I think you're going to wake up one day and wonder what you've done, wonder why you wasted so much time on all of this, and wish you hadn't. Maybe you don't believe me, but you know I'm right about this: what you're doing now isn't getting you anywhere. How many times are you going to do this before you realize it's leading you nowhere or right back to the same place?"

He almost had me there; I almost agreed with him, but then he lost me.

"There is an account for everything," he said, "for everything we say and do. I believe that account is managed by God, but even if you don't believe in that, you're going to find out that your actions will take their toll. It will cost you one way or another. You can do whatever you want, of course you can, but just because you can do something doesn't mean you should do it. This is what you do—you don't hurt yourself—you can't, I guess—so you hurt everybody else around you. That's what you do every time you go out, every time you don't come back. You think it's easier for your parents, your friends, whoever? It's not. It's the same every time, maybe worse. You should see yourself some time or imagine what it must be like to come across you in the river, at the bottom of the bluff, washed up in someone's yard. You know, if you spent half as much energy trying to live as you did trying to die, you'd have one hell of a good life."

Yeah, that's not going to work.

"That's sort of what Judge Camp said."

"Before or after he threatened to shoot you?" Don Lemley joked.

"I provoked it, I guess. I compared him to Troy Liddell."

"That must have been some breakfast," Mr. Lemley said. "What are you doing now?"

"Nothing. Reading mostly."

"What are you reading?" Don Lemley wanted to know.

"Kafka."

Don Lemley let loose one of his patented laughs, warm and embracing. "I love that stuff," he said. It turns out that Don Lemley has read more books than anyone else in town, maybe knows more about books than Mr. Coolidge. "It's what happens when you're a dispatcher for twenty years," he said. "You have a lot of time to read. Have you read *The Trial*?" I hadn't. "You have to read it," he said.

It turns out that Don Lemley likes weird stuff—writers I'd never even heard about, Russians and South Americans—and he seemed to remember all of them and started to drop by the house with books. I'd never seen Don Lemley in person before and after all the times we'd spent on the phone, I thought I had a clear image of him in my head—an older man with short gray hair, medium height, still in good shape, that's what I thought would fit the Voice of God—so I was shocked when this short, bald guy with a huge gut—a paler, heavier version of Judge Camp—stood at the door with an armful of books. The Voice of God belonged to an old, bald, fat guy. I guess it makes sense—we're made in his image after all.

He started coming almost every week, for a drop off and pickup, introducing me to writers like Karel Čapek, Robert Walser, Bruno Schulz, Gogol, Infante, Calvino, Borges, and maybe my favorite name of all of them—Joaquim Maria Machado de Assis. I spent most of my time with Don Lemley's lending library, and after a few days of this, I proposed that my father add some time back to my curfew, that he take into account the time I'd clocked in my room. He had none of it. "It doesn't work that way," he said. Of course not—it only worked one way: his way. It didn't matter—the numbers were so outrageous at this point—they were like the national debt or the distance to the farthest star, so huge as to not even be realistic, not even real. It didn't matter what I did.

I become a cat

t wasn't long after this that I began to miss the bridge. I wasn't thinking about jumping. I wasn't thinking about anything except standing there looking down at the water. Maybe if I just look, take a look, maybe it would be the last look I'd need, maybe I could just look and then go back home.

Who was I kidding?

Maddy came to see me. Her eye looked bad. Jodi had been right all along, and no one had listened to her.

"I came to tell you that I can't see you anymore," Maddy said. "My parents don't want me to."

"I'm sorry about that." I was, but I wasn't sure she was. She was still mad. "What's going on with your eye there?"

"I don't know," she said, and reflexively turned the left side of her face away from me. "I went to the ophthalmologist and he recommended a different doctor, so we went to him and he recommended another doctor, so we're going up to Iowa City."

"That's a good hospital."

"Have you been there?"

"A couple of times. But don't let that be your example. It's still a good hospital."

Maddy smiled. "You're a tough case."

"I like to think so. You'll like Iowa City. Make your parents take you downtown to see the campus. Maybe you could sit in on some classes."

"Maybe," she said. She'd almost forgotten that she was supposed to be mad at me.

She called a few days later. Actually, her father called. Here, only a few days before she'd told me that she couldn't see me anymore, now she wanted me to do something for her. "Maddy has an important appointment at the UI hospital," Mr. Leighton said, "and it's impossible for her mother and me to take her and we can't reschedule anytime soon, so we were wondering if you could drive her."

Maddy knew that I wasn't allowed to drive. "I'd like to, but I can't." I didn't want to take her even if I could. Maddy was up to something. Maybe her parents had nothing going on, maybe they had all the time in the world, or maybe what Mr. Leighton said was true, and if it were, there had to be plenty of other people who could take Maddy to her appointment, but they wanted me. Maddy wanted me. *I should want to take her,* I thought. It didn't matter what I wanted or what I thought.

"We already worked it out with your father," Mr. Leighton said. It figured. They'd already worked it out—they weren't asking me to do it; they were telling me.

"There isn't someone who Maddy would rather have take her?"

"She asked for you," Mr. Leighton said. "She was insistent. I'm sure you know what I mean."

He put Maddy on the phone.

"Will you take me?" she said.

"If you want me to."

"That's what I want."

"Okay, then."

"Okay," she said. "You have to take care of me, okay?"

"I will. I'll take you to Iowa City and bring you back, just like you want."

"Thank you," she said.

She was punishing me, I thought. She was still mad and she was going to punish me by making me do things for her, errands, chores; now that she'd broken the driving ban, she'd have me carting her all over the place and she could sit right beside me and still be mad, show me how angry she still was while I had to drive her back and forth. It wouldn't be the only time, I knew that, and for once I was right.

Maddy acted as if nothing had happened between us. When I picked her up in the morning to drive her to the doctor's, she hopped in the car and began talking in her usual way, as if the past had been erased or had never happened in the first place. She started talking almost from the moment she saw me until we pulled into the hospital parking garage an hour and a half later. She didn't talk about her eye—which looked normal that particular day, of course—nothing about the doctors or the reason we were driving. She talked about astronomy—that was her new thing—about black holes and wormholes and how space affects time or is actually part of time. I should have paid more attention, but she talked in a steady stream, almost more than my mother does in the car, which is the maximum allowed by law, the absolute maximum a person can handle.

I waited with Maddy until they came to take her in to see the doctor, then I left the cramped waiting area, filled with TV noise and mothers piling up with their sick children. I wandered the halls and watched the parade of gurneys and wheelchairs, walkers and crutches, filled with sick kids, all of them younger than I am. It was a whole city of sick—I wondered how doctors felt about it, being surrounded by so much sickness day after day. I wondered if they thought the whole world was sick. I wondered if that is what happened to Dr. Vandever—the sick people kept coming day after day and there was nothing he could do to stop it. You could heal one, but there was another one and by the time you healed that one, the first one was back or another one, on and on, all the time. Maybe that's what he thought; maybe that's what he thought when he was out mowing the lawn, cutting the grass that kept growing and regrowing, all those millions of blades of grass that kept on growing no matter what you did. I could see it getting to someone—it was getting to me as I wandered the halls and I had to find an empty, quiet room to sit in for a minute before I went back and waited for Maddy.

I was happy with my little theory until I mentioned it to Maddy. She laughed. "You know," she said, "some people know their experience isn't the same for everybody. How you think isn't automatically the way everybody else thinks. Doctors know the whole world isn't sick, the same way police know the whole world isn't filled with criminals or embalmers know the whole world isn't full of dead people." I'm sure she was right, but I wasn't so sure.

After Maddy was done with her appointment and examinations, we drove across the river to the main campus of the university, walked around downtown and grabbed something to eat, and sat outside the physics building, Van Allen Hall.

"He discovered the Van Allen radiation belts," Maddy said.

"What do you suppose the chances are of him looking through the whole universe and finding the one thing that has the same name?"

She laughed politely, but at least she laughed. "Maybe there's a lot of other stuff named Van Allen still out there," she said.

"Like the Van Allen radiation pants or the Van Allen radiation suspenders."

Maddy rolled her eyes and gave me the same mischievous look I got right before she told me about Bob, but she was too tired to continue and drifted off into silence for a while.

"Do you think you'd want to go here?" she said.

"Sure."

"What do you think you would study?"

"I don't know. Something in medicine, I guess. That would be good. But I like this side of the river."

"Maybe something in this building," she said.

"I couldn't do that. That's for you. Isn't it?"

"I'd like to study the sun," Maddy said.

"Why?"

"The sun is strange," she said, "in a good way. And we really don't know that much about it. Same thing with gravity. I wouldn't mind studying that."

"I'd like you to solve that for me."

Maddy shook her head and smiled, then thought for a minute. "If you went to med school, you'd still be here when I started. We could study together."

Maddy had to go back. Then she had to go back again. I always went with her. What had started as a favor had now become a routine. Her father never even bothered to ask; Maddy would call and tell me when she needed to be there and off we'd go.

Mrs. Leighton came with us. Once. I don't know why she had me drive, but there I was chauffeuring her and Maddy to the doctor's, with Mrs. Leighton sitting in the passenger seat, not knowing what to say to me (and I don't blame her for that, not at all), and me not knowing what to say to her, and Maddy sitting in the backseat, completely quiet for once. It was serious and somber and none of us liked it, but none of us knew how to change the atmosphere we had created. I would look in the rearview mirror and watch Maddy as she looked out the window, looking about as miserable as I've ever seen her, and sometimes, when she caught me looking at her, she'd make a face, an exaggerated grimace or frown, something for the two of us.

Iowa City is fine, but there isn't one decent bridge in the whole town. They're all too short, too close to the water—you can see the college students jumping into the river for fun—or their idea of it anyway. The Iowa River had no attraction for me, too narrow and shallow, making its way southeast until it spills into the Mississippi. There wasn't anything there I wouldn't see at home. Well, there was one thing—a hotel downtown, in the ped mall near the physics building. I looked at that hotel with some curiosity.

"That's the place," Maddy said as we walked around the ped mall.

"It's not high enough."

"How high does it need to be?"

"Ten stories is usually good."

"You're one short."

I shrugged but kept looking. There were taller buildings in town, but I wasn't interested in them—I kept looking at the hotel. Maybe it was the fact that it was just a little shorter than it needed to be. I don't know—it was like being drawn to the wrong girl, drawn to things you know you shouldn't mess with. Sometimes you're suddenly connected to someone, or something, and you don't know why.

"You want to go up there?" Maddy said.

"No."

"You're not going to leave me here by myself?" Maddy said.

"Not a chance."

"You promise?"

"I promise."

If it had been anyone else, I would have seen the promise as a trap, but with Maddy it was different. Besides, I didn't think she had anything to worry about. Of course I was wrong.

Maddy never talked about what happened in the hospital, not to me anyway. She talked about anything and everything except what happened in the hospital, how she was feeling ("Great" was her standard response, delivered in a way that you believed her, not ironic at all. She was never ironic, probably couldn't have been if she tried), or what her prognosis was. I tried not to ask her about it but tried to let her know that she could talk to me if she wanted. She wanted to talk about other things. A whole host of other things.

We took a different way home from the hospital every time—there was no sense in making Maddy see the same stretch of road over and over. So this time we went west as we left Iowa City and then south on Highway 1 so I could take her through Kalona, a small town that has the largest Amish community west of the Mississippi. I thought she'd like to see them in their horse and buggies, that it would be calm and tranquil, a nice contrast to the harsh light of the hospital and the machines and tests and whatever else they put her through. Maddy didn't care—I mean she was happy to be going a different way, happy to be going home, happy that I was trying something. Of course what I tried and what actually happened are two different things—Kalona was a nightmare.

As we drove through town, we didn't see a quaint old-timey town, we saw nothing but motorcycles. They were parked up and down the street, a convention of them intruding on the town and destroying my plans. There were rows and rows of them parked along the street, all the same kind, antique Indians, in red and green and black, lots of black. They looked stupid and out of place, and I had no choice but to keep moving. We saw one buggy as we headed out of town, a black buggy and a black horse with its black-clad driver. Maddy looked at me and said, "What year is this?"

I thought we had left the bikers behind as we headed south, but we soon heard the whining sound of them approaching behind us. I glanced into the rearview mirror but didn't see anything and suddenly there were two of them next to us—old bikes with two guys in leather jackets and black helmets with dark visors. They looked as if they should be in black-and-white movies from fifty years ago. Everything was old and out of time and place, even us.

The bikes cut us off and I had the urge to speed up and hit them, ram the car into the back wheels and send them spinning off the road, or drop them on the road in front of us and drive over them, our car grinding their stupid, vintage vehicles into the ground. They didn't belong here, but here they were, annoying and threatening and their irritating whine hanging in the air long after they were out of sight.

The road makes a noise all its own. It's a single note that stretches in all directions, low and nearly inaudible, only I could hear it loud and persistent as I drove Maddy back from the hospital. It grew louder and louder, merging into the tone that is oftentimes in my head. The noise seemed to come from everywhere—the road, the fields, the sky, the car itself, a flood of sound. Trucks whipped past us in the opposite lane, disrupting one sound with another, a welcome interruption. I wanted to slam the car into one of the oncoming trucks, any of them, the next one. My parents' fears were being realized—all the reasons they didn't want me to drive—but I couldn't do it, not with Maddy in the car.

She was looking out the window, calm in her silence.

I pulled over and got out of the car and barely made it to the ditch. I threw up until there was nothing left and stood there, my hands on my knees, and waited for it to come again. But it didn't. The sickness had stopped; the noise was gone. There was nothing but the road, a flat, silent line of tar. There was nothing but the fields, quiet and still, nothing but the sky, empty and blue. I walked back to the car. Maddy was leaning against the passenger side. "I'm the one who's supposed to be sick," she said.

I feel now (right now, I mean) the way I felt then—sick and helpless. This is worthless, a waste of time. It doesn't make any difference—nothing makes a difference. I took her back and forth to the doctors—what good did it do? I did what I could; it didn't matter. I tried to help, tried to change the way it was all going—you can't change it. The world sheds itself of people every day, like scales on the dried, useless skin of a snake, and moves on—it loses people every day, great and small, young and old—it has lost some of the greatest, those who have tried the hardest, and still it moves on. What does it care about the health of a ten-year-old girl? What does it care about me and what I want? I'm still hunched over, puking out this crap, and Maddy is still sick and still the one trying to cheer me up, and the cars and trucks keep moving past us, not one of them stopping, and it all keeps moving and moving and moving and in the end you don't have a choice.

"That's what it's like?" Maddy said as we started to drive away.

"I don't usually get sick, not like that."

"It's my fault," she said.

It *was* her fault—only in the sense that if she hadn't been there, I would have done something—I would have taken care of it, would have done something before I had to retch out the sick in the ditch, would have taken the ton of steel I was in and used it like the self-destructive weapon it was designed to be. Instead, I was sick, like some pathetic addict who misses his fix. It had to stop.

"Can I tell you something stupid?" I said. "Something I've never told anyone else? If I live too long, I'm afraid I'll die."

"Of course," Maddy said.

"I mean I'll be afraid to die. I'm not afraid now. I want to do it now while I'm strong enough. What if I get a job, get married, have a kid? I can't do it then. And what if I get old and wind up stupid with Alzheimer's or something worse and won't be able to—what if I wind up wanting to live and not being able to? I don't want my life to be over and still have to live it. It's better this way, better to do it now when I'm not afraid of any of that other stuff. That's it. That's the reason. That's it."

"What if you got sick like me; is that what you mean?"

"It's not what I meant. You know that."

Maddy didn't say anything more about it. She didn't see it the way I did, and maybe I shouldn't have said anything. Sometimes I forget how young she is, but I have the same thoughts now as I did when I was her age. Maybe she'd already thought it through and didn't want to tell me. She could keep her secrets better than I could.

The resurrection will be televised (#37)

Against the dark sky there is a darker shadow. It is motionless for a moment, quiet and still, barely perceptible on the edge of a dark cliff, standing against the dark sky, a black patch on a black background, and then it's gone. It is falling—the camera catches it as it falls and tries to stay with it, losing it a few times, falling behind so there is only the black bluff before it captures the figure again. It is unclear what or where it is, but you can tell that it is falling through the air, dropping from some height. You know it can't be good, and maybe, even before the next part, you begin to realize that the falling object is a person—you don't know who it is, but you know it's someone falling and that they have jumped from something solid into nothingness.

There's nothing more than that—the image of a person falling. You don't see the impact, you don't even see the body as it ends its descent even though the camera is right on it—it's too dark, too far away, too many other dark shapes around it—bushes, boulders, the dark hillside swallowing up everything—but the next shot is an image of the body, the camera poised directly over him, over his broken and lifeless body. There's more light—you can see blood and broken bones as the camera quickly moves across the body before stopping on the face. You can see him clearly on the ground: his face is calm, without a scratch on it, as if he had laid down on the ground, and the camera stays there on the closed eyes and quiet mouth, in stark contrast to the mangled body below. The camera moves position; the light lurches a few times, but the face remains the same. It's hard to tell how much time has elapsed—the video gets impatient near the end, jumping from night to day, then twitching with impatience more than a few times, moving closer, then back, then closer again—there's no sound, only the image of the boy, until suddenly he opens his eyes and then the short video is over.

I first saw it online. Jodi sent me a link; it was on YouTube with the title "The Resurrection." It already had over eight hundred views. There was no information about who had posted it, or no good information, but I knew who had made it. It had to be Vern and probably Ash. Just like with the cow head, they would never admit it, keep denying it and denying it, but it had to be them. Or maybe not. It doesn't really matter—whoever made it was long forgotten. I thought the whole thing would die out—all the YouTube views were probably from school, from town, people who already knew me and were tired of me already. They talked about it at school but no more or less than anything else, it seemed to me. I thought it would run a short course and that would be the end of it. But I was wrong. It started slow but then took on a life of its own, and everything, all the unwanted attention, swung to me like a bright, searing sun.

I retreated back to my room; I stopped hanging out down by the river. I thought I could stay there forever, wait it out in my room a few more weeks until school started again. I talked to Jodi every now and then, and talked to Maddy, and talked to Don Lemley, of course. He's the one who told me about the trouble. He followed it and tried to stay on top of it, but it became too big; it became one of those self-made snowballs, an avalanche, a tsunami of shortsightedness and self-importance. Mr. Lemley said that the video was being talked about in those stupid suicide chat rooms. I didn't care. I hated those places anyway.

"You have to shut this thing down," he said.

"I can't do that. Not even if I wanted to."

It was true. It was too late. The video was starting to spread. People were linking to it, posting it on their own sites. Within a couple of days it passed 20,000 views, then almost 100,000. Then two people killed themselves and said it was because of the video. Then the news picked up on it. They made it sound as if I were responsible, as if I had made those kids kill themselves, and they showed the video. At least part of it, showed over and over, over and over, as if it were the most important thing happening in the world.

I don't know why I became the one they fixated on. There are eighty-eight suicides every day in this country, and suddenly

I'm the one who gets all the attention, the one whose face they show over and over on the news. It's a twenty-four-hour news channel, and this is all the news they can come up with, the most important thing in the world to fill up all that time?

My father, who had usually been so amused by the TV, didn't think any of this was funny. "This is a mess," he said, and, like most of the people, proceeded to blame me. "This video thing is something you and your friends did when you were out drinking, isn't it? You probably thought it would be funny, right?"

He didn't believe me when I told him I had nothing to do with it. And when I couldn't tell him who had made it, it all reverted back to me. It was *my* video, *my* posting, *my* fault, *my* problem. The only person who tried to help me was Don Lemley.

"I'm bringing you a Bible," he told me. I reminded him that he's brought me plenty. "They're obviously not doing any good," he said, "yet. You have to read them. Have you read them?" I've read it—some of it. "You need to study it," he said. "Study it and learn it and learn from it. It will help you, believe me. Call me if you need to; we can do this together. If it seems like too much, call me. I'm worried this is going to get ugly."

Don Lemley's right about that, of course. It was going to get ugly, and I wanted to tell him that there wasn't anything the Bible could do about it. Instead, I told him not to worry. "Maybe it will be okay," I said. "Maybe the world will end before it gets too bad." He gave me one of his best laughs at least.

I stopped thinking Don Lemley was a nut a long time ago—at

least not a dangerous nut—he's more strident in his views than most people I know but less than a lot of religious people you hear about. He doesn't go around telling everybody what to do; he's not on street corners with a sign saying The End Is Near; he's not threatening to burn the Koran or bomb clinics or any of that. He's just waiting for the world to end so he can get to heaven. And I was about to meet some real crazies—people who wanted to save me from hell and those who want to send me there—and what I know, what I've learned, hasn't all come from the books he's given me, but from simple observation of the world in which we live—no matter how bad things are, there's always someone who wishes they were in your place; no matter how fucked up you are, there's always someone who wants to be just like you. Especially if you're on TV. Or maybe because. "When is it all going to end, Mr. Lemley?"

"Soon," Don Lemley said, and I wanted to tell him that we want the same things, each in our own way.

We had stopped answering the phone, and Don Lemley offered to field all the calls. "It's what I do," he said. So he answered the calls, mostly from media morons who wanted to get me on the air so they could humiliate me even more, I guess. They wanted my parents on so they could condemn them in front of millions of people. We turned them all down, but after the whole thing dragged on for a few more days and more suicides were laid at my feet—the media kept blaming me as they continued to show the video even more. "It's called the Werther effect," Don Lemley said. "We have to put a stop to it." When I asked him what the heck the Werther effect was, he told me to look it up. So I did. Of course it had to do with a book.

Camera crews tried to camp out on our lawn, but Mr. Lemley was good about sending cops over to chase them off. Everyone else stayed away from the house like we were lepers except Vern, of course, who hovered around the cameras, offering a story or two, hoping to get on TV, but he never was. He tried to come to the house, but my father wouldn't let him in. He was now convinced that Vern was to blame for all of this, but it wasn't all his fault. We knew that. It was my fault, and now I was going to have to pay.

Finally, after much deliberation and too much talk and too much clamor, Don Lemley thought we should have a press conference.

"I've been to one world fair, a picnic, and a rodeo, and that's the stupidest thing I ever heard," I said, throwing around a little Dr. Strangelove, but not even my father thought it was funny.

I was against it. My parents were against it. Even Don Lemley wasn't sure it was a good idea, but he didn't see any other way, and in the end we saw that they weren't going to leave us alone. Mr. Lemley arranged the whole thing. He even introduced me, with me and my parents sitting behind him. "I've know Adam all his life," he said, "but not really. I knew who he was; I knew he was a young kid with a problem, but I didn't really get to know him until recently. We've talked on the phone, almost every day, for a while now, probably longer than he'd like and longer than I thought I'd be talking with him, but I'm glad that we've talked. I'm glad that it has continued. It used to be that I would call him and ask him how he was doing and he wouldn't say much more than 'okay' and that would be the end of it, but slowly we started to talk more and more, longer and longer, and the longer we talk, the better I feel, and I like to think the better he feels.

"And the longer we talk, the longer I think we'll be talking in the future. I think we have become friends, at least I'd like to think so. Over the past number of months I think I've gotten to know Adam and to understand him a little. He is a very private person, and I will try to respect his privacy, but I want to say that he is nothing like the person portrayed on television. I don't know who that person is, and most people here in town know that it isn't our Adam. It's a fiction, a made-up character. Anyone can tell you that Adam, our Adam, would not have made that video, would not have wanted it made, and certainly would not have wanted it shown to anyone. And he would not have wanted it to influence anyone or to hurt anyone.

"It is Adam in the video, but he had nothing to do with it. It was made without his knowledge or permission, an invasion of his privacy, and edited and altered by someone for their own reasons and purposes. The fact that he has agreed to come before you today says something about his character, but I want you to know another side of him as well. He has been helping a friend of his, a friend of ours, who is ill, taking her to the specialists in Iowa City. Adam has been helping her, asking for nothing in return, not even acknowledgment. I'm sure he's not pleased that I mention this, and I only do so because I think you all should know that you know very little about him, that there is so much more to all of this than you realize and perhaps care to know."

All I had to do was say something.

I didn't know what to say. I wanted to tell them that I didn't care. I didn't see why they should care. Hadn't they read Camus? Who am I to say anything about it? Who are *they*? I wanted to tell them that I didn't see how my actions made any difference at all. If these are people who are so easily persuaded by someone else, then if it wasn't me, it was going to be someone or something else. I couldn't say that. My father wrote down some things for me to say and Don Lemley wrote out some things. I read them over and over and thought most of it sounded all right, but it wasn't what I wanted to say. I wanted to tell them that I'm not responsible for the actions of all those people, none of whom I know or met or have even given one thought. I'd like to tell them that I'm sorry, that I feel sad for the loss, but I don't feel that way at all. I don't feel anything except regret.

What I thought I was going to say was something like: "I regret that my private actions have become public. It should have never been recorded or shown to others. I had nothing to do with the video and knew absolutely nothing about it. I think all questions should be addressed to the person who made it and posted it online. I wish that whoever is responsible would come forward and face you directly. I can't control what others do—I can only take responsibility for what I've done, and I did not make the video or even know that it was being made. I wish it hadn't been, but obviously my wishes were not respected. I have nothing else to say."

I didn't like it; it still felt as if I were reading something, a prepared text, crafted by others. I should have said what I really felt—that I envied them, the ones that had jumped and didn't come back—I wish it was me in their place and they were here having to deal with cameras and microphones and accusations and explanations and talk that won't amount to anything and words that won't change anything. I wanted to tell them that people are going to die, and there's nothing we can do about it, and if someone really wants to kill themselves, they're going to get their inspiration from wherever they can find it—music, TV, online, watching clouds in the sky, watching rain in the street, watching the river, wherever. If it wasn't this video, it will be that one; if it's not one song, it will be another—there are plenty of excuses to be found, plenty of rationalizations. I don't know what they want from me—I can't bring those kids back. I would trade places with any of them who wanted to trade, but I'm still here. I'm sorry about that, believe me, but I'm not sorry that they're gone. People do stupid things all the time; they can't put it all on me. Or maybe they're so pissed because maybe, just maybe, they think it wasn't so stupid.

I looked around the room, at all the cameras facing me, at all the reporters with microphones and recorders, everybody hanging on what I was going to say. I didn't like it. I wanted them all to go away. So I said what I thought would make them leave.

"It was a hoax."

I told them the whole thing was a fake, but I didn't tell them much else. For me it was as if the air came out of the balloon, a long sigh of relief, some terrible weight had been lifted from me and I could get up and walk around and not have to worry anymore—but the rest of the room, it was bedlam. People started shouting questions, one on top of the other so you didn't know what they were asking or who was asking it. My parents looked shocked, wide-eyed and clueless, even Mr. Lemley seemed surprised, but he had a slight smile, as if he understood, as if he almost enjoyed it as much as I did.

We left the room with everyone shouting at us—stupid questions, none that needed an answer. And for all the noise and commotion and chaos there was in that room, it stayed there. No one followed us.

"Why did you tell them that?" my father wanted to know.

"I thought if I gave them what they wanted, things would go back to the way they were before."

"Now they're going to say we're liars," my mother said.

"They're going to say what they want to say anyway," my father said. "Everybody we care about already knows the truth. You might have done the right thing in this." It was the efficient way to go—my father saw that. "We denied them our essence," my father said—it was okay to joke again, he figured, and he and I laughed, but my mother wasn't so sure. She was still worried what everyone else would think. I wanted to tell her not to worry, people don't really think that much.

The truth is, the video *was* a hoax, sort of. Vern (even though he still won't admit it) got lazy or impatient or sloppy and didn't stick around until the end. The final shot of the video, the one of me opening my eyes—it's not from the bluff. It's the same shot from The Point, from the cow video he made. He did an okay job of faking it, making the backgrounds match (sort of), a good enough job that no one said anything before, but afterward everyone seemed to notice. Vern still hasn't gotten over it. "You blew it," he said, which is about the last thing he said to me. I don't know what he expected, but now he was the one who was mad. We continued to hang out, but it wasn't the same. Vern, and Ash somewhat, would hardly talk to me; some days they wouldn't even look at me or would act as if I wasn't around. I didn't care. I hope he stays mad.

Maddy called me after the press conference debacle. "My parents aren't going to let you take me to Iowa City if you keep doing this," she said. "You have to promise to stop—just as long as I keep going to the doctor. Promise me."

The hoax thing worked. We were left alone, mostly forgotten again. It had all lasted less than a week—blown up like a big balloon that hung over the whole town and then popped and vanished. Everyone lost interest and moved on—all the cameras and microphones and reporters, all those people who had seemed so concerned, so outraged, all of them who had so loudly worried about us "kids," all the types that made demands, wanted YouTube shut down, all social media stopped, the Internet policed or restricted or removed, all those that demanded change, investigations, laws, regulations, arrests, prosecutions, punishment—none of it happened and they no longer cared. Now they were screaming about some other thing—they had moved on because some celebrity had done something, stolen something or threw a hissy fit, an athlete cheated on his wife, a cat called 911—you know the drill. Something stupid happened and suddenly it was the most important story in the whole world.

A guy jumps and the world goes crazy for a couple of days and then everybody gets bored and moves on and never mentions it again. The real story isn't the one they talk about but the ones they don't. Eleven kids killed themselves yesterday, eleven today, eleven more tomorrow. It happens all the time, a self-inflicted Columbine-worth massacre every twenty-eight hours.

I talked with Felthy about it, about the other suicides. I knew about them, and I never paid attention to them, but now they seemed to be piling up, ticking off like numbers on a clock that isn't going back, no matter what. You hear about people who survived the *Titanic*, survived Nazi concentration camps, survived a war and then decide to end it all on their own. I wonder if they have more or less conviction than I have.

"I'm thinking about joining the army." I told Felthy that a soldier kills himself almost every day now—men and women not much older than I am, not much older than my brother—how much do you hear about that, all those guys who go down the same path? At most it might get mentioned for a few seconds on the nightly news or some pathetic morning show, then they cut to another person with a movie or a book or some other crap to promote. They'd all rather crawl up the ass of some celebrity than talk about things that matter. But what do you expect? It's not the news; it's all entertainment to them. Mr. Coolidge was right: crap in equals crap out.

"Why the army?" the doctor said.

"Everybody's always telling you to be yourself, that you're special, all the time how special you are, crap like that. But in the army you're not special; you're just one more guy in a uniform. Besides, maybe I'll get killed or find a better way to kill myself. And people think differently about them when they think about them at all."

"How do people think?"

"They feel sorry for them, I guess. They have sympathy. They know what soldiers sacrifice. It's not thought of as a failure, maybe, not so much anyway."

"You think it's a failure?"

"Me? No? Some people do."

"I didn't think you cared what people thought."

I shrugged. "I don't. I'm not saying I'm joining the army. I'm saying I'm thinking about it, that's all."

"What about college?" he said.

"It's not going to happen. My father says that I've put him in a tough spot. He says that the number he's been showing me, the one he knows I thought was minutes off my curfew, now he says that's the dollar amount he's taking out of my college fund."

"Is that true?"

"Is it true? I don't know if it's true that he's going to screw me on the money. Is it true that he said it? Absolutely. Time is money, he told me."

"How about a scholarship? Your grades are good enough."

"Maybe the navy. I could go out on a submarine. You couldn't get much farther away from here than that. Or I don't think I could."

"You could go into space," Felthy said. He sounded like Todd when he said it; it was something Todd would say, if I ever talked with him about this stuff anymore. I didn't. And I couldn't tell Mr. Lemley about college; I didn't want him to think my father was an asshole. Dr. Stinchcomb didn't think anyone was an asshole—it was against his profession or something. He couldn't judge anyone. That's a rule or law for him. Maybe I should be a therapist.

"I'm not going anywhere."

It was the last thing I said to Dr. Stinchcomb. That was before the video, before taking Maddy to Iowa City, even before my little run along the river and breakfast with Judge Camp. I'm not going back to see Felthy. But maybe I should give him an update—a lot has happened since he last saw me. Or maybe he's forgotten all about me. He probably sees a lot of people. He could forget about me; I wouldn't care.

I was glad to be forgotten again, glad to have to drive Maddy back to Iowa City—not because of her, but glad to get away, to do something. Maddy wondered if we'd be recognized. I hadn't thought about it—everybody at the hospital knew me already, so they were used to it, I thought, and we'd have to deal with the others, if there were any. Maddy thought we wouldn't be able to eat outside, but it wasn't a problem. No one knew me, or not many—we got a few stares, a few more looks, but no one said anything. I learned one thing from all of it—I'm not that different. The realization was a little comforting, a little disappointing, and more than a little disturbing. There are a lot of freaks in the world.

The day they gave her wings

I took Maddy to her floor and then found the nearest waiting room. It was a small, cramped closet, with eight chairs and a small couch and a large TV that played the same news over and over. There was no one in the room. I turned off the TV and then walked up and down the hall until Maddy was finished. I never knew how long it would take; sometimes it was an hour, sometimes three or four. It always seemed to take forever. I went back to the small room and turned on the TV and tried to find something to watch. There wasn't one thing worth watching, so I turned it off again and paced the hallway a few times. Doctors and nurses hurried past me—everyone seemed to move with deliberation and purpose except me. There was a lot of activity in a room down the hall, a half-dozen men and women in white coats hurrying in and out of the room. I didn't want to see it. I walked back down the hall and a phrase leapt into my head—"the day they gave her wings." I didn't know what it meant, but there it was, taking up all the space in my head, and it wouldn't go away. I went back to the waiting room and took my notebook and opened it to an empty page and started to write. The phrase was still there, but it was surrounded by other sentences. I wrote them all.

I wrote a short story about a young girl who is sick and goes to the hospital to get help, but instead of treating her, the doctors and nurse torture her and try all these different experiments on her, trying to turn her into a new species, a human-animal hybrid. The narrator tries to find the girl, searching for her in the labyrinth of a hospital. When he finally finds her, she is fine, with two small, beautiful wings starting to grow out of her back.

I know it sounds bad, but it sounds better than what I actually wrote. I threw it away, but I kept writing every time I took Maddy to the hospital and even other times, but I stopped writing fiction so much. I wrote about what I knew—isn't that what they tell you? I wrote about the people I knew—I wrote about Jodi and I wrote about my parents and my brother; I wrote about Maddy. I wrote a lot about Maddy, and then I wrote about myself.

How to lose a winning match (#38)

We were down by the angel, but we'd retreated away from her and hung out more against the trees and bushes on the hill, a safe distance from the small crowds that still circled like scavenging birds in the parking lot and close to the statue. Things had mostly died down from the whole video nonsense, but there were still groups of these unknown gawkers. Who knew where they came from. "They look downstate," Vern said.

"We're downstate," Bruce said, "about as downstate as you can get."

"I meant downstate Missouri," Vern said. "They look like hillbillies."

"So do we," Todd said, and took a long drink off a bottle of cheap whiskey he'd bought from somebody, maybe one of the hillbillies.

Most of them got bored after a while and left, but we were already bored, so we stayed.

A car full of girls pulled up near the statue around ten, and before it had completely stopped, the back door opened and Jodi tried to get out. She almost fell over as the car came to an abrupt halt, and she grabbed onto the open door to steady herself. She laughed and walked toward me, holding a tall can of Rio Loco and a half-finished bottle of schnapps. I'd never seen Jodi drunk before.

"I need to talk to you," she said, not even looking at Todd or the rest of them. I got up and followed her up the hill. She turned toward me and offered both the can and the bottle. "Which one?" she said.

I don't usually like that energy drink stuff—even though it has enough alcohol in it to get the job done, I can honestly say that I've had antifreeze that tasted better. Rio Loco was illegal in Iowa for high levels of caffeine and alcohol, but you could still buy it across the bridge in Missouri. I took the can and sat on the thin, brown grass. Jodi paced in front of me as if trapped in a narrow cage.

"How's Maddy?" she said.

"I don't know."

"You're with her," she said. "You see her, see her more than I do. Tell me."

"I don't know. They don't tell me anything, and Maddy doesn't talk about it, so I don't ask. Her eye looks better."

"It's not her eye," Jodi said.

"What is it?"

"I don't know. From what my mom says, neither do the doctors. They're talking like it might be her brain."

"So what are they doing?"

Jodi squinted at me. "I was the one asking questions."

"You know more about it than I do. What happens when I take her to the doctors?"

"Tests, I guess," she said. "And some trial medications—heavy-duty stuff, I think. All I know is what my mom tells me. I don't know. I thought you'd know more. I don't talk to her, I don't see her; they're mad at me, I guess."

"The parents. Not Maddy."

Jodi nodded. She sat on the worn-out grass near the top of the hill and looked out across the water. "My mom says they're talking chemo for Maddy."

"That makes no sense. Who told her that?"

Jodi shrugged. "I don't know, some gossipy mom in Hy-Vee probably."

"I don't believe it. Not if they don't know what she has."

"Maybe they do," Jodi said. She started to take a drink of schnapps but stopped and tossed the bottle onto the grass. She looked up at the bridge looming over us and then at the older bridge off in the distance.

"Is it easy?" she asked.

"It's the road I'm on."

"That's stupid," she said.

"Maybe." Maybe I said it wrong. It's like everything else

around here, I should have told her; it's a trap, something you can't escape—the same thing over and over, like hanging out with her and Todd and the rest of them, going to the same places with the same people day after day even though we know we'd be better off doing something else with someone different. It's an addiction—I guess that would have been the best way to put it.

"Is it easy?" she said again.

"If it were, I wouldn't be here. There's something that makes it easy and hard at the same time."

Jodi moved in front of me and furrowed her brow, examining me. "I think you're happier than I am," she said. "Isn't that funny?"

"You'll be happy again."

"I don't know," she said. "I don't know; I guess it depends on what happens with Maddy. I should have done something, something sooner."

"You're not the one. You did everything you could. That's not on you."

"It wasn't enough," she said. "Besides, it's only part of it."

"You should come with us to Iowa City."

"Maddy won't want that, and her parents wouldn't allow it. Isn't that the craziest thing—I'm out and you're in. Who'd have thought?"

"They think they know what they're doing, but they don't have a clue."

We both laughed.

"I'm more like you than anyone else," she said. "Don't you

think? I think so. Maybe you can't take me with Maddy, but you could take me up to the bridge, just for a look."

"You're drunk, that's all. Let's wait until you're sober."

"I couldn't go up there sober."

"Then you can't do it at all."

"You're such a dyke," she said for the first and only time, and rolled over laughing. I watched her, and the thought entered my mind like a parent barging into your room, suddenly and with no warning, and I thought that I wanted Jodi to go up to the bridge.

Maybe if she went up there with me, she'd think differently about me. Maybe she'd see things the way I did, appreciate me more. Maybe I'd think differently about her too. I'd never been there with anyone else; why wouldn't I go with Jodi? Maybe everything would be different.

"Do you want to see my sign?"

"I want to go to the old bridge," she said.

I took her hand and helped her to her feet and we walked to the top of the hill, directly underneath the new bridge. We could hear the traffic passing over our heads and Jodi wanted to stop and listen to it.

"Don't you love that sound?" she said. "Especially when they're right there, at the top of your head. It sounds as if they're a million miles away and right on top of you at the same time. Why is that?"

I shrugged and told her that I thought the same thing. She was back on the ground again, lying face up, facing the pale belly

of the bridge but with her eyes closed. She wanted it to be nothing but sound. I knew that feeling.

But I wanted her on the bridge. I took her by the hand again
and coaxed her back to her feet, and we walked over to the old
bridge. Just the look of it frightened her; the dark metal gridwork
was almost invisible in the dark. You could see the river below
and the darkness ahead but had to concentrate to see the iron grid
that stretched over it. It didn't look as if it could hold us, she must
have thought. And then there was the fence, ten feet of chain link
stretching above us, with concertina wire on top, and she probably
wondered how I ever got around it. Maybe I should have stopped
there, like a magician who has just performed an amazing illusion
and has everyone in awe, and then he shows the trick and all that
awe evaporates because it seems so simple, almost stupid. I didn't
care; I wanted us to go on.

She held onto the back of my shirt as we made our way
through the broken fence and walked toward the middle of the
bridge. We could see the barricade ahead of us, the barricade that
was meant to stop cars before they were dumb enough to drive
right off the edge and into the river.

"Let's go back," she said. We weren't even close to the edge—
we were in the middle of the bridge—walking right down the
center stripe between the two lanes—and in the middle of the
first section. We couldn't have been more in the middle, all alone,
no different from walking down a two-lane road at night.

"At least come over to the ped walk." I led her to the side of
the bridge, but she stopped at the railing. I crawled over and stood

on the narrow path where countless people used to walk back and forth across the river. I tried to help her over, but she wouldn't budge.

"Let's go back," she said.

"I want you to do something first."

She tightened her grip on my hand and tried to pull me toward her, but the waist-high metal railing was between us. The railing felt cold against my shirt, and we could feel a few traces of colder air sneaking from the north. It was a good view up here when the trees change into all their colors, and it was a good view when the trees were bare and the ground covered in snow—you could watch the eagles perch in the tree or fly high above the river and dive down after fish. Jodi could see all of it if she wanted.

She had a worried look on her face. She was worried about me, worried about what I might do.

"Just look at the water," I said, "just one time. Look at the bridge over there, look at the cars, and then look at the water; listen to it, just for a second."

I wanted her to see the steamboat and the parking lot, see that her friends had left, see that you couldn't see Todd and those guys; maybe they'd gone too, but where did they have to go? You couldn't see them in the dark away from the parking lot, that's all; they hadn't gone anywhere. I wanted Jodi to see it all and to know that no one could see us on the bridge, not from down there and probably not from the other bridge either. But she didn't want to look—she'd come all this way and she wanted to leave before she took it all in, before she could understand it. She'd wanted it, but not really. I knew that before we started to come up here, but now that she was here, I wanted her to just look, take one look.

She looked. I watched her looking. What I always saw as mine, only mine, from this spot, my bridge, my view, my place, my river, she was seeing—but she wasn't really seeing it the same way. It was different for her. It wasn't hers, not in the way it was for me. I was disappointed but glad at the same time. I wanted to go back. It wasn't the same.

"Let's go," she said, and I started back across the railing to go with her.

We walked down the middle of the bridge again. Jodi didn't even want to look down through the grating—she kept her head held slightly above level and held onto me as I led her back and we crawled through the fence and she suddenly grabbed me and kissed me and said, "Isn't that better than kissing Violent Cuntland?"

"You're drunk."

"I am drunk," she said. "And I like it. You should have told me about this a long time ago."

She was right about that. "I have to keep a few secrets from you."

"You can't keep anything from me," she said.

Maybe she leaned toward me, maybe I didn't care—I kissed her again and a door opened and we both fell through—the two of us together—and we kept falling and we weren't afraid because we knew that we would never land, that we would keep falling just like this until one of us stopped. I didn't want to stop;

I wanted to keep falling with her, hold onto her and never leave, never go back, but I stopped.

I opened my eyes and looked at Jodi. She looked a little drunk, a little afraid maybe. I wanted to kiss her again, but I didn't. I wasn't sure. Maybe it was better to leave it just like that for the night, to see how it might go tomorrow. We had time, I thought, but she was already walking back from it, trying to get back through the door we'd opened and closed it.

"We'll always be friends," she said. She'd sober up and regret it; she'd wake up tomorrow and wish it had never happened and I'd be no better than I was before—no, I'd be worse because of the regret Jodi would have, because she knew what was inside her and she'd be afraid of it now, ashamed, afraid that it could happen again. "There's a connection between us," she said, "like a cord that can't ever be broken. We'll always be friends, right?"

I wanted to tell her that I wanted that cord to be as short as possible, but she was already letting out slack. "Always."

We walked down by the angel without a word. I'd forgotten to tell her to look at the angel, to look at the expression on her face as we looked at her from the bridge, the only person who sees you standing there. I forgot. It was just as well.

Todd had left, but the rest of them were still there. Jodi wanted to go home, but no one had a car, so we walked. We went back up the hill so I could grab the bottle Jodi had left there, then we headed past Main and avoided everybody. We walked through the empty streets—everyone else in town had retreated for the night, the streets dark and empty and the houses cold with only the TVs flickering and shivering through the windows like a protective light. Jodi was quiet. She was sobering up, I thought, and maybe embarrassed about everything. I wanted to tell her not to worry about it, that she had nothing to be embarrassed about. Instead, I finished off the bottle as we walked to her house, and then she turned and said, "Take care of Maddy for me," as if that might be the last thing she was ever going to say to me.

"I am."

"No you're not," she said. She was serious. "You have to really take care of her. Pay attention. Don't half-ass this like you do everything else."

"Okay." I thought she would at least hug me before she went inside, but she didn't. "Do you really think I half-ass everything?"

"What difference does it make what I think?"

I should have told her that it made all the difference, but I stood there and probably had a stupid look on my face and she was already walking away from me. I should have said something. I didn't do what I should have. Why start now?

I went back down to the bridge. The parking lot was empty; the new bridge looked empty and cold, almost frozen, under the wasted lights. I went back to the spot where Jodi and I had been not more than an hour before. It wasn't the same. None of it was the same. I was glad she had been there on the bridge, glad that it had all happened, but now it wasn't the same. I had wanted things to change all summer, and now that they had, I wasn't sure if this was the change I had wanted. I left the bridge and went to the bluff. Nothing had changed there.

I played it safe. I didn't say anything about the bridge or the kiss or anything and Jodi didn't mention it either, so we ended up back where we were before. I hoped that maybe she'd get drunk again and we could try it all over, but that didn't happen. It was just as well. I wasn't sure I was still in love with her; I wasn't even sure that I even liked her then. I wanted to get away from everybody, not in the old way, but to get away to Iowa City or somewhere else, just leave town on one of those trips with Maddy and never come back. I thought about stealing my parents' car and leaving on my own or taking Bruce's, taking something and leaving, leaving for good, disappearing off the map and finding some new place where they wouldn't know about me and all the stupid things I'd said and done. There had to be one town like that somewhere, didn't there?

Sick of good-byes

'm done with this town. There is nothing left but disgust, revulsion. I hate this town. I hate the factories and the plumes of filth they spew into the air; I hate the streets and the buildings and the homes and especially the people who live inside, who allow the factories to pollute us, who allow the ugliness to pour out over the town in a great flood of unpainted houses, unmowed lawns, trash littering the streets. I hate the way this town clings to me, the dirt and the sunlight, the ground trying to hang onto me, the way the sounds stay in my ears too long, the harsh squeal of the train wheels on the tracks, the factory whistles, school bells, the closing of doors, the wind as it comes and goes and leaves me here. I hate the way we speak here, how the *s*'s slide toward *z*'s and moronic *r*'s appear where they shouldn't; I'm afraid that this is infecting me, marking me so that wherever I go in the world, people will know where I'm from. I can't hide. I hate the words the people say and how they never mean them or never think about what they mean. I hate the way people are treated and the way they treat each other. I'm done with it—sick of railroad tracks and river roads, parking lots and parks and boats and statues and bridges and bluffs. I am finished with the river. Whatever attraction I once had with it is now gone or, if not gone, then rejected, just as the river has rejected me.

"More light and light, more dark and dark"

Maddy didn't look good when I picked her up in the morning to take her back to Iowa City. Her eye was foggy and she either kept her eyes closed in the car or placed her hand over her left eye. She still wouldn't talk about it. I felt like Don Lemley asking her how she was. "I'm good," she said.

She looked worse when she was done with the doctors. It had been a short session, only about ninety minutes—I didn't know if that was a good sign or not. I was in my now-usual spot—the small room that never seemed occupied, and I had spent my time writing about Mr. Coolidge and Dr. Vandever, had hardly written much about them at all, in fact, when Maddy came in and told me she was ready to go home.

"I can wait," she said. "If you want to finish. Don't hurry because of me."

"I'm ready. It's not anything I'm going to finish anytime soon anyway."

"Will you let me read it?" she said.

"When I'm done."

"Maybe I can't wait that long," she said, and smiled.

I let Maddy pick where she wanted to go for lunch, but I already knew. We parked downtown and got a couple of falafels to go over on Linn Street and then walked over and sat outside Van Allen Hall. "We could go inside, see what class is in the lecture hall, or walk around upstairs."

"Maybe next time," she said. She wasn't good, no matter what she said.

"I know I shouldn't ask, and I'm sorry that I am, but you have to tell me—are you getting any better?"

"No," she said.

"What do the doctors say?"

"It's something in my brain; that's what they tell me. They're not sure what it is, but they're trying to find out, trying to get rid of it. I'll get better, they keep saying, but I'm not. Aren't you sorry you asked?"

"I wish I could do something."

"You do a lot," she said. "Everything. That's why I wanted you to take me. Who else would do all of this?"

"Everybody."

"Not my parents," she said. "They're too worried. My father says that if things don't get better soon, he's taking me to the Mayo Clinic."

"That sounds good."

"I don't want to go there."

"I could take you."

"I'm not going to any more doctors," Maddy said. We finished our lunch and took a walk across the ped mall and Maddy led me into the hotel, across the lobby, and into the elevator, where she pressed the button for the top floor.

"Let's go back down, Maddy."

"Let's go to the roof," she said.

"Let's go back to the car."

She ignored me and I followed her to the roof. I knew where this was going, but I didn't know how to stop it. She wanted me to help her. She was asking me to help her. What was I supposed to do? I couldn't stand by and do nothing, especially not when she was asking, knowing that I was the only one who would understand. I was going to help her, I thought. I honestly thought I was going to help her.

Maddy walked over to the edge of the roof but didn't look down. I stood right beside her, not looking down with her.

"What do you think would happen if I jumped?" she said. "Do you think I'd come back like you do?"

"I wouldn't count on it."

"What if you jumped with me?"

"I'm not going to jump, Maddy."

"Why not? Isn't that your answer for everything?"

"It's an answer," I said, "but maybe not the right one."

It was a beautiful afternoon—a clear sky that seemed to stretch above us forever, and there, a couple of blocks away, were the double silver-gray observatory domes on top of Van Allen

Hall and the moldy green cross of St. Mary's Church unnecessarily stuck there in the sky behind them, seeming as close as if we could almost jump over and touch them. But we didn't want to go across. I looked at Maddy; she was looking at the same place, the gray dome that could see the stars and the planets and look into the face of the sun. She took a picture, then tilted her head back until her camera was pointed straight into the sky and captured the great arch of blue directly over our heads. The Van Allen radiation belts were somewhere out there, hugging the earth, and beyond that was everything we could see and not see, everything and nothing. It was all there. She placed the camera on the roof ledge and turned to me.

"This is a good view," Maddy said, looking over at the silver domes.

"I like it."

"Don't you wish it could be like this all the time?" Maddy said. "Don't you wish it could be today all the time, just the two of us on this roof with this sky and this sun and everything? Don't you want more days like this, like it is right now?"

I nodded. I did.

"When I get better, can we still come back here, just the two of us?" she said.

"Right here."

Maddy squinted at me with mock disapproval and then looked back toward the silver domes in front of us. "Everything changes," she said. "Everything. So we have to keep coming back to see how much."

Whatever dark cloud had passed over Maddy was long gone; she was back to her old self. I wish I could say that I had done something to help drive it away, but I hadn't—she did it all on her own. If anything, I had brought the cloud, or was the dark cloud—I'd gotten her to the roof, put the idea in her head, but she was the one who got us back down, had looked and backed away and was standing there smiling.

"Let's go," I said.

"Okay," Maddy said, and took my hand and pressed the button on her camera and then led me to a spot on the roof. I was late in turning. Maddy is perfectly still in the photo, had turned and stopped in time to be in focus, while I'm blurred, caught mid-turn, but you can see that it's me, see that I'm smiling, looking at Maddy, who is smiling too, her hand still in mine, both blurred together. I made her give me the picture. It's on my phone and comes up every time she calls, and sometimes even when she doesn't.

Taking the cure so I can be quiet / a new skin

U up? I had a nightmare. Can I call u?

The phone rang and Jodi answered. "What happened?"

"I had a dream about Maddy," I said. I told her about our trip to the roof; I told her that I saw Maddy lying there on the bricks of the ped mall; I told her that it was my fault.

"It was just a dream," Jodi said. "Maddy's going to be all right."

"You don't know. Nobody knows. Remember when you told me that I was going to break her heart—what happens if she breaks mine?"

"No matter what happens, it's not your fault," Jodi said.

"Nobody knows that either. It could be all my fault."

"You wish," Jodi said, "but I can't put that on you."

"I promised her I'd help."

"You are."

"Not enough."

"What else can you do?"

"I don't know."

"Well, whatever you do, leave the nightmares to me," Jodi said. "That's what I'm good at. You're good at helping Maddy, whether you know it or not."

It was nice of her to say, but I hadn't done anything. I left the house and didn't want to go to the river, didn't want to go to the bluff, didn't want to see the angel who wouldn't care about any of us, who wouldn't have a single dream about Maddy or Jodi or anyone. Instead, I went to the jail; I went to see Don Lemley. He was sitting behind bulletproof glass, slumped in his stressed chair with a book propped open in front of him. He hurried out when he saw me and led me back to his post.

I told him the same things I'd told Jodi—I told him about the rooftop in Iowa City, I told him about the dream, I told him almost everything, part confession and part plea. Don Lemley wasn't going to tell anyone else. He'd helped me when I needed it; now I thought he could help me help Maddy.

"What can I do?"

"You're doing all you can," he said.

I shook my head. "It's not enough."

"Okay, then," Don Lemley said. "Let's get to work."

He asked me what I knew about Maddy's symptoms. I told him and he typed them into Google. I told him I'd already done that—that I'd been to all the worthless medical sites before, that I'd searched for what I knew—headaches, vomiting, fever, trouble breathing, eye inflammation—and they all come back with the same stuff, ranging from a common cold to cancer, pneumonia to Legionnaires' disease. Don Lemley didn't care; he did it all over and sifted through the same crap.

"The doctors know all this stuff anyway."

"You asked me what you could do," Mr. Lemley said, "but I have to get up to speed as well. And tomorrow we can get to work."

"I want to thank you for everything you've done for me."

"That's all right," he said. "I didn't do as much as I'd hoped."

"You did a lot. I want to thank you for that. And I want to thank you for finding me all those times. I know it was you, you and Judge Camp."

"It wasn't me," he said.

"I know you did. It's all right. I appreciate it."

"I might have been the one to locate you," he explained, "but I'm not the one who found you. That was your father. He went and got you, almost every time."

Here all this time I had this image in my head of Mr. Lemley coming out to the woods or down by the water, sometimes into the water, and dragging me out, picking me up, with my body in various forms of wreckage, decomposition, whatever, and carefully taking me home to my own bed. I'd carried that image with me, sometimes appreciating what he'd done but more often mocking his efforts, thinking that he was the moron for saving me, that he should leave me alone to do what I want—what business was it of his anyway? And more often than not I thought it was a game, that I could outwit him, find a place where he couldn't find me. I thought it was me against Mr. Lemley and Judge Camp. But it wasn't. It had been my father all the time. I didn't want that image; I didn't want to imagine his face as he came upon me on the ground or as I surfaced out of the dank river. I don't know how he could do it.

"How long will it take?" Bruce wanted to know the day we discovered the cow. "How long will it take to become bones?"

We didn't know. Vern thought it would take all summer; Ash thought it couldn't take more than a week. The best I could come up with was, "It depends." It had to be different in water than on land; it had to matter how hot it was, whether it rained, what animals could get to it, all of that stuff.

"We're going to find out," Darryl said, and we voted to leave it alone, which we almost did.

The cow always made me think of Zig. It made me think of him when he shed his skin, how his eyes would turn milky and he became almost listless, waiting for the right moment when he could inch his way out of the old, useless skin and leave it behind while he became something different and still the same. "Everything changes," Maddy had said, and as usual, she was right.

I couldn't sleep—I wasn't tired. So I stayed downstairs and watched the sun slide up the sky one more time and waited for my father. When he came down, I told him something I should have told him a long time ago, not that it made any difference, but at least it was something. "I'm sorry. I know it was you who found me. I'm sorry for that."

He left the room and went to his study and I followed him. He took a stack of photographs from his desk drawer and handed them to me. They were pictures of railroad tracks, a tree, a spot on the ground; some of the places I recognized, others I didn't, unintended destinations, unplanned arrivals. I knew what they were; I didn't have to look at more, but I looked anyway. I was in some of them, and in some of them I wasn't in the frame, but I was there. I knew I was there even without the date and time he'd written on them. I imagined him standing over me, finding me with the help of Don Lemley and who knows who else, standing there looking at his watch and the place where he'd found me. They were an embarrassing chronicle covering almost a decade of my failures, a sad scrapbook of unintended consequences from hurtful deeds committed by myself.

I thought of the basement and how I wanted to avoid that scene again, the grim aftermath left behind, how I thought I had avoided it, only for it all to come back in picture after picture. Most fathers have pictures of their sons playing sports, holding trophies, maybe, smiling at their accomplishments, pleased with what they've done. My father had pictures that looked like crime scenes, hidden away in a drawer. That's what I'd given him. I handed them back to him.

"Why did you take these?"

He held the pictures closed between the fingers of his two hands, as if holding a captured bird. "My job is to protect you," he said. "I want to protect you, to make sure that you're all right."

"I'm all right."

He looked down at his caged hands, but they remained still. "My job is to take care of you," he said, "and to make sure you can take care of yourself. I don't think a better paradox has ever been invented. Those two things seem always at cross-purposes. How much do I interfere, and how much do I leave you to learn for yourself? That's the big question, isn't it, and no one can tell you because no one knows. There aren't any answers; everyone's different. Your brother needed to be left alone; maybe you needed more interference. I don't know what to tell you; maybe it won't make any sense until you have kids of your own. All I can tell you is that we worry about you; we worry about you every minute of the day, worry that you'll be all right. If I could lock you up in a cage or a plastic box and carry you around, I would, but I can't, so here we are."

"It sounds miserable."

"It's the most amazing thing ever."

I didn't get it. I still don't, not entirely.

"Here's the thing about it," my father continued. "Think about your friends, think about Maddy. Don't you want to protect Maddy?"

"Sure."

"Don't you worry about her?"

I nodded.

"And how does that make you feel?"

Worried. I didn't know what he meant, but I sort of did. I liked it. I liked worrying about her, wanting to help her. If he'd said any of this to me at some other time, maybe I wouldn't have a clue about what he was trying to say, but I sort of did now. Before I could say something, he was talking again. I didn't mind.

"Now multiply that connection you have with her, or with your other friends, or some girl you might like, multiply it by some magnitude, and that's the connection I have with your mother, that's the connection you'll have when you meet the right woman. Then we both multiplied that by another magnitude when we had your brother and another again when you came along. That's the point of it, to have those connections, as painful as they are, as much worry as they might cause; they give back in strength and comfort and joy, believe it or not, and the more connections you make, the happier you are, the more point there is to getting up and getting through the day."

"So how does that explain the pictures?"

"This is where I found you," he said. "I thought that if I looked hard enough, I could figure out what hold this thing has on you."

How could I tell him that he was looking in the wrong place?

"It doesn't have a hold on me," I said, "not like it used to."

He didn't hear me, or maybe he heard me but he didn't understand. He was looking down at his hands. He finally opened them and looked at one of the pictures. It was hard for him to look. "I found you here," he said, his voice struggling to get to me.

Don Lemley called me later. He'd gotten about as far researching online as I did. "Do you think we could go and talk to Mr. and Mrs. Leighton?" he asked.

It was going to be another dead end. Couldn't he see that? But I didn't say anything to him. "I'll ask."

I thought Don Lemley wasn't going to help at all. Maybe he was just thinking of busywork for me to do, humoring me until the inevitable change occurred. I called the Leightons and they agreed to let me bring Mr. Lemley over in the evening. They knew how much he'd helped me, and what did it matter anyway? It couldn't hurt.

I spent the afternoon at the library hunting through the stacks for maybe something I couldn't locate online—a medical journal or article, something that might lead me somewhere farther than where Don Lemley was taking me. I read through more symptoms, more pathologies, more causes and no cures. I thought I knew a lot about how a person could die. I had no idea. A cough could lead to influenza, pneumonia, emphysema, congestive heart failure, cancer. Every one of Maddy's symptoms seemed to either be potentially minor or fatal, part of an inconsequential illness or part of a larger, deadly pathogen. I was ready to give up—I wasn't smart enough, astute enough, and I certainly wasn't a doctor. If they couldn't figure it out, what chance did I have? Don Lemley probably knew this all along, but he kept going.

"What did you learn today?" Mr. Lemley asked as he drove over to the Leightons'.

"Nothing."

Nothing was not an acceptable answer.

"Nothing that will help us."

"But what did you learn?" he said. "Even if it has nothing to do with Maddy—what did you find out, in general?"

"Mosquitoes kill a lot of people."

"Is that right?"

"Millions. I hate to think about how many times I've been bit, just this summer, but I guess it's different."

"A different mosquito," Mr. Lemley said. "It's the difference between pest and pestilence."

"Just think if Mormon flies carried some disease. We'd all be dead by the end of summer." I was talking, but Don Lemley was listening. I had no idea that what I was saying would matter at all, but it did, at least it did because of Mr. Lemley.

Mr. Lemley asked the Leightons to review the progress with Maddy, and Mr. Leighton took him through the timeline and filled him in on the tests and recommendations, the false leads and dead ends. The Leightons had a file they kept, with every doctor's name, every test and result. I let the grown-ups talk over the stuff

I thought I already knew and went to see Maddy. She was sitting at her desk, with Manxcat on her lap.

"Any pictures today?" She hadn't taken any pictures in almost a week.

"None." She closed the laptop and moved to her bed. Manxcat followed her and jumped on the bed and curled himself on her pillow.

"Are you ready for school?"

"I guess so," she said.

"It's my last year."

"I know."

"I think I might go to Iowa," I said. "You can come visit me." She nodded.

"You can help me with my homework," I said. "Can I take your periodic table with me?"

"No," she said.

"I might need it. Besides, I think it's time you got the one eighteen." I left her room and got the tube I'd placed outside her door. "It's from Jodi and me."

Maddy was holding the new, rolled-up chart in her lap when Don Lemley and her parents came up the stairs. Manxcat took one look at Don Lemley and jumped off the bed and ran out the door. Don Lemley looked at me with a surprised reaction, as if I had suddenly said something to him and he was trying to hear it, or understand it.

Don Lemley waited until we had said good night to Maddy

and were back downstairs when he asked the Leightons how long they'd had the cat.

"Seven years," Mrs. Leighton said.

"Have you ever mentioned it to the doctors?"

"I don't know," Mr. Leighton said. "Why? What does the cat have to do with anything?"

"I don't know," Mr. Lemley said. "Something Adam said on the way over got me thinking. You might want to call the docs and ask. It's probably nothing."

It was everything.

One of the doctors, an ophthalmologist who had looked at Maddy on one of her first visits but not since, wanted to see her again as soon as possible. Manxcat had made Maddy sick, had transmitted something to her, a parasite or something, that started in her eye and migrated into her head. It was like a third world disease right down the street, and while it had plagued the Leightons for months, it was taken care of quickly and relatively easily. "Almost impossible to test for," Mr. Leighton said the doctor had told him, "and very rare that it has gone this long and this far." Her parents drove her up the next morning. It probably never crossed their mind to see if I wanted to go along. It didn't matter. What was I going to do up there anyway? Sit around nervous with everybody else? They took more blood, ran more tests, and said that Maddy was going to be all right. She was going to need some heavy-duty medication, but they said she was going to be all right.

○ ○ ○

We were in Maddy's room—she was in delay mode again, scanning the room with her camera and talking about everything she saw. It was way past her bedtime. She had the camera held in front of her and was looking at my forehead. "I wish I had a scar," Maddy said.

"Where?"

"Intersecting my left eyebrow," she said, drawing her finger down her forehead into her dark eyebrow, "or under my lower lip."

"Why?"

"A memento," she said. "Something to remember all of this."

"You think you might forget?" Jodi said.

"I won't forget. But I'd like everyone else to remember."

"They'll remember."

"Not for long," she said. "Not when I get old."

"Scars don't always last anyway. Look, you can hardly see mine anymore."

"I can still see it," Maddy said. "You better not lose it."

"It's time for bed," Jodi said. "You have school tomorrow."

"We're going to turn out the light. Go to sleep."

"How old are you now?" Maddy asked me.

"You know."

"I don't know," she said. "I don't even know if you know. I mean, maybe you're not the age you think you are. Maybe time is different for you."

"Different how?"

"What if time stopped or slowed all those times you were

dead, you know, like people in outer space who are in suspended animation or who travel at the speed of light and when they come back to Earth, they've only aged a little but everyone else is older or dead."

"Or apes have taken over the whole planet."

"You wish," Maddy said. "Maybe you're a lot younger than you think; that's all I'm saying. All those hours, days you weren't around, you weren't aging, so it adds up. Maybe you're not even old enough to drive."

"I think I'm old," I said. "I mean, I've been dead—you can't get any older than that."

"You can joke about it, but maybe you should think about it."

"I don't know the answer, so I try not to think about it. If you want to solve it for me, go right ahead."

"Maybe I will," she said. "Maybe we're the same age—maybe I'll find out that I'm older than you."

"I wouldn't be surprised."

EPILOGUE
("dying is an art, like everything else")

This is what I know about time. Time is not a river, but it is like one—it twists and turns, runs straight as an arrow, then circles back on itself; it collects in deep pools and shallow eddies; it trickles in weakness from drought and floods with unbearable force. It is swift and slow, muddy and clear; it diverges, dams, meanders, has hidden treacheries and blind curves. It has shoals and rocks and rapids and currents and needs to be navigated carefully. It seems to repeat itself, rising and falling, always running, but it can't repeat itself because it's never the same. It is exactly like the farmers describe the river—it does what it wants and there's nothing we can do about it. You either sink or float, and the whole river is always working on you, constantly working. It eats away at everything.

I see my past playing in my head over and over in a loop that always winds up the same. I don't like what I see. It was a waste of time—I know that—but it's a bigger waste of time thinking about it. I have it all out now, so I can move forward.

I am moving forward, inch by inch some days.

The thing is, I'm not better, I'm not happier; I'm different. I've always been different, I know, but now I'm different from how I was. I'm like an element on the sun that Maddy talks about, changing from one thing to another while keeping the same form—I've changed properties, I guess. And sometimes it seems that everything that's happened to me has happened to someone else, like an actor who sees himself on film and doesn't recognize himself or an athlete who looks at his old uniform, his trophies, old pictures from his playing days and thinks it couldn't have been him that did all those things, that it had to be somebody else.

I'm not saying I'm done with it; I'm not even saying I don't think about it still—I do, almost every day, but it's not a calling, it's lost its interest (more or less), lost its pull, its inevitability. There are other things that are more interesting—like this, writing it out. I wish I could have shown this to Mr. Coolidge, all these pages, instead of blanks. I think that's what he meant—let's go—let's get to work. I wasted too much time for him—I don't want to waste it anymore. Don Lemley's going to take a look and Maddy, of course. I gave Maddy my word—if I can't keep that promise, I don't deserve anything.

Don Lemley still believes in the end of the world. He has faith. He doesn't know when it's going to end—he's not quitting his job, selling his house, and moving to Brooklyn anytime soon—but he still thinks the whole thing is coming down, maybe in his lifetime, probably in mine, or yours. Sometime soon, he says. Maybe. At least it's getting closer, closer than yesterday, and a lot closer than the day before that. I tell him that he has a new problem—I plan on staying around for a while. "That's not my problem," he says, and lets loose a laugh that suits his voice, something you want to keep hearing.

"Thanks anyway. You don't need to call me anymore. I'm done with all that."

"I'm glad to hear it," he said. "How about if I called you every once in a while still, maybe bring a book by now and then? Would that be all right?"

"Yes sir. I look forward to it."

We still talk almost every day except he doesn't always call me—I call him—and now when I tell him that I'm doing all right, I think he believes me.

I never wanted to have a story to tell, I never wanted to have anything, not a chapter, not a paragraph, not a sentence, not a single recorded word. I never wanted to create anything, to be remembered or acknowledged, to leave any mark, not a scratch, smudge, smear, nothing. I wanted to be like a grain of sand on the beach, unnoticed and unimportant, one of billions of other grains on one beach that is one of a billion other beaches on a speck of a planet that is only one among uncountable billions, wanting nothing and achieving nothing.

That's not entirely true. I wanted. I wanted to avoid the natural course of things. I thought it should be that way, but I know that what I do won't change—that I can't change the natural course—but I can change my wanting to change it. I thought I wanted nothing, but I wanted too much, and I thought that what I wanted would put an end to my disappointments and suffering, but it was part of them, as big a problem as anything else. I'm just a small speck—the fact that I can sit here and write one word is amazing, and even if nothing comes of it, even if it is drowned out in the din of all the other words or ignored and unnoticed, it is still an accomplishment. This is my way forward, my way out. Each sentence leads somewhere, a bridge, a road, a river, leading somewhere away from here, a line thrown in hopes of catching something. I inch forward. I think about something Jodi told me the night we went together to the bridge—"You can keep coming back to the same spot, over and over, not getting anywhere, or you can change everything and get a different result." Some days are still dark, but it's not the same—sometimes that tone still echoes inside me, but it passes. Everything changes. Even this. I think about Maddy and me on the roof; I think about my father's hands holding the pictures; I think about those hands holding me.

Maybe it won't last the year, long enough for me to graduate and get out; maybe it won't last a month. What do I know about time anyway? All I know is that for now I don't feel the need to go down to the bridge or the bluff or any of that—they don't call to me, or I don't hear them. I don't need the hours when I'm gone; it's not all I want. And who knows, there might even be the end of the world. We always have that going for us.

I was introduced to suicide at a young age, and it has never left me. I have known too many people—teachers, physicians, neighbors, colleagues, friends, and family, more than a dozen in all—who decided to take their own lives. I have recalled the too few conversations and arguments, the silences and missed signals. Most kept their thoughts and decisions quiet, hidden and out of reach, leaving a gulf of lost opportunities and unanswered questions. I wish there had been more time to talk, more time to wait for talk. I wish there had been more time. If nothing else, this novel is my unqualified investigation into those hidden thoughts and emotions, and a journey through a very fictional character's struggle with one of life's most basic dilemmas: what to do with the time we have been given.

Luckily, I did not take this journey alone. I want to thank the following for insight, support, inspiration, and a patient tolerance for my unceasing questions and uncontrollable need to take what I can use whenever and wherever I find it:

Arielle Asher, Audrey Cooper, Ellen Cooper, Tom DePrenger, Jen Fowler, Beckie-Ann Galentine, David Halpern, Christie Hofknecht, Jacob Hurlburt, Roxana Hurlburt, Trevor Ketteman, Gina Maolucci, Emily Romero, Paul Rutkowski, MD, Julie Strauss-Gabel. And thanks to my father, who introduced me to the writings of Camus and Kafka (and plenty of others).

The National Suicide Prevention Lifeline (1-800-784-2433, 1-800-273-8255, suicidehotlines.com, suicidepreventionlifeline.org)

Gregory Galloway